Help me...

®

Ned Harrison pushed the palm aside and plowed through the underbrush, looking for the property boundary stake. He walked toward the creek in the general direction he reckoned, and found the stake with orange surveying tape ahead and a bit to his left. He walked to the stake, looked to his right along the property's waterfront, sketching an image in his mind of where he could construct a dock and boatlift. Interesting possibilities with this property.

He began to make his way along the creek's edge for three hundred twenty one feet—107 paces. The survey stake that marked the southern border of the seven-acre property was right where it should be. He turned around, studied the creek and the property along it, again sketching a brain image of where he could build a dock. His boat, a 22-foot Key West center console, rested easily between its two lines, one leading to an anchor off the stern holding its backend in deep water, the bow line double hitched to the base of an old palm tree. He could step right onto the bow from the bank, but the hull floated without touching the bottom.

He unrolled the plat of the property, studied it briefly, and turned and began walking away from the creek along the southern property line. He swatted palm leaves and plowed through underbrush making so much noise he didn't hear the car drive onto the property, ahead and to his left. He stepped into the clearing and was surprised to see a black Mercedes sedan. He froze in his tracks when he heard a woman and man arguing and saw violent movement inside the car. The passenger door flew open and a brunette woman spilled out, falling onto all fours.

The driver, a tall, neatly groomed man, exited the driver's side, ran around the car and grabbed the woman by her hair with one hand and hit her with his fist in the back of her head with the other. She collapsed, doing a face plant in the dirt.

"You bitch! You won't be bringing me down. You won't be *spilling any beans*!"

The man turned and walked quickly to the car, leaned in and began to dig through the glove box. The woman struggled, clumsily getting to her feet. She began to stumble away from the car and straight toward Ned, who was standing at the edge of the brush. Ned took a couple steps toward the woman and shouted, "Hey!" His voice was drowned out by the roar of a pistol. Blood sprayed from the right side of the woman's chest from the bullet's exit point. She was knocked to the ground by the blast.

She raised her head, looked at Ned and said weakly, "Help me."

The man walked to her and kicked her in the side of her head. She fell motionless, without even the motion of breathing.

"Bitch! Guess you won't be going to the press after all."

Ned edged back into the brush, concealing himself behind the palm leaves. The gun wielding man looked around, then walked quickly back to the car, jumped in and spun out in a cloud of dust and careened toward the main road.

Ned waited until the car squealed onto the pavement, then stepped from the underbrush and ran to the woman. He gently rolled her over and felt her neck for a pulse. He found one. She was taking rapid and shallow breaths, and was bleeding profusely. Ned ripped her shirt away from her wound. The exit hole was high on her chest and about the size of a quarter. He yanked off his shirt and wrapped it over her shoulder and pressed hard on the entry and exit wounds hoping to slow her blood loss, without great success.

Her eyes fluttered open and she faintly muttered, "Help me. Help me." She took a couple rapid breaths and asked, "Am I going to die?"

"You'll be fine. I'm going to get you to a hospital. Just hang on."

She looked up at him, a look of pleading on her face, and drifted into unconsciousness. Ned struggled to get her onto his shoulder and began trudging toward his boat as quickly as he could manage.

*****

The well-groomed Senator Evan Lee slammed on the brakes of his Mercedes and began banging his fist on the steering wheel. He was sweating profusely, his mind racing, dread flowing through him like high-pressure water. What the hell should he do now? What the hell should he do?

He thought back over the scene. She had threatened to go to his wife and to the press about their affair and his use of government money to finance their extravagant weekend trysts. He couldn't have that. He just couldn't allow her to derail his political career. Not now. Not with the White House this close. He dealt with her the only way he could. And he saved others from doing the dirty work.

Someone would have killed her anyway; too much money and power were at stake for some very rich and very powerful supporters. They wouldn't have allowed her to screw it up. Neither would his wife.

Then the thought of the woman's body hit him. Damn! The body! He had shot her with a gun registered to him. He couldn't leave her for some local sheriff to find; if the bullet was still in the woman, or if the police found it somewhere, ballistics could lead them directly to him. He knew he could likely out-maneuver a murder investigation team through his well-placed connections in state and federal government, but not if he became too hot, too much of a risk for his political connections to touch. He had to go back and get her. His people could handle it from there. He spun the car around and raced back toward the scene of the crime.

He whipped the Mercedes onto the dirt drive onto the vacant land and lurched toward the clearing on the rough, bending set of ruts until he skidded into the clearing, creating a cloud of dust that took a few seconds to clear. When it did, Senator Evan Lee's heart sank. This couldn't be. Was he in the right place? Yes, but what the hell? The woman was gone! He jumped from the car and ran to where she had fallen; blood everywhere, but no body. Damn! Where the hell did she go? How?

He began to walk in mindless circles. She had to be alive. She had to have wandered into the woods. She couldn't have gone far. He ran back to the car and retrieved his pistol and resumed his search. He found a few large spots of blood near the edge of the clearing. He walked into the woods. Ten yards farther there was another spot. She couldn't get far before she bled out. So much blood. He would find her any second now and drag her back to his car and drop her into the trunk.

Then it hit him. What had she said right after he shot her? "Help me?" Had she really said that? He ran the scene back through his mind. It had all happened so quickly and he had been in a state of panic and blind rage. Had she really said "Help me?" Who was she saying it to?

The sound of a boat motor roaring up to speed shattered his thoughts. No! No,no,no! Had someone been there, had someone seen what happened and taken the woman and fled by boat? This was bad, very bad. He ran back to the car and spun back toward the road, fishtailing as he hit the pavement. He took his phone from his pocket and pressed a speed-dial button.

"Chris! I, I, we have a problem, a big problem. I need help and I need it now. This is bad, very bad."

*****

Ned turned on his VHF marine radio and tuned to channel 16 and said, "Coast Guard, Coast Guard, this is the Allyson Two, over."

A few seconds later there was a reply by a professional-sounding male voice. "Allyson Two, this is the Coast Guard, over."

Ned replied, "Coast Guard, I have an emergency and need assistance. I have a woman with a gunshot wound and request that an ambulance meet me at Maybank Creek Landing immediately, over."

"Roger, Allyson Two. We will dispatch emergency personnel to Maybank Creek Landing. What is the name, age and the vital signs of the victim, over?"

"Unknown, Coast Guard. I stumbled upon her and she is unconscious. I can't check her vitals as I am in route to Maybank Creek Landing in a small boat, over."

"Roger, Allyson Two. Do you have any weapons onboard, over?"

"Negative, Coast Guard, no weapons onboard, over."

"Roger, Allyson Two. Emergency personnel are in route to Maybank Creek Landing; ETA of 14 hundred, over."

"Roger, Coast Guard. I will be approaching in a 22-foot Key West boat with a light blue hull and white deck. ETA of ten minutes, over."

Ned put the microphone back in its clip and adjusted his course with his left hand. He had laid the woman on the sole of his boat and was pressing firmly on her chest wound, pinning her down and putting pressure on the wound in her back. Still, a frightening amount of blood streamed back along the sole and drained out the stern scuppers. He drove the boat and operated the throttle with his left hand alone, but right now he only had to handle the direction of the boat since the throttle was maxed out and the four-stroke Yamaha was spinning 5,150 rpm. He glanced at the speedometer. Fifty-three miles per hour – best he could do. A few minutes later he saw the landing off his port bow. An ambulance was backing up to the walkway that led to the dock.

Quickly, a crew pulled equipment from the vehicle and scrambled toward the dock. Ned blew his horn seven quick times and sharpened his turn toward the dock.

His concern grew on how he would navigate to the dock with one hand. A thought came to mind when he was fifty yards out and closing fast. He slid off his right Merrill shoe and stepped firmly on the woman as he removed his bloody hand. He pulled throttle back steadily and fully into reverse, coming to a sliding stop alongside and a foot away from the dock, sending a wave breaking over it as the ambulance crew scrambled up the gangway with their equipment away from the collision they expected.

Only a couple seconds passed before one of the medics was onboard and looking at the woman. He quickly began giving orders to his partner, mentioning I.V.'s and "bleeding out."Ned was looking down at the woman's pale face when he felt something tugging at his leg. He heard a voice say,

"You can lift your foot from her now, sir."

Ned lifted his foot and jumped to the stern and made fast a line, then scrambled to the bow and did the same. The two medics were frantically attending to the woman. Ned stood back and watched. He began to feel the after effects of a massive adrenalin rush and the cold, sharp cut of reality returning. It was a familiar feeling. He was replaying the event in his mind and plucking out the details.

Two police cars skidded to a halt at the end of the pier. The officers ran down the pier to the dock and approached his boat, the officer in front with his hand on his weapon. Ned turned his head to the officer, a tall, fit black man in his forties, standing tall and strong, wearing a look that suggested that he was a well-seasoned professional. Ned guessed the man to be about 6'2", 205 pounds. He was built strong and lean, and had piercing jet-black eyes. He had some grey beginning on his temples, and short-cropped hair. Ned guessed he had been a college athlete, or that he could have been.

"Yes, officer?"

With a calm, gentle delivery, the man said, "I need to ask you some questions, sir. Mind if I come aboard?"

Ned moved to the bow and sat facing the stern. "Absolutely."

The officer stepped aboard and stood in front of Ned. "Sir, are you armed?"

"No."

"Do you have any weapons onboard?"

"No. I mean I have a knife or two, but no guns."

The officer, who sported an efficient poker face, sat on the console front seat and said while facing Ned, "I'm Detective Sam Strickland. Now, tell me what happened."

Ned went through the event and answered questions along the way. No, he didn't know the woman or the man who shot her. He didn't get a tag number but could give a description of the man and his car, and he told the officer precisely where the woman had been assaulted. Officer Strickland listened carefully to Ned's description and said, "I think I know the place you're talking about and I believe I can drive us there. Ned, is it OK if I call you Ned? "

"Sure. I have a plat of the property that will have the name of the road it's on." Ned moved to the console and retrieved the map from its resting place wedged between the GPS and the windscreen.

"Ned, let's take a look at the scene. You ride with me."

Sam Strickland led the way to his unmarked squad car. When they arrived at the car, Sam said to Ned, "Please ride with me up front." Ned slid into the passenger seat. As Sam drove out of the parking lot, another patrol car with two officers followed them. When they arrived at the land, one of the policemen began photographing the scene and leaving little markers on the ground where there were shoe prints and blood spots.

Ned showed them where he had been standing, and they retraced his steps to the water where he had tied his boat, then they retraced his path back to the clearing, photos being snapped along the way. Ned described what he saw, when he saw it and what the shooter looked like in detail. As they made their rounds, Sam noticed a shiny object in the clearing. He bent over and gave it a closer look ... an ejected shell casing. Sam saw a twig a few inches away, and slid one end of it into the shell casing, tilted it so it would stay on the twig, and picked it up. When he stood, he turned to hand it to one of the officers, but they were engrossed in photographing the blood pools and footprints. Sam slid the shell casing into a baggie, then into his front pocket. He would log it into evidence when he got back to his office. It could prove to be a valuable.

Every modern firearm sold in the United States has one round fired from it before it leaves the factory. The shell casings are scored by each gun; every one is unique like a fingerprint. The marks on each shell casing are recorded along with the serial number of the gun. A shell casing found at a crime scene could be matched with the manufacturers' records, and the owner of the gun can be traced via the corresponding serial number.

After Ned finished the third re-creation, Sam said, "Ned, would you mind coming to the station and giving a formal statement?" Ned agreed to go with them, but asked about his boat.

"Detectives are going over the boat now. It will take them another hour or two, and we should be finished and have you back to the dock by then."

They began to drive away. Ned had a thought.

"You better make sure someone stays with the boat until we get back."

Sam turned and asked, "Why is that, Sam?"

"Because the person that did this may want to know who found the woman. He may know that there's a witness and he may not take kindly to that. It won't be hard to find out who that is if they find the boat and get the numbers off the side."

Sam picked up his radio microphone and called one of the officers on the scene.

"Stay with the boat until we return, and cover the numbers on the bow."

The simple but questioning reply was a simple "Yes sir."

*****

When they settled into the interview room, Sam prompted Ned to tell the story on his own, uninterrupted. Sam made notes on questions to come back to. Once Ned finished, Sam ordered that the recording equipment be turned off and the transcript be typed up for Ned's signature before he asked blankly, "Pretty good eye for descriptive detail, Ned. How do you remember it with such clarity? Most people lose the details in the fog of the event."

"I'm pretty observant."

"I'd say." Sam paused, appraising Ned. "What line of work you say you're in?"

"Retired." Another pause.

"Young for that, aren't you?"

"I worked very hard to make it happen."

Sam pressed, "What kind of work was that?"

"I worked for the government." Ned was silent for a moment, thinking about details that hadn't been covered that weren't necessarily tied to the case, but things he was curious about anyway.

"Where'd you get that knife you had in the console of your boat?"

"Gift from a friend."

"I've seen one like it before, back in my service days."

Ned locked eyes with Sam. "You want to know about what I saw, or what I own?"

Sam smiled. "Alright, just curious. No offense intended. You just strike me as unusual, different from our normal witness." Ned didn't reply, just stared blankly at Sam.

As Sam drove Ned back to his boat, they rode in silence for a few minutes before Sam spoke.

"Ned, you watch yourself. I don't know who you saw, but he doesn't seem like the kind of person who will like having a loose end out there. He's proven himself capable of killing at least once. He might not mind doing it again. I try to always listen to my instincts, or that voice in the depths of my brain, and I have an uneasy feeling about this."

Ned said, "I hope you're wrong, but I've been thinking the same thing. The shooter had the look of someone of money and power. Expensive clothes, expensive car, and carried himself in a way that suggested power … a man who was used to getting what he wanted. In my experience, when that type of person sees you as a threat to their power and riches, they get a little upset."

Sam smiled again and he gave Ned another appraising look.

"Ned, my instincts also tell me you retired from a job that leaves a man with the type of skills to take care of himself. Just keep a low profile until we figure out who we're dealing with."

Ned replied, "I'm pretty good at keeping a low profile, too."

Sam smiled. "I bet you are."

Ned casually said, "Something about the man looked familiar to me, but I can't put my finger on it."

Sam looked at Ned with arched eyebrows, and said, "He looked familiar to you? Don't you think you should have mentioned that to me?"

Ned said, "I'm not sure it has any substance. It could be that he looked similar to someone I saw in a movie or on the street somewhere, I just don't know. If I figure it out and it means anything, I'll let you know."

"Let me know when you figure it out whether or not you think it means anything."

When they arrived back at Maybank Creek Landing, Ned and Sam stepped from the car and walked together toward the boat.

Sam handed Ned his card and said, "Ned, you think of anything, my cell number's on my card. Remember, this could be nothing more than a crime of passion, but I've not yet met a perp who loves witnesses. Makes them jumpy."

Ned let that resonate as they walked, thinking back on the shooter's face and its familiarity. As they arrived at the boat, Ned looked down to find dried blood covering the rear of the cockpit, and dirty shoe marks all over the boat. He hadn't thought of the mess he would find. He always kept his boat clean. Always. He shook his head as he thought about the task awaiting him. He turned and asked Sam, "Can I clean this up now?"

"Yes. Samples and photos have been taken and the boat has been gone over with a fine toothed comb. It's yours again. Sorry for the mess. You like this boat?"

Ned said, "Love it. It will scoot, handles great and that Yamaha is a dream. I installed full electronics. It's designed well. I love it."

Sam asked, "Ever take it offshore?"

"I have, but I don't like being out of the harbor unless I'm in something much bigger. I don't care for being beaten to death by rough seas, and I'm not particularly fond of what the ocean can do when she's angry. She eats small boats."

Sam laughed. "I'm with you on that. Where do you keep it?"

I'm staying with a friend on the Ashley and I keep her at his dock while I'm here, in a garage when I'm not. I lived in Charleston a long time ago. Since then I've lived in several places, and now spend most of my time on some land I have in the hills of Southwest Virginia or at a similar place in Colorado."

Sam said, "Now you're looking for land here. Moving back to the Holy City?"

Ned answered, "I won't sell either of my places in the mountains, but the Low Country has always held a place in my heart. I was born in Beaufort, so maybe the salt was in my blood when I came into this world."

Sam said, "It happens."

Ned asked, "So what about you. Are you a Charleston native?"

Sam answered, "Grew up on the water near Edisto. My family has farmed there since the end of slavery ... before the end, actually. I was the first to go to college. After a stint in the Navy, I came back here and have worked as a detective ever since."

Ned said, "Navy. What was your job there?"

"Naval intelligence."

Ned said, "I know, you could tell me what you did, but you'd have to kill me?"

Sam laughed. "That's right, so don't ask any questions."

Ned laughed and said, "I won't if you won't." After a brief pause, he said, "Well, I guess I'll be moving on."

They shook hands, and after one last reminder to call Sam with anything that came to mind, they said their goodbyes and Ned casted off. Ned eased the boat backward into the river, shifted to forward, idled until outside the "No Wake" buoys. After going a few hundred yards out from the dock, Ned called his friend Steve, with whom he was staying while in Charleston.

Ned had set up camp in Steve's forty two foot trawler that is docked behind his house on the Ashley River. Ned gave Steve a brief summary of the day's events, and said, "I should be back at your dock in an hour or so. I'll explain more when I see you, but I'd like to tie up my boat on the inside of your dock so she can't be seen."

"Tie it in the inside slip; that should do the trick. Did you get a look at the shooter?"

Ned replied, "I did. I get the feeling I've seen him before, but I can't place him. Maybe he just looks similar to someone else. I don't know."

Steve said thoughtfully, "Don't focus on it for a few hours. Sometimes when you stop trying to dig into your mind for that nugget of information, it floats to the surface on its own. It'll come to you. Got to run. See you in an hour."

"Great. Meet me on the dock with a cold one ready?"

"You got it."

Ned pushed the throttle forward. The Yamaha dug in and the boat quickly planed. Ned headed up river toward Steve's dock.

Chapter 2

Ned had the entire boat covered in soap foam when Steve walked down the dock. As Sam began to hose down the boat, pink suds in the cockpit began to flow out the stern scuppers and pretty soon the boat was free of blood and dirt. Steve stood on the dock raptly listening as Ned recounted the events of the afternoon.

The story lasted longer than the washing and they walked up the ramp from the floating dock and sat under the roof of the pier gondola. Steve stepped behind the rough wooden bar and poured himself a single-malt scotch, and a Canadian whiskey and water for Ned, who sat on the wooden bench seat that extended the perimeter of the gondola and finished his story.

Steve asked, "And you say the shooter looks familiar?"

Ned answered, "He does. Vaguely."

Steve paused as he sifted through his thoughts, and said, "Well, it'll come to you, probably when you aren't trying to remember. But it's a little discomforting to know that someone you've seen before just killed a woman and, if he doesn't already, he'll soon know there was a witness. I doubt he'll be happy. The question is what he will do then. Turn himself in, run, or something else?"

Ned and Steve had a second drink and enjoyed the sun setting over the river. The alcohol and the beauty of the surroundings rinsed away some of the tension of the afternoon's events, and as dusk arrived they walked up to the house to cook dinner.

Steve said, "I'll be meeting my plumber and my electrician at the house down the river tomorrow morning and I'll be busy with that most of the day. What do you have planned?"

Ned answered, "There's another piece of land I want to look at a few miles down the Edisto River from Elliot's Cut, and another about a mile up the Ashley from here. I'm going to run over to each in the boat and take a look and snap a few photos of each."

Steve said, "Sounds great. There're sandwich makings in the fridge if you want to take some lunch with you. What time are you planning on leaving?"

*****

The Senator paced back and forth across the office with a near-empty glass of vodka in his right hand and a cigarette in his left. He couldn't stop moving, couldn't stop smoking and couldn't stop drinking. He slugged down the remaining vodka, walked quickly to the bar and poured himself another.

He said, "That's it. That's what happened. It was just a freak accident. That's all it was."

Chris Johnson sat in the corner watching the pacing, drinking and smoking bundle of nerves that stood in front of him. He had listened to the story at least three times, but something still seemed incomplete. In every crisis there was a solution. Also, in every crisis there is a detail capable of obliterating even the most carefully planned crisis management plan. Sometimes the detail was unexpected or overlooked, but in this case there couldn't be that crippling detail. The stakes were too high. The life of the man in front of him stood in the balance, but there were more people whose plans would be ruined. Very powerful people … the *most* powerful people.

Chris had made a name for himself as the best in the PR business. He had kept executives on the path to greatness, he had even helped *the* Chief, as in the Commander and Chief, reach his goals, and retain his office after an endless string of self-induced PR blunders. He knew the ins and outs of a crisis, and he knew how to handle them. It was always the surprise detail that was the land mine. He hadn't yet identified it, but he could feel it looming. He spoke. "Alright, ease off on that booze. Just calm down, sit down, and start from the beginning again."

The Senator protested, "Damn, Chris, I've told you what happened over and over again. I'm tired of this shit. Just tell me what we're going to do next."

He swung his hand in the air and said, "Fix this shit!"

Chris was unabashed. He said, "From the beginning. Tell me again." He paused before adding, "And this time leave out the bullshit and insert the truth."

The senator slugged the contents of his nearly full glass. He blurted, "Goddamnit, Chris, it's what happened."

Chris sighed. It was going to be a long night. He would get the truth, even if it took all night, which it may, judging by the last three hours. Unfazed, he said, "From the beginning."

*****

Dinner completed, Steve and Ned were carrying dishes to the kitchen when Steve turned on the TV to catch the weather forecast for tomorrow. Ned, walking to the kitchen with his hands full of plates and silverware suddenly stopped, dropping two forks that clanged to the hardwood floor.

He froze, staring at the TV before blurting, "That's him! That's the man I saw shoot that woman today. That's him."

Steve took a few quick steps until he could see the screen. He looked intently at the TV, then at Ned. He asked, "Are you sure? Are you absolutely positive?"

The sound was muted on the TV. The man was addressing the press core. He said a few words and stepped into the passenger seat of a black Mercedes before it drove off.

Ned said, "If I had any doubt, it was erased by the car. That was the car the man was driving. That was him!"

The TV switched to a commercial. Steve wore a look of fear. He asked, "Ned, do you know who that is?"

Ned answered, "No. Must be a celebrity, but about the only time I watch TV is when a football game is on. He does look vaguely familiar. Who is it?"

Steve's look grew darker. "Ned, that's Senator Evan Lee. He's the front runner for president in the election in two years."

Ned felt a thick dread flowing into his body. He said flatly, "That can't be good. I've heard a lot about him, and none of it was pleasant."

Ned pointed at the television. Steve turned up the volume as the newscaster said, "Locally, we learned this afternoon of a woman shot on the Ashley River, and a good Samaritan that saved her life. Sara Gonzales, 24, of Charleston, was found shot on the bank of the Ashley river. A visiting fisherman found her, called authorities and rushed her to a landing where she was treated and transported to MUSC hospital."

The newscaster paused, looking toward his support staff. "We have an update just in. The woman has died from her wounds. We don't know yet who the Good Samaritan is, and we are sorry his efforts were in vane, but we thank him for his efforts.

Chapter 3

There it was, the detail that could sink the ship. There was a witness! Chris Johnson smiled to himself in satisfaction that he had uncovered the first little, tiny critical nugget of truth. He roared, "There was a fucking witness? It took you five hours to tell me there was a fucking witness?"

The senator stammered something insignificant. Chris Johnson let it flow through his brain, looking carefully for anything important, discarding the bullshit.

Chris poured himself another cup of coffee and stirred in the milk. He sat back in his seat and looked at the amount of remaining memory on his voice recorder. Another three hours before he would have to switch to a second unit.

He jotted in his bound notebook, leaned back in his chair calmly and said, "So, a man was in the woods watching you. Tell me everything about him. His hair; the color, straight or curly, short or long? His height; tall or short? Fat or fit? Pale or tanned."

The senator's answers were vague – at first. Chris kept drilling deeper, persistently chipping away, gathering more and more detail. After another 30 minutes of painful drilling and the description was no longer vague. Chris ended his interrogation with a summary.

"So, we have a man in his forties, brown hair, six-feet-two, 190 pounds of lean muscle who looked confident, not scared, and comfortable being outside. Probably a skilled boater, an outdoorsman, likely owns firearms and knows how to use them."

The senator smiled. "I think some of that is conjecture on your part, like owning firearms and such, but isn't it very good that we now have a good description of the man?"

"Not conjecture. The man came by boat, not car. He showed no fear in a dangerous situation. He is physically fit, had no scratches or cuts after walking through thick brush and moved quickly. He also looked intently at you. He didn't panic and run off screaming, he *looked* at you. Think about it.

"You were in a panic and had lost your head. You lost control, but with some work you know what the man looks like. That means he remembers more about how you look than you remember about him. You have a problem. A big one."

The senator's face dropped and turned deep red. He gulped. "What should I, what can I ... I need another drink."

Chapter 4

Jimmy Rogers worked the levers on the backhoe like an artist flicks his brush. The movements were measured, but so practiced they looked like casual flicks of the wrists. He maneuvered the shovel of the machine to within fractions of an inch of where he intended. Each deliberate move in Jimmy's mind transferred from his brain to his wrists in quick but smooth synchronicity. The machine, however, lacked grace and made its moves in jerky, powerful lurches. As he worked, small roots broke free with snaps and flying dirt. The larger mass of the old oak stump moved but refused to release its grip on its century-old home in the edge of the field at the bottom of Wicker Mountain.

Appalachian Mountains, southwestern Virginia, 48 miles west of Blacksburg, seven miles south of the Appalachian Trail; Jimmy Rogers' 546 acre tract, bordering the headwaters of the Cutthroat River on its south, adjacent to Ned's 324 acre tract to its west.

In disgust at his inability to coax the stump from its perch, he retracted the bucket, raised the stabilizer leg on each side, turned around in his seat, jammed the machine into forward gear and drove it 75 yards and parked it next to his blue Ford 150. He shut down the engine of the backhoe, jumped off and walked to the bed of his truck. Jimmy's blue coon dog looked up at him curiously from his lounging spot on the shaded open tailgate. Jimmy paused and looked at the dog.

Jimmy said, in the Appalachian accent he always reverted to when he was back in his home mountains, "So you're going to give me that look, huh? Don't act all innocent, just go ahead and say you told me so. I know you didn't believe I could get that old stump moved, so just go ahead and say it." Jimmy paused again. "That's right, you DID tell me that. And now we all bear witness that you have officially recorded your 'I tole you so.' Now that I have you on record, let me now officially tell you, again, that you are wrong. I ain't defeated. I never lose. I was just giving that stump a fair chance."

Jimmy leaned into the back of the truck and drug out a big steel box. He hoisted the box onto his shoulder and took a step toward the backhoe before stopping and turning to the dog. "Now it's time to get serious. It's time to give that stump a little nudge. By the way, you got a light?" Jimmy smiled at the dog, winked and hoisted the box up beside the seat of the backhoe.

Jimmy drove the backhoe over to the stump. After arriving, he taped together three sticks of dynamite. He stretched out the attached fuse and cut it at two feet. He lay on his stomach and reached the dynamite down beneath the stump. Rolling to a sitting position, he leaned back and dug the lighter from his pocket, flicked it and held the flame under the end of the fuse until a smart sparkle erupted.

Back at the truck, the blue dog never lost his gaze on Jimmy. He watched with dog interest as the backhoe came back toward him as fast as the machine would go, dirt flying as it bounced over the rough ground, Jimmy whooping at the top of his lungs. Jimmy slid the machine to a stop beside the truck, jumped down and dove head first into the back of the truck.

Jimmy grabbed the dog, pulled him close and covered his ears just as a huge boom erupted, sending a volcano of dirt and rocks 60 feet into the air, a large oak stump atop the chaotic rubble. The noise was deafening the first time it passed over them, only slightly less so the second and third times it echoed off the mountains around them. The sound of dirt and rock rained down on the truck, and there was a loud crashing as the stump broke through branches in the nearby trees, followed by a ground-shimmering thud.

Jimmy smiled a big smile and said to the old blue dog, "Don't you never, never, ever say 'I tole you so' to ole Jimmy again, cause I never give up. Never!"

The dog licked Jimmy on the chin, walked to the back of the truck and jumped out. He sauntered over to the back wheel of the backhoe, looked up at Jimmy, put a dog smile on his lips, hiked his leg and peed on the tire.

Jimmy slapped his leg. "Always got to have the last word, don't you?" Just then Jimmy heard a vehicle coming down the gravel road that led up to Ned's house. Jimmy watched through the window of the truck's bed cover as a red Jeep roared down the mountain, across the field and over the bridge they shared and onto the paved road. The Jeep's tires squealed as it accelerated onto the pavement and headed south down the mountain. He couldn't make out a tag number, but it didn't look like the Jeep was from Virginia. It looked more like a Washington, DC tag, which wouldn't be all that unusual for Ned. But Ned usually let him know when someone was visiting. The last he had seen Ned was two weeks ago. He was leaving for South Carolina the next day and had asked Jimmy to keep an eye on things, like he always did when Ned was away, which was a lot. But Ned hadn't mentioned guests.

Jimmy crawled out the back of the truck. "Well, Blue, guess we best ride up to Ned's and see what gives? Come on. Ride in the cab with me. I don't like it that those folks skedaddled right after the sound of me nudging that stump free. Might mean they was running 'cause they weren't supposed to be there, and that explosion scared 'em off. "

*****

It didn't take Jimmy more than a first glance at Ned's house to see that the Jeep hadn't been driven by guests, not the invited kind, anyway. The front door of the house had been beaten up, but hadn't given way. The "guests" had taken a large rock to it, but must have looked for easier entrance. Jimmy stopped the truck, leaned over and opened his glove compartment.

He retrieved the long, heavy .45 revolver, popped open the wheel and checked that all chambers were loaded, clicked it back into place and stepped out of the truck. He took one step before the window next to him exploded and a gun roared from inside the house.

Jimmy dove back into the cab of the truck, started the engine while lying across the seat, pushed the dog into the floor and jammed the truck it into reverse and floored the accelerator and spun the wheel. Out of the corner of his eye Jimmy saw a rifle barrel pointing out from the second floor window. Jimmy steered the truck with his left hand, jammed it into drive and pushed the accelerator with his right foot and swung his gun toward the upstairs window and squeezed the trigger twice. Just before the truck spun away from the window, Jimmy saw the rifle tumble to the ground. Jimmy kept going until he was around the bend 75 yards from the house and out of view. He stopped the truck and grabbed the 12-gauge shotgun from the rack behind him.

He slid from the truck and edged into the woods. He said to himself, "This is my turf, boys, and I don't take kindly to you being on it. And in my friend's house, too. That beats all." He addressed the dog. "Blue, you stay put."

Jimmy jumped across a small drainage culvert and began edging his way up the side of the mountain and to his right toward the house. He moved tree to tree, careful to minimize his exposure. He didn't know who was inside the house or why. He didn't know their motivation. It was probably some desperate meth heads, so they could be high or suffering from a bad need of the drug. Meth-heads were famous for acting like they were bullet proof, leaving all caution behind and behaving as if they were impervious to pain. They could be very dangerous people.

Jimmy moved tree to tree until he was 50 yards from the house. He lay back against the trunk of an old oak. He eased open the chamber of the 12-gauge shotgun until he saw brass. He opened the wheel of the forty five. Five rounds remained. Four shells were in the shotgun, and those were loaded with buckshot. Jimmy concluded that he was adequately armed as long as he didn't get into an extended firefight with several people, and he didn't intend for that to happen.

Jimmy eased his head around the tree and took a quick look at the house before ducking back. He sat still and surveyed the image in his brain. The rifle was on the ground beneath the window he had shot toward. There was no one in the window, nor in the other three he saw from his perch. The door looked battered but closed, so whoever was in the house didn't enter – or leave – from there.

That raised a question. Ned had made the place very secure to prevent what had apparently happened; someone had broken in. All doors and frames were steel reinforced; same with the windows. In addition to their steel reinforced frames, the small windows used bulletproof glass, and the large windows across the front of the house had wire grid panels that rolled closed at the flip of a switch. They were closed.

The exterior walls of the house were made with mountain rocks, supported on the interior by an 18-inch poured concrete sub structure. The easiest ways to break in would be to cut through the metal roof or up through the floor. Jimmy began to move again and circled around to the opposite side of the house. The door on this side was also damaged but hadn't given way. There were no ladders to indicate anyone had cut through the roof, the basement door was intact, and no windows had been successfully breached. So there was nothing to indicate that anyone had made it into the house ... except for the person in the house.

Jimmy walked 60 yards, stopped behind the trunk of a tree and thought it over. He pulled out his cell phone to call Ned, and then to call the law, but he was interrupted by the sound of a door opening. He peeked around a tree and what he saw surprised him. It was a woman running from the escape tunnel as fast as she could. And the clincher? She was running directly toward him. He looked at her hands. No weapons. The woman was covering ground quickly. Thirty yards away. Twenty. Ten and Jimmy was still so surprised he hadn't decided what to do. Then she was five yards away. Jimmy kicked his leg out from behind the tree and caught the woman on her right shin with the hard heel of his boot. She cried out as she flew through the air. Jimmy laid his weapons on the leafy ground and jumped on her back. He yanked both her arms behind her as she continued to kick and scream.

After another thirty seconds of struggle the woman exhausted herself and began to quiet down. Jimmy began to speak, "I don't know who you are, but I don't like you breaking into my friend's house, and I'm especially bothered that you shot my truck window out with that rif…"

The woman shouted, "I'm a friend of Ned's! I didn't break in, and the only reason I went in is because they were chasing me; they were going to kill me. I'm a friend of Ned's!"

Jimmy held his grip on the woman. He noticed she was quite beautiful with long auburn hair pulled into a pony tail, and she had tanned skin and light blue eyes, a color Jimmy couldn't remember seeing before. "How'd you get in the house?"

She said, "My key! I have a key! It's in my right front pocket."

Jimmy held his grip on her. "Then why'd you shoot at me?"

She said, "Men were here trying to kill me. How do I know you're not just another one of those assholes?"

Jimmy asked, "Who was trying to kill you? Who are you?"

She said, "Let go of me! I'll tell you everything, but we've got to get out of here. Now! They'll be back."

Jimmy slowly loosened his grip on her. He rolled off her and grabbed his .45 and pointed it at her. "You just stay right there and start talking."

The woman took several deep breaths and said, "I'm Kara, a friend of Ned's. We used to have a thing a few years ago. I stayed here with him a few times, and he showed me the tunnel and gave me a key to the house."

That's when Jimmy knew she was a friendly. Ned was very selective about who knew about the tunnel, even more so about who he gave keys to. The only reason Jimmy knew about the tunnel is because he built it. Ned swore Jimmy to secrecy before he talked about his plans for a secure and secret escape route.

He made Jimmy swear on his ancestors and sign contracts that included stiff penalties if he divulged anything about it. When Jimmy needed help, Ned was at his side. No other workers were allowed onsite when the tunnel was under construction and no one else saw the blueprints.

Jimmy asked, "How'd you get up here? I don't see a car anywhere."

"The hard way; I walked. Enough of this! Who the hell are **you**?"

Jimmy lowered the .45. "I sold Ned this land. I built his house. I live on the adjacent property. I watch his house for him when he's gone and I share whiskey with him when he's here."

Jimmy wiped his hand across his forehead. "Now that we got the pleasantries out of the way, who was in the red Jeep?"

"There are three of them and they're bad people. They must have followed me here from DC or figured out from some cell-phone calls I made. I don't know. But they know where I am, and they want what I have."

"And that would be what?"

"Knowledge, and if they get hold of me, they won't stop until I am dead or I tell them. And then they'll kill me. So, enough with the friendly chit chat shit, I have to get away from here. Now. Where's Ned?"

Jimmy took a slow, deep breath, and let it out slowly. The best thing he could do would be to get back in his truck and go home. Forget he ever saw this woman. As tempting as it was to do the logical thing, he knew he couldn't. Not Jimmy. Not only would he be letting down his friend and neighbor, but it would fly in the face of everything he believed in: loyalty, being a man, doing the right thing. That's the way he was raised. That was the code among the good people who grew up in the mountains of southwestern Virginia.

Jimmy pulled himself up and stood facing the woman. "Well, Kara, I guess you best come with me. We have several miles to walk. It won't be easy in these mountains."

Jimmy paused and looked Kara over, giving her silent approval for her clothing and hiking boots. "But I guess you won't have any trouble with it."

Kara stood and brushed herself off. "No, I don't mind a walk, but seems like a waste of that truck of yours."

Jimmy smiled. "So, we take my truck. Those bad boys that's sniffin' after you see us, follow us and come snatch you. I don't see much future in that; for either of us."

She said, "I see your point. Let me grab my backpack." She walked back toward the tunnel and disappeared into the rhododendron thicket that hid the tunnel entrance. A few minutes later, she returned with her pack on her back. She walked up to Jimmy as he let out a whistle. A minute later, a dog ran to his side, tail wagging. Jimmy said, "This is my partner, Blue. Hand me the pack."

He took it, hoisted it and dumped the contents onto the ground. He leaned over and began rummaging. He found a cell phone, removed its battery and threw both as far down the mountain as he could. He searched every nook and cranny, standing when he finished, holding a small black disc.

"Looks like your friends gave you a GPS." He threw it against an oak tree, then picked up the two pieces and stomped them flat against a rock. Kara asked, "What did you say you do for a living?"

"I didn't. Let's get moving." He started walking north.

Chapter 5

Jimmy led as they scrambled up steep mountainsides and slid down others. They skipped over three streams, stopped at two springs along the way and drank deeply from the cool, pure water that flowed up from the depths of the earth. The woman talked little and had no trouble keeping up with Jimmy, even passed him on the climbs on many occasions.

Jimmy kept running different scenarios through his head. If the guys in the Jeep returned, they could easily find out where Jimmy lived by looking through his truck and finding the registration in the glove box or tracing the tag number. They might want to pay a visit, but he wasn't too concerned about that. Finding out where he lived was one thing. Actually getting to his house was another. The winding, two-mile gravel road was challenging enough. The extra features Jimmy had added would stop any unwanted vehicle, short of a tank, and even a tank had no better than even odds of making it all the way to the house.

Jimmy thought through the measures he would need to take to make sure his home was fully secured. Lock two gates along the driveway, turn on the vehicle sensors and alarms, let the dogs out of the pens, and run the water pumps to top off the two cisterns.

After two hours of tough hiking through the mountains, Jimmy stopped, casually scanned their surroundings and said, "I'll lead from here. Stay back 20 yards. When I hold up my hand like this, it means stop, drop and cover. No questions, comments or arguments."

Kara brushed back a strand of hair from her forehead with the back of her wrist and looked at Jimmy, took a deep breath and asked, "You done something like this before, Jimmy? You don't seem to be a stranger to people wishing you harm."

Jimmy, who had continued to scan their surroundings, showed a quick smile that disappeared as suddenly. "I grew up in the mountains. A man learns as a young 'un to take care of himself. You learn to hunt, live off the land and store your food for winter.

"You also learn to protect it so that when those what've been too lazy to do for themselves get hungry, they don't come take yours."

Kara looked at him quizzically. "Come on. You mean someone would actually come steal your food?"

Jimmy stopped his continuous scan of their surroundings and looked directly at Kara. His eyes got big and he answered frankly, "Your food, your whiskey, your money, wife, kids, cows, horses and even your land. Same as they will in the city, just out here it might take the law a day or more to show up when you call, so people take their time as they steal what they want. And if you haven't experienced that in the city, just wait until a big storm knocks out the power or a riot gets out of control. When people get greedy, they steal. When they get hungry, they'll kill you for a loaf of bread. When the lawmen think their families are threatened, they won't be coming to your house to stop someone from stealing from you or even killing you; they're going home to protect their own. Count on it."

Kara cringed a little, and said, "You make mankind sound so primitive. We're pretty different, the two of us. I don't think that way."

Jimmy smiled. "It is primitive, even cruel at times, and you had best accept it. Anyway, you shot out the window of my truck just a few hours ago because you thought I meant you harm." Jimmy winked. "We don't seem that different after all, now do we?"

Kara thought about that for a few seconds, then visibly shivered. "No," she said reluctantly, "I guess we all do what we have to do."

Jimmy took exception. "No ma'am! Not all of us. Most people are sheep and just go along because it's easier. Think about what's happened throughout history. Some people just go along until they are hanged or shot or burned up in big ovens, all because they hope that if they go along, someone will be nice to them. Well, if you had just gone along a few hours ago, you said yourself that those what was after you would've killed you. Based on what I saw today, you aren't a sheep. No ma'am. Sheep don't shoot at people."

Jimmy continued his scan, but looked at Kara again when she said, "Then I guess we're a regular match made in Heaven, Jimmy."

He laughed, quietly. "I reckon so. Say, before we get married, let's get to the house and fix some dinner. All this talk usually gives me a headache, but today it's making me hungry. Now remember, if I raise my hand like this, it means stop, drop and cover."

Kara smiled. "Got it, and let's go already."

As Jimmy made his way carefully ahead, moving easily and quietly from tree to tree, Kara wondered to herself what was coming next. She had always been a decent judge of character, but now she was deep in the mountains with a man she didn't know, without a chance of help from anyone. If he had ill intentions, she was in for a bad time. But Jimmy seemed genuine. He seemed to be one of the good guys, and he said he was a friend of Ned's. He knew about the tunnel entrance, and if Ned had let Jimmy know about that, Jimmy had Ned's trust, and that meant something. But she wouldn't feel comfortable until she talked to Ned.

*****

Ned and Steve stood on the deck of Steve's house sipping coffee and looking out over the river. Ned's phone rang. It was Jimmy. Jimmy told Ned what had happened and described the damage to Ned's house, then the signal faded and the call was dropped. Ned hung up the phone. He decided to spare Steve the details so he could honestly say he knew very little should anyone ask. He said to Steve, "Someone tried to break into my house in Virginia and I have to go back this afternoon."

Steve asked, "How long will you be there?"

Ned said, "Not sure. I'll have to inspect the damage and either make the repairs or arrange for someone else to take care of them. There must be more to it.

My neighbor Jimmy, the man who called, was brief and almost cryptic, like he didn't want to tell me much over the phone, but then the call was lost. Signal is sketchy up in those mountains. I'm not sure what's going on, but something is."

Ned turned to Steve and said, "If anyone asks, it will be best for you if you tell them that you don't know where I am or when – or if – I'll be back."

Steve said, "Got it."

Ned said, "I'll pull my boat out and get packed.   Drive up this afternoon."

Chapter 6
Washington, D.C.

John Blackmon answered the cell phone curtly, "John."

There were several seconds of silence before a deep voice said, "The kickoff team has failed. Coach is putting you in the game. Last known location is in southwestern Virginia. Coordinates will be texted to you. The man in New York sent a personal request for you. He said this is mission critical. Subject is a female who disappeared from NSA."

"Critical? NSA? Tell him the price is triple. No negotiating. Send me the particulars. You have the banking information. Once I see the right numbers, I'll go in the game."

The line clicked dead. John Blackmon had a bad feeling about this, bad feelings about the man in New York, really. The girl in Virginia was the second job the man had hired him for in the last three months. The man seemed to be taking on water faster than was sustainable, and ships usually sink when there are too many leaks. The man sure seemed like a sieve.

John would do this last job. He would charge three times his normal fee, and then he could finally have enough cash to amply fund his retirement. All bets were off then; his phone would be turned off for good. The senator and all the other majorly flawed people who had come to power could go find someone else to clean up their messes. The man in New York was definitely one of the flawed, and a dangerous one, at that. He just might control the current president and the next, but on the other hand, he could very well make history as the man who brought down the American system by unintentionally doing something outrageous that exposes the corruption in the positions of power. It had worsened progressively over the decades, but now anyone who had enough money could get anything they wanted out of Washington, no matter how inappropriate it was. And people that lacked the cash couldn't get anything done, no matter how noble. The man in New York wasn't simply responsible for a long line of corrupt officials; he just might be the worst man yet to ever influence the future of America.

John shook his head at how bad things had become. After a minute, he chuckled as he thought to himself that maybe he should spare the free world of its demise by taking care of the man in New York. Delicious thought.

John's fantasy was interrupted by the buzzing of his cell phone. He picked it up and looked. A text had arrived. GPS coordinates. He sighed, took one final sip of his morning coffee, and stood to go prepare for his mission.

*****

Ned finished packing a few clothes and sat on the dock bench. His cell phone rang.

"Hello."

"Ned, this is Sam. I need to have a word with you. Can you take a minute?"

"Sure. What's up?"

"Ned, it is critical that what I am about to tell you remain confidential. It is very important. In fact, it could be life and death information. Do you understand?"

"I think it's pretty clear that this is confidential information. OK, this will remain confidential – with one condition."

"Which is?"

"That if it comes down to my freedom, liability or life, or that of other innocent people, all bets are off. Otherwise, I agree to maintain confidentiality."

44

"What did you say you used to do for a living?"

Ned grinned. "I didn't. So what's on your mind?"

"Not on the phone. You know, NSA and all, and we're dealing with people who might be powerful enough to access such information. I'll bring you a cup of coffee. Are you on land or water?"

Ned answered, "Either, actually, but water is more convenient for me."

"Good enough. Pick me up in 20 minutes at the dock where I last saw you. That way we can be assured of privacy."

Ned eased his boat next to the Maybank Creek dock and Sam stepped aboard. Ned slid the shifter into reverse, backed up ten yards and swung the Key West smoothly around before shifting to forward gear and adding power until they were on a plane. Ned took the paper coffee cup from Sam and steered the boat into the middle of the river. Once the dock was three miles behind them, Ned eased back on the throttle until they were at idle speed.

Ned turned to Sam and asked, "So what's up?"

Sam took a breath and began to speak. "It was reported on the news last night that the woman you brought in died from her wounds.

"That is false. The woman is still in intensive care and is hanging on by a thread, but she is there under a false ID. We learned a few things yesterday that lead us to believe that she could be at risk if her attacker learns she is alive."

"I see. And just who is this attacker?"

"Sorry, but I'm not at liberty to say at this time. What I can say is that the person or people we think are possibly involved are powerful people. They also have a reputation of ruthlessness. For those reasons, we want to protect the victim."

"Powerful person, huh? What makes you think that?"

"We received an anonymous call from a young lady in Virginia. She said she knows who the victim is and who shot her. Said it was a lovers' rift of some kind, and that the shooter was well connected in Washington."

"That's interesting. So why are you telling me all of this?"

"Well, Ned, because I think you could be in danger as well. If these people are so connected, they might find out who the witness is. So what I am telling you is that I want you to get out of town – out of the state – until you hear back from me. Touch base with me from time to time, but don't call from an insecure cell phone or regular line."

Ned interrupted Sam. "I know how to make a secure call, or as close to secure as can be with today's technology."

Sam paused again, staring at Ned before deciding not to ask the questions he knew he wouldn't get answers to. "Don't tell me where you are going, and don't tell anyone else that can't keep it a secret. Just go."

Ned asked, "OK, I'll do just that. Anything else?"

"Just one thing. Watch yourself. If these people involved are who we think they are, this could be a rough ride for all of us."

Ned said, "Watch yourself, too. I'll be leaving this afternoon."

After Sam stepped back onto the dock, Ned eased back into the river and pushed the throttle forward, all the way. Once at top speed, he thought to himself, so Sam has probably narrowed down his list of suspects, and the senator was likely a recent addition to the list. It seems like people are intimidated by the senator, so he must be very powerful, very connected, very slippery and very dangerous. I'll just have to learn what makes this senator tick, and what makes him squirm. Even the best of them have weakness that can be identified and exploited. Politicians, without fail, have the most glaring weaknesses and closets full of skeletons they somehow think no one knows about. I have some research to do when I get to Virginia. I need to find the senator's weaknesses and rattle a few of those skeletons. This could be fun.

Chapter 7

Once he could see his house, Jimmy turned toward Kara and put his finger to his lips to let her know to be quiet, and then motioned her to sit on the log beside where he stood. When she sat, Jimmy took a seat beside her and began to scan his house and the surrounding area. Blue, a few yards in front of them, turned and watched them sit, then whimpered once. The dog looked longingly toward the house, then back at Jimmy, and reluctantly came and sat between Jimmy and Kara. Jimmy rubbed the dog's neck, but never stopped scanning the area for signs of other people.

Kara also scanned, but mostly kept her sights on the house. It looked strikingly like Ned's, with the mountain-rock walls and metal roof. It was also a two-story structure, and while there were plenty of windows, those on the first floor were all high off the ground. She noted that they would be difficult to enter, and concluded that it was an intentional feature. There were no trees or bushes within 40 yards in any direction, nor were there any boulders, depressions or other features common to the area. It was as if the entire perimeter had been cleared.

She whispered, "Why is the house so alone in the opening when the area is so rich with trees and other natural features? Don't you think that's a bit odd and unnatural?"

Jimmy spoke without affecting his gaze. "Two reasons: First, forest fires are fairly common around here, and when the big fires get loose, they burn everything in their paths, including houses. No fuel, no fire. That's also why there's a metal roof, so that embers can't fall on it and set the whole place on fire, and that's why there are no bushes or other fuel near the house. And second, so I can see anyone coming way before they get to the house. In my experience, those who have bad intentions are reluctant to be out in the open, and as you can see, the house is in the open. No shadows to stay in, and no trees, rocks or gullies to hide in. If they are still dead set on coming after the house, their chances of arriving are diminished if I don't want them to get there."

Kara thought a few seconds before responding. "Makes sense, if you expect an all out assault or a raging inferno. And, Jimmy, you said 'in my experience.' What was that experience that made you design your house like a fortress?"

Jimmy smiled. "Aw, I'm an old mountain country boy. That's just the way we think. Probably goes back to the days of moonshining when the Revenuers used to come and burn people out of their homes, or when a competitor wanted his to be the only still in the mountains. They would kill people to make sure they got all the business because they had to feed their families, too. The more liquor business you took from the other man, the less they had to feed their families with." He looked at her and smiled, "You remember our conversation about what people will do if they're hungry?"

Kara shivered. "I remember, and I guess you have a valid point."

Jimmy said, "One that will come in handy if your friends from Washington find out you're here." Kara shivered again, and slid a little closer to Jimmy. He might be as foreign to her as an alien, but he was certainly a good ally to have.

After a few more minutes, Jimmy stood and said to Kara, "Let's go check the gate and see if anyone has come in since I left this morning. But stay quiet. We'll keep to the woods as we make our rounds. I want to double lock the gate and set the alarms, along with a few other things that will make us more secure."

Jimmy winked and started through the woods quietly, as if he were hunting. Kara was amazed at how quickly and silently he moved, and she tried to step where he stepped and keep his quick pace. It was impossible for her to do, but she surprised herself at how much quieter she was than when she hadn't been trying to maintain stealth. She watched Jimmy carefully, noticing that he walked a little like a cat. He was careful to place each foot on a rock or on bare dirt as much as possible, and he reached down with his foot and felt what was beneath his shoe before shifting his weight. It reminded her of when her pet cat would stalk prey. She wondered if they were stalking, or if they were the prey.

Chapter 8

After the long drive to Virginia, Ned turned onto his gravel driveway and started up the mountain through a thick canopy of various hardwoods and hemlock trees, as well as the laurel thicket that was so dense and dark that it felt like a cave. He bent over and reached into the glove box and retrieved his pistol, a .45 Smith and Wesson model 1911. It was heavy and felt that way in Ned's hand, but in return it packed a heavy punch to anyone or anything on the bad end of it. Ned slowed to a crawl and slid the pistol from its holster and ejected the magazine. He checked the chamber to ensure it was empty, then confirmed that the magazine was full before reinserting it into the handle of the gun. He slid the pistol back into the holster, leaned the gun barrel down into the cup holder in the console and resumed his drive.

A half-mile later he rounded the curve to find Jimmy's truck, but no Jimmy. He surveyed the house, taking note of the open upstairs window and the bullet hole in its frame and the rifle on the ground. He turned the truck around and parked it a few feet away from and parallel to Jimmy's truck. Now he was protected on two sides.

He stood from the vehicle and quietly looked around. He unfastened his belt and slid it through the holster, then refastened the belt. The pistol sat on his right hip. He leaned into his Toyota Land Cruiser, retrieved his cell phone and dialed Jimmy's number. No answer. So he got out and quietly, stealthily circled his house, careful to stay concealed in the trees, never getting closer than 50 yards from the house.

Ned slid the rack on his pistol and chambered a round. He surveyed the house, approached it carefully, picked up the rifle and moved quickly to the house where he leaned against the rock outer wall. The rifle was his. It was the Winchester 30-30 he kept by his bed. It was easy to identify by the long scratch in the stock that had come from a hunting trip ages ago.

Ned circled the house carefully and circled it again, taking a wider radius the second time. Aside from the footprints near the vehicles, the bullet hole and the rifle, the only evidence he found of other people was the area of turned up leaves and scattered debris near his hidden tunnel entrance. There had been a struggle. Ned sat with his back against a large oak and pieced together the scene. Someone had run from the tunnel and a struggle ensued. After looking around, he saw broken bits of plastic next to a tree a few feet away, and disturbed leaves indicating that two or more people had walked away through the woods ... in the direction of Jimmy's house. He pulled himself up and walked over to the broken bits of plastic, picked up a few of the pieces. He wasn't sure, but it looked as if the plastic had come from an electronic device. He thought for a few minutes before turning and walking back to his house for a close inspection. The front and side doors had been damaged, as if someone had taken a sledge hammer to them in an unsuccessful effort to get into the house. Two of the windows had similar damage.

Ned removed his keys from his front pocket and unlocked the two locks on the door closest to the drive. As he turned the key, he heard the heavy, spring loaded steel rods slide from their four points of contact in the steel frame. He put his keys back in his pocket and pulled the pistol from its holster. He slowly opened the door and stepped in, quickly stepping to the side, his back to the wall. He stood and let his eyes adjust to the dimly lit room. After a few minutes, he could see that someone had eaten.

There was a half-eaten plate of food on the table and a half empty glass of white wine on the table. He made the rounds of his house, inspecting every door and window, and checking every closet and likely hiding place.

Nothing other than the kitchen looked disturbed, until he got to his upstairs bedroom. He walked over and closed and secured the window. He moved to the bathroom. Someone had showered. A used towel hung on the rack. Ned felt it. It was dry. There were also hairs on the counter and in his hair brush. Long, auburn hairs. He slid the pistol back into the holster and pulled his phone from his pocket. He dialed Jimmy's number. No answer.

Ned looked closely at the food on the table, and touched the bread. Hard, maybe a day or two old, but not dried out. He had a decision to make. He could stay here, or he could drive over to Jimmy's. He preferred to do the latter, but he knew about Jimmy's protective measures, and he didn't want to be the victim. Jimmy had laser motion detectors, cameras, an electrified gate, three different heavy steel barriers he could swing across his driveway and lock, his dog, and then there was the defense arsenal Jimmy kept in his house and a couple of other strategic places on the property. Ned knew that Jimmy was never a threat to pick a fight, only to finish it. He had heard stories about times in Iraq and Afghanistan when Jimmy had to fight his way out of impossible situations. Jimmy had fought literally down to tooth and nail to save his fellow soldiers and himself from enemy fighters, and he had come through it each time with nothing more than cuts, bruises and stories he couldn't tell.

Not long after they had met, Ned and Jimmy went to town one night in southwestern Virginia for supplies. Jimmy walked out into the dark parking lot ahead of Ned and was putting groceries into the back of

Ned's truck when four punks emptied out of a nearby car and circled around behind him. Ned had just walked out of the store to see the event unfold. He could see one of the punks pull a gun on Jimmy and point it in his face, and another of them took a step toward Jimmy with a big knife. With speed that surprised Ned and belied Jimmy's appearance, in a smooth motion Jimmy swiped the gun aside with his left hand and took it from the punk.

He side-stepped the lunging knife, cocked his knee and kicked the punk holding it in the chin, sending him back three yards in an unconscious heap. Pointing the gun at the punk directly in front of him, Jimmy kicked him in the balls with his right foot, and with full rotation of his upper body, landed his left elbow squarely on the nose of the punk who was rushing him from his left. The one remaining punk raised his hands over his shoulders as he backpedaled into the corner of a parked car and sprawled backward on the ground.

By that time, Ned was a few feet away. The punk got to his feet and turned to run, toward Ned, while looking back to see if Jimmy was coming after him. Ned's instincts took over and he planted an elbow into the punk's chin. The punk crumpled backward and fell motionless.

The punk Jimmy had kicked in the balls struggled up to his feet. He reached in his back pocket and retrieved a knife, but Jimmy put a looping right-hand punch on the punk's forehead, sending him a few feet over on his side, motionless. Jimmy took the magazine from the gun and slid it into his back pocket. He racked the slide so that the chambered bullet landed in his right palm, and he put the bullet in his front pocket.

After that, Ned always felt confident that it would take an inhuman effort or very large weapons to defeat Jimmy. He was a good neighbor to have, and a good ally, but not the person you want to walk up on in a dark alley without identifying yourself.

That was a factor as Ned considered his options. He could stay put and keep calling Jimmy. He could walk to Jimmy's, following the tracks he saw in the woods if that's where they led, or he could drive over. Ned decided to drive over, after some preparation.

Ned walked upstairs to his bedroom and into his closet. He reached to the top of the shelving unit and clicked the release, and pulled it until the unit swung back into the closet. Ned then put his right hand in the sensor, heard the muffled click of the lock disengaging, and pulled the heavy steel vault door until it swung open. He reached inside the door and waved his hand to activate the motion sensor, lighting the room.

He walked into the cedar-lined steel vault, which had two tall cabinet doors along the left wall that held his long guns and ammunition, and smaller rows of cabinets on the right that held his pistols, ammunition, several knives, binoculars, cell phones, two satellite phones, GPS navigation units, handheld weather radios, shortwave radios and FM communication radios, as well as passport and ID packs and satchels of cash and other survival gear. Four full backpacks hung on each side of the door; the two on the right were for extended stays in the mountains, and the two on the left were for short, quick jaunts.

On the far end of the room on the left was a large desk with unrolled maps of the area laid out on one side, and on the other rested a large shortwave radio transmitter, satellite phone and a control unit for his security system and other apparatus. Mounted on the wall were two flat screens, one for security cameras, controlled by a keyboard on the desk, and a CPU built in beneath it from which he could control all security features in the house, including locking the doors and gates. In the ceiling in the far-right corner was a door with a rotating handle like in a submarine. He hadn't had to use the door, and hoped he never would — it was only for emergencies. The hatch door led to the attic, which was built with dropping panels that served as gun turrets if needed.

Ned selected an automatic shotgun and buckshot shells, and a Browning X-Bolt .270 rifle and three magazines of ammunition. He also selected a HK .45 Compact pistol, three full magazines and an ankle holster. Checking all three weapons to make sure the chambers were empty, he loaded each, slid the HK into an ankle holster and attached it to the inside of his left leg, and put the extra magazines and shells into one of the small backpacks that hung on the wall. He closed up the cabinets, turned off the light, stepped out of the room and locked it up.

Ned slid into the seat of his truck and put the backpack on the passenger seat beside him. He removed the full-sized .45 from his hip holster and stuck it barrel first into the console cup holder. He took a deep breath, started the truck and started down the driveway. He hoped he wouldn't need any of the weapons, but someone had been in his house, damaged the exterior trying to get in, and left a slug in the upstairs window frame.

The question was, who had been in his house and how had they gained entrance, since the attempts to break into a window or door had failed. It had to be Jimmy, since he was the only person he knew that had a key, but why was Jimmy's truck at his house, and the most burning questions: Where was Jimmy now? Who had walked through the woods? Why had any of this happened? He had no answers, but he intended to change that.

*****

Detective Sam Strickland leaned toward the woman as she lay in bed. She was no longer in intensive care; she'd been moved to a private room. Her eyes fluttered as she tried to wake up. Sam said, "Miss? I am detective Strickland, and I would like to continue our conversation if you feel up to it."

She opened her eyes, frantically scanning the room as if she was looking for someone in particular that meant her harm. Seeing no one but the detective, she asked, "Who are you?"

"Detective Sam Strickland of the Charleston Police Department. I'm here to help you. You're safe here. There are two undercover policemen in the hall, and at least two near each entrance to the hospital. There will also be someone with you in the room at all times. You are as safe as we can make you."

The woman tried to sit up, but winced in pain and laid back. She appeared terrified, and looked Sam in the eye as she said, "You can't keep me safe!"

Sam leaned in, "Why do you say that, ma'am?"

The woman's eyes were wide with fear.

Sam continued, "We know it was someone powerful who shot you, but we aren't sure who. If you tell us, we can arrest him and get this whole thing over with."

The woman burst out with a sarcastic laugh. "Arrest him? You? You're just a city policeman, you can't arrest him." Sam leaned back in his chair. "Why do you say that?" The woman replied, "He's way too powerful. He'll find out who you are and do to you what he tried to do to me." Sam said calmly, "I seriously doubt that a man will complicate the mess he's in by killing a policeman. Shooting a woman in a lovers' quarrel is bad enough, but he won't get the chair for that. Killing a policeman is a different ball game." The woman laughed again. "Lovers' quarrel? You think this is a crime of passion? Is that what you think? Detective, you're in way over your head."

Sam sat up straight and said, "So if it isn't a lovers' quarrel, what is it?"

The woman's face sobered with seriousness and fear. She said, "This is about power. Getting power, and keeping power, both of which result in large amounts of money that ultimately belongs to other people. He didn't shoot me over a lovers' spat, he shot me because of what I know."

Sam felt a chill. "What is it that you know that someone would kill you   for?"

The woman said flatly, "He shot me because he found out that I know about the four other people he and his goons have killed during the past three years. I saw the last one, and he himself pulled the trigger. They made him do the deed. I suspected something sinister was going on,   so   I   followed   him   one   night." Sam discretely reached into his front pocket and pushed the record button on the compact recorder.

The woman continued, with a look of regret on her face, "I thought he was fooling around with yet another woman, so I followed him in downtown Columbia last Thursday. He and two other men drove to a house in the old rich area downtown. I parked a block away and sneaked into the yard of the house and hid in the shadows until I found a window I could see them through. I got close enough to see them and hear their voices, but I couldn't hear their words. I'll never forget what I saw. I think they made him do it, but I saw the Senator put a gun to the back of a man's head and pull the trigger. When it happened, I gasped, and he must have heard me. He looked up and I think he must have recognized me, because when we were in the car in Charleston, he started asking me where I was last Thursday.

I told him that I was home, but he didn't believe me and he lost his cool. He started yelling that he was going send me away for good, and that I could never speak of it and never come back to the U.S. I got mad then and told him I was going to the press and the police. He punched me in the side of the head, and I jumped out of the car and started to run."

The woman looked down at her bandages and a tear ran down her cheek as she said, "That's when he did this to me? And he'll find me and finish the job, or his people will. He is connected to this man in New York who pulls all the strings, and he is a bad man."

Sam's heart sank a little, although he was only mildly surprised by what the woman told him. Trying to comfort her, he said, "We told the news that you had died from your wounds. In fact, your funeral was this morning. We couldn't find any family members or close friends, so only our people and a few reporters showed up, but you had a nice funeral. You're safe, miss."

The woman didn't smile or cry, just said, "No, detective, I'm dead, or will be soon, and so will anyone else they suspect I talked to. That means you." The woman looked him right in the eye and said, "Get your affairs in order, because your funeral will be soon."

Chapter 9

Ned stopped his truck several yards short of the locked gate on Jimmy's driveway. He dialed Jimmy's number again; still no answer. He would have to walk in to get to Jimmy's house. He backed up his truck and parked on the right side of the gravel and dirt road, taking care to get over as far as he could so he wouldn't block the road. He got out of the truck and slid his .45 back into its holster. He reached in and grabbed the backpack and his rifle, and locked up the truck. The gate across Jimmy's road was five feet high and he would have to climb over it.

Ned walked up to the gate and looked to his right at the small electrical control box. On the box, a small green light was lit, which meant the gate had not been electrified. Ned maneuvered his rifle between the cross bars, turned it and leaned it butt down against the fence beside the gate.

Many a hunter had shot himself or a bystander while climbing over a fence. That was one of the first lessons Ned learned when he began hunting as a young boy. He could still hear his father's voice when they approached a fence, "More hunting accidents have happened when climbing a fence with a gun in hand. We don't have accidents, and we don't climb fences with our guns."

Ned climbed to the top of the tall gate and swung his leg over to the other side. He paused and waved in the direction of the security camera Jimmy had hidden in the nearby hemlock tree. "It's me, Ned, and I'm coming to see you." As Ned swung his other leg over the top of the fence, his lofty perch gave him an earlier view of the roof of a vehicle a half-mile back. Atop a fence was no place to be with people approaching, especially since he had had uninvited company that left damage and a bullet hole in his house, so Ned hastened his pace, jumping the last couple of feet to the ground. He picked up his rifle and quickly moved into the forest, making sure to get higher and hidden behind something that would conceal and protect him. He disappeared into the shadows just before the black Ford car slid to a stop a few feet short of the gate. Two men got out, one from the front passenger seat and one from the back on the same side of the car.

Ned reached into this pocket and switched his phone to silent mode, and raised his head a little higher from behind the gray, lichen-covered boulder. He got his binoculars from the backpack. He wanted a good look at the men, and the glasses would shrink the 60 yards that lay between him and them. He looked at the first man. Dark hair, clean cut in a suit, all business. He looked like an FBI agent. Ned looked at the second man. Similar build and description, but the man had his face turned away from Ned. Then he turned. Ned's pulse hastened. These men weren't FBI; these were bad men.

Ned recognized the man who turned, and his memories of their prior meeting were not good. This man was a killer, and he liked to kill slowly. He would experiment with ways to inflict pain and prolong the agony. Ned had seen one of his victims in Afghanistan. The army had contracted this man to interrogate terrorists, and the man always got results. The only problem was that the people he interrogated always died during the process.

Ned had come into an abandoned building during the war to find this man torturing an Afghani civilian suspected of being a member of Al Qaeda. A woman and three young children lay mutilated on the floor nearby, and the prisoner had just died. He wore a look of frozen terror as if his eternity would be spent in a hell similar to the one he had just suffered.

The man Ned now looked at through the binoculars had tortured the man's family one at a time over the course of three days while the man sat tied to a support column watching the carnage until it was his turn. Ned had been struck by the medieval nature of the scene and by the calm coolness of the look in the interrogator's eyes. The man simply had no conscience, and that's why the Army hired him. And now the man was in Virginia, on Jimmy's property, wanting in. By instinct, Ned picked up the rifle and aimed it, but the man ducked into the back of the car, and the other man got into the front of the car and closed the door. Ned couldn't see even a profile of the men through the tinted windows. No shot.

They sat for several minutes. Ned imagined they were talking on the phone, getting instructions from whomever was giving them, and Ned wanted to know who that was. Then the car backed up until it was behind Ned's truck. His license number; they were going to find out who the other visitor was before they made a decision. After another five minutes, the car made a three point turn and backed up to the gate. The driver got out and walked over to look at the gate and lock. He had a look of disgust, having concluded that he didn't have the proper equipment to break through, so he walked back to the car, leaned over and told his companions the bad news.

The two passengers got out of the car and clumsily climbed to the top of the gate. The man who looked like the FBI agent jumped the last three feet to the ground and landed awkwardly, letting out a yelp. He sat there for a minute or so, and finally stood up and took a couple of gingerly steps to make sure he could still walk. The interrogator clearly admonished him, although Ned couldn't hear what was said. Then the two of them began to walk toward Jimmy's house, still a long way off for the injured man. Ned stood quietly, slid into the backpack and picked up his rifle.

Ned was going with the men to Jimmy's house, but he wasn't walking with them. Ned would stick to the woods, never losing sight of the men, never allowing them to see him. The day just got more interesting.

*****

Jimmy walked back into his house after checking his security measures, bolted the door behind him and walked through the mudroom into the kitchen. He was greeted with the welcoming aroma of bacon and the pleasant sight of a pretty woman.

Kara turned and said, "I hope you don't mind. I was starving. Breakfast food was the best alternative of the food you have that isn't frozen, although I'll say that you have an impressive supply of meats and vegetables in your freezer."

Jimmy replied, "The closest store is 43 miles away, and winter storms can lay you in for days at a time. Last year we were socked in for 17 days before the roads were passable. It took me two days to clear my road, and I had a bulldozer. I'd be a mighty thin man if I didn't lay in a good supply of food."

Kara replied, "If that happened in Washington, most people would order Chinese or Italian or whatever they wanted and have it delivered. So what would you do out here?"

Jimmy laughed. "First of all, if I couldn't get in or out with a bulldozer, and the main roads were impassable, the only way someone could deliver anything would be by helicopter. Bulldozers are a lot more common than helicopters around here. Anyway, even in good weather, no one would deliver food way out here. When you live this far from town, the only time people will show up with food is if you die and they are holding a wake. I think I prefer my freezer."

Kara served two plates and set them on the table. She asked, "You going to eat?"

Jimmy didn't reply, he just sat down and started eating. He didn't speak again until his plate was cleared of food, then he stood and grabbed dirty dishes and pans and took them to the sink and began washing them.

His chore was interrupted by a shrill beeping alarm from a small alcove off the kitchen. His motion alarm at his gate had just sounded. Probably a deer or bear, but in light of what he had seen earlier in the day, he was going to check. Jimmy walked into the alcove and looked at the monitor mounted on the wall to see a man climbing his gate. Jimmy touched the controls and zoomed in on the man, now straddling the top of the gate. It was Ned, and he waved at the camera. Jimmy swung the camera until he could see Ned's truck parked on the side of the road. He swung the camera back to Ned in time to see him tense up and look intently down the road, then hastily climbed down from the gate, grab his rifle and quickly head straight into the woods toward the camera, then beyond it. Someone else was coming.

Jimmy called to Kara, "You might want to come see this."

Kara walked in to see the screen filled with a view of a truck parked alongside the dirt road just beyond a gate. She said gloomily, "We have visitors. And so soon!"

Jimmy turned slightly and said, "That truck belongs to our friend Ned, but he's just run into the forest. It's the next visitors that might be a problem."

Kara asked, "What next visitors? I don't see anyone."

Before Jimmy could reply, a black Ford roared over the crest of the hill and into view, skidded to a stop in front of the gate, and two men got out. Neither Kara nor Jimmy spoke again until the men were standing by the gate and Jimmy zoomed in on them. He asked, "You know these men?"

Kara felt a chill. "I've never seen the man in the suit, but the other one, the cold looking one, was one of the men who tried to get into Ned's house. He's an evil looking man. I actually shot at him, but clearly I missed. He's bad news, which means the other guy is, as well. This is bad."

They watched until the two men began their walk down Jimmy's long driveway, leaving the one man – whom Kara had never seen – sitting in the car. After they were out of view, Jimmy turned and said, "We have about 30 minutes until they get here.

We could make a run for it, but this house is stone and metal for the most part, and the window glass will reject or slow down most bullets and nearly all people. I built this house before I built Ned's.

"When Ned saw my house, he snooped around for a while and asked me to build him a home similar to this one. I did. Anyway, we have a lot more protection here than if we run off into the forest, but we always have that option if it goes badly. Like Ned, I have a hidden entrance to the house, and there are three heavy steel doors between the mouth of the escape tunnel and my house. It's a serious advantage for us, and it can be a great hiding place and an exit in case we decide to take to the woods. I doubt we'll need to, but keep your gear nearby."

Kara hadn't taken her eyes from the screen. She asked, "Are there any other cameras closer to the house?" Jimmy turned back to the control panel and pushed a button to switch the view to the next closest to the house. No one there. He pushed another button and the picture showed two men walking with guns in their hands, one scuffling along with a limp. Jimmy moved his hand to a stick control and swung the camera until it was pointed into the woods.

Kara asked, "Why did you do that?"

Jimmy answered, "I'm looking for Ned, but as I suspected, I can't see him."

Jimmy turned to Kara and said, "You better come with me." Jimmy led Kara up a flight of stairs, then into his bedroom closet. Kara heard latches and locking mechanisms click open.

Jimmy said, "Follow me," and he led her into a vault identical to the one in Ned's home. He looked at Kara and asked, "You have any experience with guns?"

She brushed back a strand of auburn hair and replied, "I didn't always live in the city. I grew up on a farm in North Carolina.

"My dad taught us to shoot as soon as we could bear the weight of a gun."

Jimmy asked, "What was your weapon of choice?" Kara replied, "It depended on the job at hand. I used an automatic 12 gauge shotgun for bird hunting or to run off trespassers, carried a 9 millimeter on my hip any time I was out on the land, and hunted with a Winchester 30/30. It was my favorite."

Jimmy raised his eyebrows. "I underestimated you."

Kara replied, "Many a man has done the same, and it often works in my favor."

She smiled and winked. Jimmy reached into a cabinet and pulled out a Winchester 30/30. He cocked the handle to check the chamber and handed her the weapon barrel down. He reached back into the cabinet, turned and handed Kara four boxes of shells.

Jimmy stepped over to a different cabinet. Kara heard the unmistakable sound of a pistol slide racking as Jimmy checked the chamber. He handed her a 9 mm 1911 Smith and Wesson pistol, and a leather belt and holster. He said, "There are eight loaded magazines of 10 rounds on the belt." He turned again, reached and handed three boxes of shells to Kara and said, "Here is more ammo if you need it."

Jimmy selected his own weapon. He strapped on a Smith and Wesson 1911 .45 pistol with a belt holding eight magazines. He stepped over to the larger cabinet and selected an automatic Remington 750 Woodsmaster with shoulder strap, and a shoulder belt with another eight loaded magazines. He also picked up a short Beretta 12 gauge shotgun and box of buckshot shells.

He turned to Kara and said, "I'm going to open the hatch at the top of the ladder in the corner. Once I do that, I want you to climb up into the attic and let me hand you these rifles and the shotgun. I'll check each chamber to make sure it's empty, and will hand you the weapons stock first. The important thing here is to keep your hands and fingers away from the triggers. Got it?"

Kara nodded and stepped toward the corner, checking chambers as she stepped. Jimmy climbed up and wrestled the hatch door open, then stepped back from the ladder.

Kara started up, and Jimmy noticed again how nicely she was built. He thought to himself that she was almost as attractive from behind as she was in front, and that was good. He shoved aside the thoughts and got on with the task at hand. Kara looked down through the hatch and said, "Ready."

Jimmy checked the chamber on the Winchester and handed it up to here stock first. He looked at her hand placement, and she was following his directions.

He did the same with the shotgun and the Remington, then handed up extra boxes of ammunition. He also handed up two small packs, just like the ones Ned had in his weapons vault. The packs contained knives, food and water, flashlights, lighters and maps of the area.

Jimmy looked at his watch. Six minutes had passed. They had to hustle. Jimmy climbed up quickly and shut the hatch behind him. He picked up his rifle and shotgun and walked over to the south wall. He leaned the weapons there, and walked back and retrieved the ammunition. He led Kara over to the east wall. Jimmy reached up and slid two bolt locks free and swung down a one-foot wide panel that was about eight horizontal feet long. It rested like a shelf against three supports.

Jimmy said, "These walls are stone all the way up to this shelf, and there is a quarter inch sheet of steel on the inside. If any bullet passes through that, it's coming from a tank or fighter aircraft. Not many of those around. The north and west walls are the same, and we'll get to those if we need to. And listen, this is important. Ned is in those woods somewhere, so make sure who you're shooting at. You have a scope on that rifle. Use it and be sure."

Kara looked out over the driveway to her right, and the open lawn and forest in front of her and to her left. Jimmy hustled over and opened the south wall shelf, which overlooked the open south lawn, the driveway, the barn and woods beyond.

Jimmy could hear Kara sliding cartridges into the Winchester, followed by the racking of her pistol as she chambered a round. Good. She was ready.

Jimmy did the same, followed by sliding five shells into the shotgun, which he leaned back against the wall when he finished. He concentrated his gaze on the driveway and the nearby woods. As he racked a round into the chamber of his pistol, he heard Kara say excitedly but muted, "Here they come!"

There they were, the two men, one limping. They stopped 80 yards out and had a conversation. After some discussion, the limping man handed the rifle to the man with the cold expression and headed toward the barn. The cold one headed up into the woods on the east side of the driveway. Jimmy said to Kara, "Keep your scope on the man in the woods. I'll track the other one."

Kara said, "He's moving toward us from tree to tree."

At that moment, Jimmy watched the limping man emerge from the other side of the barn. He had passed behind the barn, and was trying to flank them and approach from the rear of the house. Jimmy quietly moved to the west wall and lowered the shelf. He looked down to see the man about twenty yards from the house, and he had something red in his left hand. Jimmy looked a little closer. A gas can! They were going to try and burn them out. The man edged closer to the house. When he got to it, he began dousing the back door with gasoline, and backed up while pouring a trail of gas. When he got twenty feet out, he pulled a lighter from his pocket and began to bend over to light the gas covered ground. Jimmy couldn't let him do it. He clicked off the safety of his rifle and aimed carefully. He put his index finger on the trigger. The man sparked the lighter. Jimmy began to squeeze.

*****

Chris Johnson had been on the phone with several connections. First, the most important one; the money connection and power behind the throne, Nicholas Bedekoski.

This was the man he was most concerned about, and he was the man to whom he had, and always would, devote his loyalty, although he would never say that to the senator. Mr. Bedekoski was an eastern European immigrant who had made billions trading on various commodities.

No matter what he invested in, he won. Not because he could see the future of financial markets, but because he had so much money and so many unscrupulous connections that he manipulated the market to his favor.

His favorite was betting on currency futures, mostly that a chosen currency would lose value, and that's where the bulk of his money came from. He would short the currency, then release pre-prepared information to selected members of the press. The stories ranged from a rumored grave illness of a country's leader to a fabrication about the upcoming decisions of the Federal Reserve Board related to currency policy. Illegal? Absolutely, and ruthless as well. Many people had been ruined because of his actions, but he didn't care. He had two goals that he would stop at nothing to achieve: to own or control the most money of anyone in the world, and to actually control the world through the guise of fairness, which in itself was a guise for concentration, consolidation and controlling all the world's sources of wealth.

The Trojan Horse of the system was to create a world where everyone had enough money, food and housing to live a good life, without the divisions of wealth in today's capitalistic societies. But in reality, the end result of such systems was always the same – a privileged few owned all the wealth and freedom while everyone else existed on the scraps those in power would toss them to keep them in line.

Bedekowski was always amused at how many people would do anything he asked, no matter how unthinkable, only so they could remain part of or earn their way into his good graces and to be on his list of the privileged when he ran the world, which he was certain to do. His last remaining domino was the United States, and he was very close to having that in his pocket as well.

He already 'owned' the press, all the universities and the preparatory educational system, had made great strides in the Supreme Court, Congress, and he also owned the last of the three branches of U.S. government, the executive branch. He would continue to own that after the upcoming election was over and Senator Evan Lee took his oath of office.

Evan Lee was the perfect candidate. Most important, he was charismatic and had a unique ability to make crowds and TV audiences believe him, and more incredulously, like him. He came off as a smart, strong, principled leader, which couldn't be further from reality.

Bedekowski chuckled to himself at how gullible people were, especially these dumb Americans. These people live in the richest country in the world with, until lately, the most independent, self reliant citizens. That was before he began his work three decades ago to dismantle the country from within. Now the entire country was weak, lazy and stupid, the majority looking for a free ride no matter the cost. And the senator was about to help him seal the deal once and for all.

After the election, all U.S. powers would be granted to the United Nations, and he had owned that organization since its inception. He would keep a puppet leader in place there, and the senator was naïve enough to believe it would be him, and that he would actually be the one making the decisions, with the riches of the world at his beckon call. He would be able to do what he wanted, any time he wanted, with the woman he chose that day, and cost or laws wouldn't matter. That's what the senator thought, and he couldn't have been more wrong. Bedekowski had special plans for the senator, and they were not similar to the senator's.

Bedekowski was thinking about all of this when his private phone rang. Only a few people had that number and they knew the threshold any call had to meet before they dialed the number, so this was an important call. He picked up the phone, but didn't say anything. The line was "secure" according to the Homeland Security leader, but Bedekowski knew more about the National Security Agency (NSA) and their capabilities than any of those stupid political appointees in government. He knew because he had a hand in the creation of the agency, and he used them often to recover or obtain information that was otherwise unobtainable.

He used their services often in his financial endeavors, but as much as he used them, he didn't trust them. If he could pay them off or threaten them or their family members with violence, so could someone else, and when you're the richest man in the world, you have enemies.

So the voice at the other end of the phone spoke. "Chris Johnson here. We need to meet immediately. I will be at our usual park bench in NYNY at 7 p.m. tonight."

That was it. The phone went dead. Bedekowski knew that Chris Johnson was the one in charge of making sure the senator didn't do anything stupid enough to jeopardize his soon-to-be presidency, and Bedekowski knew what a colossal job that was. If Chris needed to see him, that meant that he hadn't been able to perform his job successfully, and that he would have to make another of the senator's blunders disappear beneath the radar. It's not that he couldn't do it, he had saved the asses of many a politician in the past, and two of them had been presidents. Both of them stole countless amounts of money through their positions in office, and both of them were womanizers, but one – and ironically the smartest – had a nasty habit of seducing underage students, which by U.S. law was considered rape. And the man, as most egotistical men have done at some point, let his genitals override his brain and he had an ongoing affair with a young intern.

The most powerful man in the world had had sex with young women numerous times in the White House, in the Oval Office, no less. And, the most powerful man in the world let a young intern outwit him. She kept evidence, and the press was the first to know about it, so it was too late for him to prevent release of the information, and the girl had given the information to the one news organization he didn't completely control.

The senator was of that womanizer ilk. He often let his brain function defer to the rise in his pants, and he had had to clean up several disasters in the past. This was certain to be yet another of the long line of philandering politicians. He looked at his watch. Five hours until he met with Chris.

Chapter 10

Ned watched the man he met in Iraq walking through the woods, going from tree to tree and keeping his stare locked on the house below. It was obvious the man wasn't used to being out in the mountains, and he didn't appear to be very experienced with a gun since he had his finger on the trigger of the rifle. Must be that the Iraq vet liked to torture incapacitated prisoners, but wasn't comfortable out doing the fighting where the opposition could shoot back.

The man was making so much noise Ned could take the luxury of watching the house and still know where the man was and whether or not he was moving. Ned saw the other man limp behind the barn and emerge on the other side with a gas can in his hand. Ned watched as the man poured gas on the door and into the yard, and bent over to light it. Ned knew that if he took a shot he would give away his location and the other man would know where he was. But he couldn't let the man with the gas can complete his mission and set Jimmy's house on fire. He took careful aim, let out half a breath and began to squeeze the trigger.

That's when he saw the gas can tumble backwards and heard the gunshot. Jimmy, or someone in his house, had shot the gas can. The man with the lighter turned and began running as fast as he could with his injured leg. He was headed for the woods a hundred yards to Ned's left. The threat neutralized for now, Ned turned his attention to the Iraq veteran. The man was still in the same spot looking at the action from behind a large hemlock tree. Ned decided to go have a little chat with the man, and began easing his way over. He would approach the man from behind.

Three minutes later Ned was 10 feet behind the man. Ned put his rifle in his left hand and picked up a rock the size of a grapefruit. He reared back and threw the rock at the man's head. There was a boom with a hollow ring as the rock made impact with the back of the man's head. The rifle the man held tumbled to the ground, and he went limp like a ragdoll.

Ned walked over, picked up the man's rifle, crutched his own under his right arm, and racked the chamber of the man's gun until no more bullets ejected. Then he swung the rifle into the side of a hemlock tree so hard that the barrel bent about 30 degrees. No one would ever shoot that rifle again.

Ned leaned his rifle against a tree and pulled out the .45, which he moved to his left hand. He stepped over to the man, who was bleeding from the cut the rock left on his scalp. The man was unconscious but breathing. Ned holstered the .45 and went through the man's pockets.

He found a wallet with a few hundred dollars in it. He put the cash and the wallet in his own pocket. He also found a large knife with a five-inch razor-sharp blade. He had seen that knife before in Iraq, and he had seen what this nasty man liked to do with it. Ned finished his search, finding nothing more. He took the knife over to a rock, picked up another and beat the knife until the blade was a bent scrap of metal. He threw what remained of the knife off into the woods, and turned back to the man and pulled off his army-issue boots. Ned removed the laces, which were tough, woven cordage, and used them to tie the man to a foot-thick tree, his hands laced behind him and around the tree, and his feet tied to another tree a few feet away. Ned stood. If the man came to any time soon, he wouldn't be going anywhere. Ned turned and started in the direction where the limping intruder had gone. One down, one to go.

*****

Kara said to Jimmy over her shoulder, "I see Ned in the woods, and I can see the other man, too."

Jimmy came and stood to her left, watching as the limping man ran behind the barn, then circled into the woods in Ned's general direction. Kara showed Jimmy where Ned was. Jimmy kept his binoculars focused on the limping man until he couldn't see him through the trees. Jimmy thought he was hiding behind a clump of boulders about 80 yards up the mountain, but he couldn't be sure.

They both watched Ned hit the Iraq torturer in the head with the rock, search his pockets and tie him to a tree. They watched as Ned headed off toward the limping man, like spectators at a football game. They grew tense when they saw what happened next.

*****

Ned eased from one tree or boulder to another, careful of his footfalls to stay as quiet as possible. He saw the limping man run into the woods and had an idea of the area the man was in, but not his specific location. Ahead and down to his left, there were several large boulders that it would be easy to hide between. The boulders were three or four feet high, and several feet apart in an irregular circle. Ned had seen the place before, and thought at the time that it would make a good place to take shelter in a windy storm or, the most unlikely of scenarios, under attack. Ned inched his way toward the boulders so he could survey the area in all directions while having good protection from all sides, save for a few gaps on the eastern side, the side closest to him.

Ned was about ten yards from the eastern gap when he saw disturbed leaves and ground. He looked down hill and saw several more places that had been disturbed. A person had made those disturbances, and they might be hiding in the middle of the boulders. He decided to back off by about 30 yards and see if he could gain a vantage point to see inside the boulders. He climbed, moving northward up the mountain. He stopped to take a look. Nothing but the outside surfaces of the boulders. Higher and more westerly. Still nothing. About forty yards to his west was a little ridge running perpendicular to the slope of the mountainside. It jutted out, the last 20 yards or so being a solid rock that jutted out at an angle. He made his way to the small ridge. He moved out to the rock. It was big enough to lie on. If he leaned away from the circle of boulders, it would be a good place to lay down and still have some protection from any shots coming from the boulders. Ned edged his way out, sliding on his belly, his arms and rifle out in front of him. He eased his head up just enough to see into the circle boulders.

He raised up a little higher. He saw a man crouched in the boulders, a pistol in hand aimed in the direction of the house.

The man was expecting his threat to be from the house. He wasn't expecting anyone to be on this ridge above him, and Ned had a very good vantage point and firing position.

Ned heard noise from down the mountain, and the man in the boulders heard it, too because he tensed, raised himself a little higher and to his right, and aimed the pistol in the direction of the noise. Ned looked toward the noise to see Jimmy coming up through the woods toward the circle of boulders, but Ned also saw another person coming … a woman. She wasn't making nearly as much noise. She was on Jimmy's right flank, and had a rifle. She moved as if she was fit and comfortable in the mountains, but she was still too far off for Ned to get a good look at her face.

Jimmy was now 60 yards downhill from the boulders and moving quickly. Jimmy sounded like a mule that was making a desperate escape and running wildly through the woods, but he moved up the hill with amazing speed. Jimmy was strong, even called himself a pack mule at times. But the problem was that he was making so much noise that he couldn't hear anything, and he wasn't looking carefully at the boulders to see the man aiming a pistol at him. If Jimmy kept coming, he would be in the firing line and within range of the man in the boulders.

Jimmy changed course and angled to his right in a northeasterly direction. The man in the boulders crouched down again thinking of his next move, since the man could no longer see Jimmy. Then the man moved and took a crouched position. He was going to wait for Jimmy to come around the boulder by the western entrance and ambush him. Ned could no longer see Jimmy, but he could see the man awaiting him. Ned looked for the woman, but could no longer see her, either.

Ned could hear Jimmy getting closer to the opening in the boulders. He shouted, but Jimmy didn't hear him. The man in the boulders did. He scrambled back into view looking for the source of the person who shouted. He saw Ned and raised his pistol to fire. Ned clicked off his safety and began to squeeze his trigger when he saw the man turn quickly and aim toward the opening of the boulders. It was Jimmy, who began raising his pistol. But the man had the drop on him. Ned fired, and the man crumpled to the ground.

Ned had just placed a rifle shot to the back of the man's skull just above the neck. Jimmy's voice pierced the momentarily silence after the rifle shot as he shouted, "Holy Hell! Good shot!"

Ned made his way down to the boulders, finding Jimmy and woman standing there. Jimmy looked at the woman, but had to stare for a couple of seconds to make sure he was right before saying in a tone of disbelief and surprise, "Kara?"

The moment was interrupted by a loud explosion from the direction of the gate. Ned said, "I think we have another problem, or two. I tied one guy up and left him about 200 yards that way," as he pointed with his left hand."

Kara said, "We watched you from the house."

Ned continued, "We better go see what he has to say, if he's awake, and then go check out the source of that explosion. You two follow me at least thirty yards behind, Jimmy on the uphill, left side and Kara down and to the right."

Kara smiled and said, "It is great to see you."

Ned smiled back and they embraced. Ned said, "It's been a long time … too long, but not so long that I forgot how beautiful you are. You look great, and you're obviously still taking care of yourself. I'm really wondering how and why you're up here in the mountains hunting down bad men, but we can talk about that later."

Kara's smile disappeared and with a serious expression replied, "Until a few minutes ago I was the prey, not the hunter. But I'm afraid it was only a temporary change. Those men were here to kill me. There'll be others. There will always be others."

Ned considered that for a few seconds, then said, "We'll help you sort this out, but first let's go take care of the matter at hand."

They made their way back to where Ned had his prisoner tied up, to find only the remains of the laces that had been cut cleanly, with a sharp knife.

The man was gone, and there was a trail of disturbed leaves leading easterly toward the gate on the driveway. A trail that two people made. The three of them moved in the same spread out fashion they had already used and went to the gate. When they arrived, they found marks where a vehicle had turned around and spun out in a hurry, and the smoldering remains of Ned's truck. He said, "Looks like your friends left their calling card."

Kara said, "Sorry. They're bad men, and they'll be back."

Jimmy said, "Let's get back to the house and figure out our next move. It's too dangerous to be out here in the open with these crazy people around."

They turned and started walking, and as they walked, Jimmy and Kara filled in Ned on what had transpired.

Ned asked Kara who and why people were after her, and she explained, "You see, NSA, which is where I've worked for almost 10 years, has access to every electronic communication of every person in the United States, and most around the world. Emails, phone calls, texts, credit card transactions, roadway toll transactions, anything electronic. We also capture images of every piece of mail that goes through the postal service. All that information is stored in a huge data base in Utah, and we have programs that search key words and alert us when anything is tripped."

Jimmy said, "I knew it! Tyranny at it's finest."

Kara continued, "Be that as it may, it's reality, and that's just the tip of the iceberg. If you piss off the wrong people high enough in government, with a simple order they can sick the IRS, SEC, EPA, and any other government operation, including, Jimmy, the Forest Service."

Jimmy asked, "Is it true that they all have SWAT teams?"

Kara answered, "It's true. Even the Post Office is arming up and it's completely out of hand. The system has spiraled out of control and is there to be used as weapons by those high in government.

"For years abuse was only an occasional occurrence, but now we have an administration that not only doesn't adhere to the Constitution, but holds it in disdain. That's an entirely different discussion, but the point is that they abuse the information to influence, ruin and even kill anyone of their choosing. That has become their modus operandi.

"So I was working one day when I was reviewing some of the reports of tripped communications. It's a fluke, but I stumbled upon a transcript of a conversation between a U.S. Senator and the most powerful and most unscrupulous person on earth, Nicholas Bedekowski. They were discussing arrangements to affect two political elections, one at the state level and one in the U.S. senate. They weren't too deep into details, but the next week the state-level candidate was ruined when information was released to the press that he had beaten his wife during a divorce several years prior. But worse than that, the senate candidate's opponent was killed a few days later in a mysterious plane crash. The cause of the crash was never found because the FAA suddenly closed the investigation. That never happens unless someone of very high pay grade orders it, and it's only happened one other time to my knowledge, over twenty years ago."

Jimmy was enthralled, shaken and validated by the conversation, and said, "I guess I was right all along about how corrupt the government has become. My house out here off the grid is looking better and better."

Kara continued, "So, I started doing some digging and it turns out that Nicholas Bedekowski had similar communications with several other senators and congressmen, and worse, he had similar conversations with the current president. So, this goes all the way to the top. I've kicked the shin of the most powerful and ruthless people on earth, and they don't like it."

Ned said, "The missing links for me are what information you have, and how do they know you have it?"

Kara said, "OK, I'll supply the links. As a matter of routine, I gave my boss a summary of this and all other communications I reviewed. He didn't comment on it, so after a couple of weeks I thought it had been filed without ever being read, like most other government reports.

So I did even more digging, and found many, many communications that all point to the same people with the same motives and the same results, which are that the people that get in their way end up ruined, dead or they disappear."

She continued, "But my boss didn't ignore the report, he sent it up the chain. That's when I had a visit that I'll never forget. I was sitting in a booth at a Washington restaurant when this small, ugly man sat down in front of me and started talking. He told me my name, where I live, about each of my family members, the amounts in my bank accounts, everything. As soon as he started talking, I knew I was in a bad spot, and I turned on the video record function of my phone. He wasn't looking at me then, but at the door to see if anyone came in behind him.

"The man then looked me in the eye with this steely, cold stare and told me that I had better erase the NSA information, never say a word to anyone about it, or that he would send flowers to my memorial service. I told him he was too late because I had already filed the report, and he laughed at that and said that the report was never created, and did not exist."

Ned asked, "But what's different now that made him he switch from warning you to hunting you down?"

Kara said, "I wanted a copy of the video on my phone, so I emailed it to myself and put it on three thumb drives. I sent the drives to three different people, one a friend of mine who works for the Washington Times with the promise that they would never look at it unless I was killed or I contacted her and asked her to print it. Three days later, she was found in the NSA parking lot with her throat cut ear to ear. I thought that my secure NSA email was just that, but clearly not.

"So I decided that I was probably going to die anyway, so I did more research and found another similar communication where Mr. Bedekowski arranged a meeting with a senator that had been very vocal speaking out against him. They were going to meet at the Washington Memorial the next night, so I rented an expensive video recorder and hid in the shrubbery.

I saw, and filmed, Mr. Bedekowski walk around behind the senator and slit his throat so badly that the senator's head almost fell off. And

Mr. Bedekowski was smiling this evil smile as he did it. He liked it. He relished it. The next day the headlines read that the senator was killed by a jilted gay lover, all of which was total fabrication, of course.

"I was so shaken by the act that I took off running. I went straight to my house, grabbed my backpacking gear and drove to the bus station. I travelled to several different cities across the country, then hitched a ride with a trucker that was going from Kansas City to Charlotte. That killed my trail for awhile, and I had another trucker drop me off where the Appalachian Trail crossed the highway, and I hiked a few hundred miles to here. And that, my dear friends, is how I got into this tight spot, and now I'm sorry I got the two of you involved."

Jimmy was speechless. Ned was concerned, very concerned, and knew that leverage was the only thing that would stop Mr. Bedekowski, then a thought struck him. In a very long shot, he asked Kara, "Who were these senators the man was talking with?"

Kara didn't have to think about it, she reeled off the names. "Senator Breck from Nebraska, Senator Adams in California, Senator Nathanial from Illinois, and Senator Lee from South Carolina."

Ned said, "Well I'll be damned. You won't believe this, but I was in Charleston, S.C. looking at some property a few days ago. While I was on this secluded land, a car drove up. A woman was in the passenger seat, and a man was driving. They fought, and there was something said about spilling beans, and he shot her. The man was Senator Evan Lee."

Ned could see the surprise in Kara's expression, and the gears turning in Jimmy's head as he processed what he had heard and formulated an action plan. After pausing for a moment, Ned said, "My friends, we are all in the same boat. Two of us are enemies of one of the most powerful persons in the world, and Jimmy, you are in the boat because you're with us."

Jimmy said, "Holy shit! I should have listened to my mother and moved to the city, anywhere, and I wouldn't be here right now and neither would you."

Ned said, "Our boat is taking on water and the sea is rough, that's true. We have two choices; we can throw up our hands and lose before the game even begins, or we can take this on, and in the process, ensure that we survive this and better the entire country by taking down some very bad people. I choose the latter option."

Kara said, "I agree, but fill in the blanks for me because when I look at the ledger sheet, I see some formidable deficits. We have the three of us, some small arms, two impressively impregnable homes and the forest to use as shelter and for hiding away; a few vehicles, maybe some cash if our bank accounts haven't been seized by these assholes, and three brains, which are probably our most valuable weapons. In the other column of the ledger I see some evil minds, the powers of the FBI, NSA, CIA, IRS and every other federal agency that exists, and some very influential people who are both ruthless and of massive wealth. So what do we have that can overcome all of that power and will?"

Kara and Jimmy turned to Ned, who looked Kara in the eye and said, "Leverage, and we have plenty of it. Leverage! That's what we need, and it's what we have."

Jimmy piped up, saying, "We have more tools in our tool box than just leverage. Between the three of us, we have connections in the military and CIA from my career and from Ned's, we have your knowledge of the NSA and all that intertwines with, and most important, we have a will to win that very few people have and some skills and mindsets they aren't used to combating."

Kara wore a puzzled look and said, "Please elaborate on these skills, and what about these military and CIA connections."

Jimmy smiled, glanced at Ned and said, "You see, Kara, I look like an old and backward mountain man, which I am when you get right down to it, but I spent 20 years in the military doing things we didn't officially do. In fact, I didn't officially exist and nothing I did is officially acknowledged. I ended my career in military intelligence, and two of the colonel's I served with are still active.

"So, when our friend Ned here came snooping around looking for land to buy, I checked him out." He looked at Ned and asked, "Stop me if I start to say something you don't want revealed. I'll keep it basic and vague."

Ned nodded. Jimmy continued, "So, first I Googled Ned and came up with a big fat zero. Then I decided to cut to the chase and check the IRS records, which is a trick I learned during my career. Back then I reported to the biggest asshole of a commanding officer that ever existed, and he used to break into the IRS system to dig up dirt on anyone who stood between him and whatever goal he was trying to achieve. He summoned me to his office one day and said that a complication had arisen and he needed me to retrieve some files from the IRS, and he gave me the procedures and a password. He was trying to get me to do his dirty work so he could create plausible deniability, but I'll keep the story short. Using his password, I managed to create another user and gateway so that I can access their files at will and if anyone ever discovers it, which they haven't in 12 years, it will appear as if my former commanding officer is the one doing it and he will take the heat.

"So anyway, I looked for Ned there, too, and according to the IRS, Ned didn't exist. So I checked military files, and found nothing there, either, so I figured that meant that Ned was working black for the CIA or some branch of military, and we had that in common. The next time I talked with Ned I asked some questions that I got canned answers to, the same canned answers we had been drilled on, so I knew then that Ned was likely ex-CIA. I still don't know what Ned did in his career and I don't need to know. But I know he has skills that will come in handy in a tight spot.

"And then we have you and your access to the NSA computers. I need to ask you this: Did you have a shadow computer and email identity at NSA?"

Kara first shook her head, but then relented and said, "I have been with the NSA for a long time, and I worked closely with the former director for more than 10 years. Being a political figure, he taught me early in our relationship that we always had to have leverage on those who opposed us.

"He taught me to have duplicate email accounts under fictitious to communicate the information we wanted to remain confidential and not easily connected to us. I learned from him how the high-stakes political game is played, so I created three pseudo-accounts. I used my primary account for typical work, and used my fake accounts for anything we wanted to keep out of the spotlight of a public inquiry or a snooping adversary. I never used the third account, so even if someone were able to access or delete my primary and my secret account, the way I structured it, someone would have to know about it to find the other account. I haven't used it since I set it up, so I can't know with certainty that I can still get in through a back door, but I probably can."

Ned said, "That's an impressive list of assets the two of you have; they will be a great help. I also witnessed the senator shoot someone, and if we can tie the people who came after us today to any of the people pulling the strings, we'll have that as leverage or for evidence should we need to go the legal route, which I doubt is the direction we'll take since these people are so connected and influential. If they are that powerful, they'll have influence over judges and decision makers.

"We have some work to do, but we can't do it here, and we can't do it in my house, either. Today's visitors will be back, and they will bring others with them. Professionals. They'll probably burn our places to the ground, but we are leaving within an hour. We have to go some place they can't find us."

Kara and Jimmy looked at him quizzically, and Kara asked, "And where will that be?"

Ned answered, "We're going to Colorado. I have a house there, too, and it's more remote than this one. I need to call a friend with a plane, and we have to get to an airstrip that's a few miles from here, but we'll have to walk. My truck went up in smoke and Jimmy's truck is at my place. And they know about Jimmy's truck."

Jimmy smiled and said, "We won't have to walk. I have an old Jeep in the barn than is registered to someone who lives in Chesapeake, Virginia, and that person doesn't really exist. And we don't have to worry about our houses, either. I'll call in my cousins. They really are mountain people, and they won't let anyone set foot on our land."

Jimmy walked over to his landline phone and dialed a number. He began speaking, "Hulden, Jimmy here. Fine, and you? Good. Hey, I need some help up here. Some men have decided they don't want Ned or me to live here, or live anywhere, for that matter. But those men came here and to Ned's house, and they tried to set my place on fire and they were shooting at us. Ned and I have to leave town for a while, but we would like our houses to be here when we get back."

The person on the other end of the phone was highly offended and shouted so loud that Ned and Kara heard him say, "I'll make damn sure nobody sets foot on your land or Ned's. I'll get the boys, and we'll make them sumbitches disappear if they come back."

Jimmy replied sullenly, "Huldon, you need to know that these are bad men and they'll be heavily armed. And they're federal men. I want you to know that before you get involved. And one more thing. There's a circle of bus-sized boulders a couple hundred yards east of the house, just up the hill. There's a man there that needs tending to. He won't bother you. He hasn't moved since he lost his head."

"I'll take care of the trash, don't you worry." Then there was another shout on the phone, "I doubt them sumbitches will have four .50 Caliber fully automatic machine guns like we do!"

Jimmy replied, "They might, and they might even bring in helicopters, so you need to either stay away or be prepared for that."

Another shout, "We'll be prepared for that, by God, and they've never seen anything like what a mountain militia has ready for them. Helicopters aren't shit to a stinger missile. Federal bastards? Bunch of pussies playing with toys and think they rule us like slaves. They's about to learn different. We don't have to get ready, we've BEEN ready."

Jimmy chuckled and said, "Obliged, Huldon, and be careful. These men mean business."

The reply was an even louder, "SO DO WE!"

Jimmy heard the phone slam down, followed by a dial tone. He turned to Kara and asked, "So, NSA woman, how many red flags did that phone call raise?"

Kara said, "Many, but 'militia' and 'machine gun' alone were enough to trigger red flags. It just might trigger a visit from a federal SWAT team."

Jimmy asked, "From which agency?"

Kara answered, "Could be one of several, such as BATF, FBI, Homeland Security, maybe a couple of others like Forrest Service and IRS. You name it. Like I said, just about every federal agency has a SWAT team now, and most have itchy trigger fingers, anxious to use the 40 hours of training they got."

Jimmy smiled. "Exactly! Forty hours! They're toy soldiers. A week of training and they think they're Rambo. The feds won't catch Huldon or his boys, mountain boys that have been fighting since they were born. First it was family against family fighting for land, moonshine territory, water, timber, gold or pastureland. Then the feds stuck their noses into mountain lives, and that stopped the families from fighting each other and united them against the revenuers when they came into the hills during prohibition trying to destroy the stills, which was the only way some of these people were surviving.

"Up here, if you threaten a man's livelihood, you threaten him and his entire family with starvation, and you also threaten his pride. Mountain people won't stand for that. The federal boys will get their asses kicked just like they have for almost a hundred years. There are caves and tunnels all through these mountains; Huldon and his boys know about all of them."

The bell rang in Kara's head. Ned was already ahead of her. She smiled herself and said, "That's a great idea, Jimmy, and one I hadn't thought of. Well done."

Ned said, "OK, Jimmy, let's gather whatever we're taking and hit the road. I'll call my pilot friend."

As Ned dialed the number using the landline phone, Jimmy began taking weapons and ammo to his truck; he included the backpacks. Ned kept his pack with him, his rifle close by and his pistol on his hip. It was habit when an imminent threat existed.

Ned's pack contained a couple of sets of fake IDs, credit cards and $10,000 in cash, in addition to ammunition and a few other handy items. It wouldn't be the first time he had used similar items, and it wouldn't be the first time he had faced seemingly overwhelming odds of surviving the onslaught of people who wished him harm, including government men. Those had been from foreign governments, but they were similar the world over.

He hoped it would be his last confrontation with people who wanted him dead, and he intended to do whatever it took to save himself and his fellow combatants. It was the way he had been trained, the way he had lived his life, and the reason he was still alive after a long career and several attempts to erase him from the earth by people in power who saw him as a threat because of what he was capable of and what he knew.

Within 10 minutes, Jimmy had pulled the old green jeep around to the front of the house and Ned and Kara got in, each still with their holstered pistols on their belts. Ned told Jimmy which airstrip, and they headed up the driveway. Jimmy stopped the truck three times on his way out. Each time, he retrieved a shovel and a tire strip and strung the strip across the driveway and covered it lightly with leaves and dirt to offer some measure of camouflage. He also locked the gate behind them as Ned and Kara swept their eyes across the area looking for any type of threat. They expected some, but saw none.

Jimmy knew the strips and locked gate would do nothing more than slow someone down and make their day a little tougher, but that was the most he could do short of lethal booby traps, and he didn't want to set those because his cousins and friends were coming to protect his place. They were prepared for the strips and the locks. Nothing more was necessary.

Chapter 11

The man drove into the parking garage of the Medical University of South Carolina after a nine-hour drive. He had traveled through the night, fueling himself with coffee and protein bars. He parked in a dark area void of any activity and turned off the car. He climbed into the back seat and removed his shirt, shoes and jeans. He opened the bag on the seat beside him and pulled out green pants and shirt, and a white coat complete with a MEDU pass card that said, "Dr. Johnson." He saw the irony and the clue the ID contained, and he smiled again when he looked at it. He removed a stethoscope and a clipboard from the bag, as well as a syringe, which he slid into the right pocket of his white coat.

The man walked directly to the woman's room, showed his ID to the policeman on duty and entered. The woman was sleeping. The man removed the hypodermic needle from his pocket, pulled off the hard cover and jabbed the needle into the port on the woman's IV tube. He pushed the plunger until the clear liquid ran through the needle and into the IV tube. He slid the cover back on the needle, wiped the entire syringe clean of fingerprints and dropped it back into his coat pocket. He acted as he was writing notes on the patient as he opened the door to leave.

He smiled at the policeman and said, "All is well. She is sleeping comfortably. Have a good day." He walked to his car, throwing the coat, along with the syringe in its pocket, into a trashcan along the way. He got into the back seat and changed back into his own clothes. He threw the stethoscope and ID under the car beside him and backed out of the parking space. At the garage gate, he smiled at the attendant, gave her his ticket and paid the $3 fee with cash. The gate opened, and the man drove out, never to return to the Medical University of South Carolina hospital. He didn't know it at the time, but it was the last visit to any hospital he would ever make – alive.

Ten minutes later, Chris Johnson pushed the "talk" button on one of the prepaid cell phones as he walked down a hall of the South Carolina State House. He didn't speak.

The male voice on the other end said, "The wall is black," the code the man from Washington used to signal that the mission had been completed. Chris Johnson pushed the "end" button and casually dropped the phone into the trashcan at the corner as he entered the atrium. He smiled to himself, knowing that one threat had been eliminated, and the other was soon to follow. The man on the other end of the phone was driving directly to western Virginia to take care of the last existing threat. Neither the man nor Chris Johnson knew yet that the threat had now multiplied to three, and that the threats were now in route to an unknown Rocky Mountain hideaway. He walked into the office that the senator occupied only a few weeks per year.

The rest of the time he spent in Washington with the U.S. Senate in session, and Chris Johnson was ready to get out of this small town and back to the center of power where the movers and shakers were moving and shaking. There were some formidable people in Washington that knew how to pull the strings of American politics, but none of them were as good as Chris, and he prided himself on that. He was referred to as the Puppet Master in most Washington circles, and he wore the label as a king would wear the crown. Only a few knew that he was also a mere puppet, with one ruthless man controlling his strings.

Chris spoke to the senator's receptionist without slowing down. He opened the senators' door and walked in without the courteous show of respect that was common when entering someone's office. Chris didn't need to show deference to the Senator. In fact, the opposite was true. After all, the senator was only the face of power. The real power was with the money man that pulled Chris's strings. That man was the power behind the throne and the one who decided what results he wanted. It was up to Chris to make it happen, and he always did.

The senator straightened in his chair quickly, a look of surprise on his face until he realized it was Chris. He should have known. Chris was the only person who would barge into his office. Chris slammed the heavy wooden door behind him and swaggered over and sat in the chair in front of the senator's desk. He leaned back in his chair and put his feet up on the desk.

The senator said with heavily laced sarcasm, "You do realize that "Mi casa es su casa" isn't to be interpreted literally?"

Chris didn't hesitate before saying, "Let's get down to business. You have one less thing to worry about today; I'm working on the other one and will complete that task within the next 24 hours. Now, Mr. Bedekowski wants to see us tomorrow, so be ready to fly at 7 a.m."

The senator looked at his calendar. He picked up his phone and pushed a button for his receptionist. "Clara, please clear everything on my calendar for tomorrow and bring the Adams file in."

The senator hung up the phone, looked at Chris and said, "I want to see her legs and rack more than the file."

Chris just shook his head before saying, "Your brain is permanently in your pants. When will you ever learn that chasing skirts will be your downfall? If you haven't realized that after what has happened these last few days, I fear there's no hope of improvement."

The senator said abruptly, "That's why you're around, Chris, so just focus on doing your job and stay out of my private affairs."

Chris quickly said, "You're a senator. You have no private affairs! Get that through your thick skull and clean up your act. One day you'll do something I can't fix. You may have already."

The senator let out a cocky laugh; quite a change in his demeanor from a few nights ago when he was whimpering around the office scared to death. Now the senator felt on top of the world, bulletproof. He was back on his game.

*****

Sam Strickland called the chief of police into his office. He showed the video of the woman telling the entire story of her tryst with the senator, the details of the day he shot her, the man rescuing her and saving her life, and the connections the senator had. It was the last factor that made her say at the conclusion of the video,

"I will be dead soon, and the senator's connections will be responsible for it. And you will die, too, detective, as will everyone else who knows about this. The senator's people are powerful, ruthless, and they will stop at nothing. They believe the senator will be the next president. He thinks that, too, and he believes that he's the one in charge of the entire effort. But he's just a stooge. The real power is a man in New York, and he pulls all the strings. I don't know his name, but I know he is the real power. I hate to say it, but you're going to regret getting involved in this. They'll kill you, too."

The chief of police was pale after the video concluded. He said to Sam, "This is way above your pay grade. Way above mine. Let this go, Sam. I'm officially taking you off the case. Now give me that video."

Sam ejected the DVD from his computer, put it in its plastic case and handed it to the chief. He asked, "Who will you pass this to, the FBI?"

The detective snapped his words, "Don't you worry about that! Don't mention this to anyone, especially that we have a video from the victim. You're off the case. In fact, you are on vacation for the next two weeks. I don't want to see you; I don't even want to hear your name. Now get out of here. You listen to me, Sam. Let this go. I know about the senator and his people. They squash people and don't bat an eye, and they won't hesitate to shed you. This has to be handled by people with more power than us. Both of us would see our careers and our pensions disappear if we chased this, and from what I've heard, that would be the best case scenario."

The chief walked out of Sam's office with the DVD, and Sam knew the chief was going to destroy the disk and do nothing more. Sam mused at how it had become accepted that people with power, people like the senator, could be corrupt and break the law at will, and no one would hold them accountable. It pained him how much values had depreciated over time. He turned off his computer and slid the case file into his briefcase. He leaned down under the desk and turned the dial on the safe until it opened. He removed two copies of the video, leaving a third in the safe, and closed and locked it.

He reached on the shelf behind him and got and 8.5x11 envelope. He wrote an address on the envelope, slid the original DVDs into the envelope and scratched a note on a piece of paper. It read, "Robert: Please store this in a secure place. Do not watch it, ever, and if something happens to me, send it to someone you trust in the media that will do something with it."

Sam signed the note and slid it into the envelope and sealed it. He wasn't sure how much postage it would require, so he put on eight stamps to be safe. He bent back down to the safe, reached in and removed a small plastic bag. He held it a couple of feet in front of his face and looked at the shell casing the bag contained, and asked himself if he should log it into evidence. But like the day the shooting had occurred, Sam had an overpowering feeling that under the circumstances, and considering the power of the people involved, he would be better off keeping the shell casing as an ace up his sleeve.

He put the shell casing and the envelope in his briefcase, walked to his car, got in and drove two blocks to a Post Office. He dropped the envelope in one of the blue mail boxes and drove home. As he puled into his driveway, his cell phone rang. He picked it up and heard the voice of one of the officers who had been guarding the woman's room. "Detective, the woman died. The doctors went in to check on her and found her dead. She just didn't make it."

Sam replied, "Thanks," and ended the call. He called the lead doctor on the woman's team and spoke with him. The doctor said, "She just didn't make it. It's not uncommon for someone with her injuries."

Sam said, "Do an autopsy. That's an official order. You'll get the paperwork soon, but do the autopsy now." Before the doctor could protest, Sam ended the call and went into his house. He was going to pay the senator a visit and see if he could get him to crack. He knew it would likely result in the end of his job, but he couldn't let this stand.

He packed a bag, got in his car and drove onto interstate highway 26 heading west.

As he drove, he dialed a number and waited as it rang. Ned answered, and Sam filled him in.

Ned said, "You better come with us. You're in more danger than you know, and we will fly down and pick you up. I'll call you back in a few minutes with a location." They ended the call. Ned turned to his pilot and said, "We need to pick up another passenger in South Carolina. Where should I tell him to meet us?"

The pilot started to protest, but gave it up as soon as he saw the look on Ned's face. He resigned himself, put the plane on autopilot and began to look at the charts. After a few minutes of study, he told Ned, "Tell him to meet us at the East Cooper Municipal Airport in two hours."

Ned made the call, and the pilot put the new coordinates into the autopilot. The plane turned 240 degrees and straightened up in a south/southeasterly direction. The pilot did the fuel calculations and determined that they would need to top off the tanks when they landed to be able to make the westerly trip without a stop. He got on the radio with the East Cooper airport and made the arrangements. He turned to Ned and asked, "Any more people we need to stop for. We'll only have room for one more after this one."

Ned replied, "Last one. What time will we land in Colorado?"

The pilot did the calculations, gave Ned the time, and leaned back in his seat. Ned hoped they could pull this off without giving away their destination. He knew the information was safe with the pilot. Anyone else, he wasn't so sure.

Sam turned his car around at the next exit and drove to Mt. Pleasant. He was standing by his car with a briefcase in his hand and a small duffle bag over his shoulder when the Hawker Beechcraft King Air 250 twin-engine plane landed. The plane taxied to within 50 yards of Sam and shut down its engines. Sam walked to the aircraft. The door opened and Ned stuck his head out to greet Sam. Sam handed him the bag and briefcase and stepped into the luxurious passenger compartment. A fuel truck drove up to the plane and began filling its tanks.

Ned said, "Welcome aboard, Sam. We'll talk after we land, but I'll be the co-pilot for the duration of the flight. This is Kara and Jimmy. They will bring you up to speed. If you want anything to drink, the fridge is right over there."

Sam asked, "You mind telling me where we're going?"

Ned replied, "Colorado. Make yourself comfortable. The faster we get out of here, the better." Sam sat down facing Kara, and said, "Sam Strickland. Pleasure to meet you."

Ned made his way back into the co-pilot seat and said, "We're ready when you are, captain."

After the fuel truck pulled away, the pilot worked through his checklist, started each engine and reviewed the gages, pushed the throttles forward and taxied to the end of the runway. He received radio clearance, pushed the throttles to maximum power. The props roared and the plane quickly accelerated. The pilot pulled back on the stick, the nose of the plane rotated upward, and the wheels left the tarmac.

Chapter 12

Two hours after Ned, Kara and Jimmy boarded the plan for Colorado via South Carolina, Hulden and seven of his cousins walked across the southern border of Jimmy's land. Between them, they carried 10 pistols of various calibers; four assault shotguns, six Browning .270 rifles, and two illegal, fully automatic .50 caliber rifles. They also had two shoulder RPG launchers.

As planned, they spread out strategically. One covered the east and west sides of the house from the safety of the surrounding forest, and one covered the north and south approaches. Four of them took strategic positions along the driveway, and the other two were slightly behind covering each flank of the main group.

On Ned's property, another eight cousins took similar positions. They were considered the "B" team. They weren't as well trained, nor did they have the military experience the "A" team had. The "B" team leader, David Payne, was the only one of them who had seen live action, his as a sergeant in Iraq and Afghanistan. He had become an expert in countering guerilla tactics, which meant he had been required to become intimately familiar with the tactics used by civilian fighting forces. He had learned well, and his skills and experience landed him on a terrorist watch list by his own government, the very government that had ordered him to learn the skills.

He discovered that status when he tried to board a commercial flight from Richmond to Jacksonville. He was surrounded by a team of TSA agents with guns drawn. The handcuffed him, harshly ushered him to a holding room and interrogated him for five hours. It was near the end of the ordeal that David Payne learned why they had taken him prisoner. It was at that moment that he learned that the government that had risked his life for considered him not a hero, but an enemy.

That moment changed everything for David Payne. He never had cared for blowhard politicians who were in office to serve themselves rather than their country, but he had always respected the office of the Commander in Chief since he ultimately took his orders from him.

But now the president had backed, maybe even demanded, the idea that military veterans were patriots when they were overseas fighting, but enemies of the State when they came home. That convinced David Payne that the current leaders of the country wanted two things: First, to eliminate anyone who could possibly defend themselves and/or pose a threat to politicians' power, and second, to achieve complete control of the citizenry.

That day, David Payne had driven all the way to Huldon's house in the mountains of western Virginia and had pledged his loyalty to the Virginia Appalachian Militia. They had one goal: to prevent the tyranny of the federal government who had turned on its own citizens. David Payne was ready for anything that happened today. In fact, he had been itching for a way to show his displeasure with the present government, which he couldn't have imagined twenty years ago. Huldon had been warning him for years that the government was trying to achieve total control, but he found it too farfetched.

Huldon had told him of the existing plans to have one world government run through the UN. He had described the domestic prison camps that had been built, the stockpiling of weapons by various federal agencies, the SWAT assault teams that had been formed by agencies that couldn't possibly need them in the normal course of their business, and the proposed legislation to disarm citizens and to seize all private retirement accounts.

David Payne had blown off all those warnings at the time, but he had seen many of Huldon's warnings come to life. Things had been adding up for David Payne, but the day at the airport and the encounter with the TSA agents had pushed him over the edge. He considered it his patriotic duty to expose and defeat the efforts within the government to turn its citizens into slaves of the State, just as had happened with all other attempts at a Marxist government.

He had concluded that such movements' stated goal was to spread wealth and raise the standard of living of all the citizens, while the true goal was to consolidate and control all sources of wealth and turn everyone but the ruling class into peasants, all under the guise of fairness and workers' rights. He would do his part to make sure none of that ever happened in the United States, or he would die trying. He just didn't know that time was today.

He got his troops into positions and waited. To his surprise, the first assault came from a single person, a man with Washington DC plates on his car. The man had driven up Ned's driveway. Since it appeared he was a civilian and posed no obvious threat, one of the militia members had walked into the driveway and stopped the vehicle.

As the militia member bent over to talk to the driver, David Payne watched through his rifle scope as a bullet ripped through the head of his friend and fellow militia member. The driver had shot him point blank. David Payne centered his crosshairs on the ear of the driver and pulled the trigger, leaving headless the man who had administered the lethal dose to the woman in the Charleston hospital bed.

David and two of his fellow militiamen went through the car and determined there was nothing there of value to them. There was no information, but the man had carried a .45 pistol on his hip and had a rifle and shotgun in the trunk. David was sure the man had come to kill Ned. He was also sure he had been unprepared for what awaited him. There would be more like him who would be unprepared for what awaited them on Ned's property and Jimmy's.

They moved the car to a vacant lot 30 miles away and burned it, leaving the driver's body slumped over in its seat. David Payne knew there would be a second wave, maybe even more. He braced himself for the coming battle. He both dreaded and relished it. He ejected the spent shell in his bolt-action .50 caliber sniper rifle and loaded a new round in the cartridge to replace it. He was ready for whatever the feds brought.

At about the time the group of four hit men approached Jimmy's house, Ned and his fellow passengers touched down on a private air strip near Deckers, Colorado. They de-boarded and piled into the four wheel drive Tahoe Ned had parked in the nearby barn/hanger. They headed northwest on roads, some paved, some of them dirt, through rolling land that was more remote than Kara had ever imagined possible. She thought to herself that the people who decried overpopulation had never been to areas like this one. They saw a total of three vehicles containing a total of five people the entire one-hour drive. They saw more deer than people.

As they climbed the last steep mile of a rough dirt road, Kara looked for Ned's Colorado house, finally seeing it from a few hundred yards away on the point of a knoll. The house was well hidden in the pines and firs, and built of similar design as his Virginia house. There was a barn-like structure that Ned pulled the Tahoe into.

They got out and walked toward the house. Kara soaked in the scenery, the absolute quiet, the air so clean that it felt crisp and refreshing. The house and barn were of similar colors as the surroundings, and the place would be hard to see from any distance. The roofs were a bit steeper and there were snow-melt contraptions near the edges of the roofs. Ned unlocked the doors to the house and let everyone in, and Kara noted that this was almost like being in Virginia, but the air was thinner and cooler and the views revealed a harsh, in your face, stunning beauty compared to the mellow scene in the Virginia mountains. She walked over to the rear of the house and opened curtains that covered almost the entire western wall.

As they parted, a view emerged of jagged, treeless peaks across an expansive valley of grass that looked like it would be fine cattle land. The distant rocky peaks sat atop shoulders of mountains covered with evergreen trees, and the tree line was as stark as if someone had drawn a horizontal line across the mountains at a specific altitude and said, "No trees above this line." It was incredibly beautiful, and incredibly remote. She imagined what it would be like in the dead of winter, and knew the answer from her memories of the Colorado ski resorts.

It would be a winter wonderland, and it would be isolated. She felt a bit intimidated by that, and shivered at the thought of total isolation, although the prospect of separation from civilization offered a level of comfort in the present circumstances. She noticed that Ned had walked up and stood beside her.

Kara said, "It's so beautiful and quiet, it's almost disconcerting, but that has its appeal."

Ned smiled and put his arm around her shoulder and pulled her closer to him. She melted into him and felt safe.

Ned said, "It is indeed. When you walk outside sometimes, especially when everything is covered in snow, it's so quiet it takes some time to get used to. But after you're here for awhile, it grows on you and you face a harder adjustment when you get back to a city."

He looked at her again and smiled, "After a couple of days, you might wonder what attracted you to the city."

126

Ned looked back to the distant mountain range, and he felt a warmth flow through him. He noticed how good Kara felt snuggled up against him. It reminded him of times long ago, and he wondered for a moment why they had gone their own separate ways. He wondered if Kara felt the same way. The way she leaned into him was a clue, but he was reluctant to let himself go there under the circumstances.

Their plane would have long ago departed, the pilot flying solo back to Virginia, sworn to secrecy. Ned had known the pilot for years, and he knew he could trust him. It would be difficult for anyone to find them now.

Ned had told each of them before they left Virginia and South Carolina to turn off all cell phones and leave them behind. Each of them had done so without argument. All but Sam Strickland had tossed their phones out the truck window along a rural Virginia road. Sam had dropped his to the ground at the Mt. Pleasant Municipal airport and stomped on it until it lay in many pieces. They were safe in the Colorado house, untraceable by any NSA monitoring technologies – for now.

It was time for a powwow. They needed to share all information and assemble an accurate picture of their situation. Ned gathered them in a den equipped with wood and leather furniture. The fireplace was the focal point of the room, and Ned lit the previously-laid fire to knock the chill from the air. Ned got their attention and said, "Alright, let's discuss what each of us knows, what we've experienced, what our useful professional experiences are, any governmental, political or other contacts we have that could possibly help us, and we'll form a plan from that."

Ned wanted to reassemble the events in the order they had happened, so he led off with an account of his experience in Charleston. After he finished, he asked Kara to speak next, followed by Sam, then Jimmy. It was a sobering discussion. The talk gave them a very good view of the situation in its entirety, but there was still something missing. The feeling that there was a piece of the story still astray gnawed at Ned. He knew there was something, but he just couldn't put his finger on it. Or someone. He needed to know what – and who – he was dealing with.

*****

Chris Johnson and Senator Evan Lee boarded the private Leer jet bound for New York City. Mr. Bedekowski awaited them, and they intended to make his wait as short as possible. Patience and understanding were virtues Mr. Bedekowski lacked, and the results of one of Bedekowski's offensives were often very unpleasant. Chris Johnson and Senator Lee had no desire to witness his wrath.

During the flight, Chris and Senator Lee reviewed the events of the past few days, and Chris coached the senator on his responses to anticipated questions. They weren't sure what Mr. Bedekowski wanted to discuss, but they intended to be prepared for anything they could anticipate.

A limousine picked them up and drove them to a large building in Manhattan. They rode the elevator to floor 103. When the elevator opened, they emerged into an atrium, not a hallway. Mr. Bedekowski was the only occupant of the top floor of the Zwiser building, and his wealth was reflected in the furnishings. The décor was cold and sparse, but a couple of original Picassos were displayed. The warped depiction of reality in the paintings seemed to fit the owner of the art. Picasso had a way of making everything look melted, displaced and bizarre, and the fit between art and owner was striking, and likely intentional. The art tended to affect the equilibrium of the observer, as did Mr. Bedekowski.

They were shown into a dark, marble-floored room. There was one window on the wall they faced, and they could see nothing but the white glare of the New York daylight. They waited almost 20 minutes in the cold room, made that way by the radiant chill of the marble and the stark décor of the room. A door opened and a dark silhouette walked in and sat at a large, barren marble desk across the room from them.

Chris and Senator Lee squinted to see the person who sat at the table, but they couldn't see any features, only the outline of the man's features.

The man was short in stature, way too round for his height, and only had hair on the sides of his head. The hair was long and covered most of his ears. He looked more like a clown than a powerful man. In a cracking, deranged sounding voice, the man said, "You had pleasant travels, I presume?"

The senator started to respond, but Chris jumped in and said, "Yes, sir, a pleasant trip. Thank you for your hospitality…"

The man behind the table interrupted him, "Senator, my sources tell me you have, to quote them, 'stepped into another pile of shit'; a large one, at that."

The senator started to protest, but Chris Johnson grabbed his arm to silence him, and Mr. Bedekowski slapped his hand on the table, creating a stunningly loud noise that seemed amplified by the marble floors and walls.

"I don't want to hear your babble. I am NOT one of your lapdog reporters or an uneducated member of the brainless public. You should know by now to leave your bullshit behind when you are in my presence. You have one purpose; to do and say exactly what you are told. Your most recent mess is notable. It could, if it became known to the public, or worse, to our opposition, derail the work I have dedicated my life to. I won't have it. You are but a puppet, and you are replaceable. Now just sit there and listen ... if a politician is capable of doing so."

Silence mingled with the cold of the room, and the result was a chill that penetrated to the bone, as was intended. Chris Johnson sat silently, still maintaining his grip on the senator's forearm. The senator tried to twist his arm free, but Chris Johnson gripped event tighter to emphasize the need to sit quietly.

Bedekowski continued, "My men have taken steps to eradicate your ... problem ... and I tell you that this is the last of your messes I am willing to clean up. It is late in the election game, young man, but it's not too late for you to suddenly develop health problems and drop out, or for even worse fates to fall upon you. You'll notice that the Governor of Nevada has emerged as a potential challenger to you in the upcoming primary. That is not coincidence. I arranged that as I arranged your rise in prominence.

"You will also note, I trust, that no more of your trysts or your clumsy malfunctions will be tolerated. Senator, you have the primary requirement of winning election from this stupid American public. You have charisma. Now, I control 30 percent of the election results through various means that the American public is too stupid to see or acknowledge. The remainder is influenced by charisma. But don't live under the misconception that you are an extraordinarily gifted man. As a result of many decades of infiltrating the media, the institutions that control election results and the courts that decide any disputes, I sit at the desk that pushes the buttons that determine who has power, who succeeds, who we punish, and who, for lack of a better word, disappears.

"I studied at the hands of the best in the Soviet Union, Cuba and Eastern Europe. I took what they taught me and added my own genius to the wheels of power. Now, my fingers can touch anyone, anywhere, and I am proud that I am on the brink of controlling … everything.

"We control the food supplies, we control the money supply, and we recently have taken control of the health maintenance of all of America, just as we have done in all other communist countries, including our neighbor to the north.

"We have two things standing between us and our ultimate goal of one controlling government: we need one more American president, and we need to disarm the American public. You can be that next president, or you can be gone. It's up to you."

The man stood and said, "Now get out, and keep your pants zipped up until after the election."

Bedekowski was gone from the room before Chris Johnson and the senator could regain their breath. They stood, the senator on weak knees, and made their way to the elevator. When the doors shut, the senator started to speak, but Chris Johnson silenced him with a motion of his hand. Chris knew there were cameras in the elevator, the limousine and in the plane. As he left the building and walked toward the car, Chris said, "Not a word until we're back in Columbia. We'll talk then."

The senator shivered and felt a penetrating dread. He had many times before made deals with the Devil, so to speak, but he wondered now if he had gotten in bed with Satan himself. Bedekowski had talked about controlling the World. The senator had heard such talk before, but always dismissed it as fantasy, even when he thought about the prospect of becoming that World leader. But now, Bedekowski made it sound real. The senator wiped cold sweat from his brow. He felt as if he had become a puppet character in a bad James Bond movie, only this time it was real. Was this the story he had half listened to in his youth when his mother had forced him to attend church every Sunday. Was this Revelations coming true? Was Bedekowski the Anti-Christ, or was he, himself, that one leader that would unite the world in its final days? He shivered again and wiped more sweat from his brow and suddenly felt nauseous. He rolled down the window and vomited, the rushing wind blowing it along the side of the car.

Chapter 13

After telling the others of their plans, Ned and Kara climbed into the old Toyota Land Cruiser with Colorado plates. The engine turned over slowly at first, then roared to life. Ned kept solar chargers hooked up to the batteries of the vehicles and the generators to keep them charged, and a rancher who lived on an adjacent ranch came over every few weeks to start the engines of the vehicles; the snow blower, the small Cat bulldozer and the generator; and to check on the house. Ned had tried on numerous occasions to pay the man for his troubles, but typical of most rural neighbors, he refused to accept payment. So, every winter Ned had a load of hay delivered to the man's ranch, and every Christmas sent a feast of smoked salmon, smoked turkey and an array of vegetables and desserts to the ranch, anonymously. The rancher had said on more than one occasion that he knew Ned was responsible and that no payment was acceptable for helping out a neighbor. Ned, while declining to acknowledge that he was responsible, asked the man, "How would a man feel if he offered a gift to his neighbor that was refused?"

As Ned expected, that left the man speechless, aware of the conflict an answer would create in his value system.

Kara wore her hair up and tucked inside a baseball cap that sported to logo of a local fly fishing shop. She was dressed in jeans, a leather jacket and cowboy boots, all of which Ned provided from one of the guest-room closets. Ned wore similar attire, and explained that he had several different sizes of clothing, both male and female, for guests who couldn't possibly anticipate the proper attire for the environment. He wanted everyone who visited to be comfortable and properly equipped, and wanted them to blend into the environment as to escape special notice. Ned had learned a long time ago that stealth was always an advantage, and one of the best ways to attain that was to hide in plain sight by blending in with the locals. If asked, the people in the area wouldn't recall seeing someone of the description provided by an outsider, even though they would be reluctant to give information to an outsider, anyway.

People in rural areas had an inherent distrust of outsiders, and that trait was in direct correlation to the remoteness of their surroundings. The more rural, the less trust they granted. It was a distrust outsiders and city folk had earned throughout American history. In their experiences, rural folks sensed condescension from city folks, and the city folks always wanted something from them with nothing to give in return.

Ned slipped the vehicle into gear and rolled it out of the barn for their two-hour each way trip to Fairplay, Colorado. There was little more than a ranch supply store, a gun store, small hotel and a few local diners and burger joints, but there also was a grocery store, which was their destination. After descending the mountainside, Ned took a right onto the long two lane road that meandered along the valley. There were few vehicles, and they drove along for long stretches without seeing another human. Cows and mule deer dotted the landscape, and they passed an occasional sign for a national forest, campground or stream or river. But the scenery was stunning, ranging from rolling grasslands to the distant peaks of the Rocky Mountains to the northwest.

They talked about what they had been doing in the years since they had last seen each other, and what they had planned for their futures. Kara smiled often and talked freely, but she had an underlying look of fear. Ned took her hand and said, "We're going to get through this and everything will be fine. We'll both grow old." Although he felt it, he didn't say that the flickers of hope had re-ignited within him that they would grow old together. But he felt it, nonetheless.

They shopped in the small town grocery store, filling two carts with staples and fresh foods, something not at all unusual in such rural areas where most of the population was spread across many miles and people came to town to shop no more than twice a month. Meats, vegetables, fruits, snacks, baking supplies, milk, juices, spices, charcoal, soaps and shampoos, aspirin, Advil, allergy medications and first aid items; bread, beer and wine, toothpaste, and on and on their list went until they had checked off every item.

It took them 10 minutes to load the items into the back of the vehicle, and another 10 to fill up with gas at a nearby station.

They stopped at a roadside ice cream shop and ordered a chocolate milkshake with two straws. Neither of them normally consumed such, but when Kara saw the shop's sign, it reminded her of a time they had together long ago, and with such an uncertain future, she didn't know how many good times she would be able to re-live. So they stopped, sat at an outside picnic table and leaned toward each other and sipped the straws. It was much like a time so many years ago, and they both realized it. As they finished the last of the milkshake, Ned smiled and said, "Kara, we are going to be OK. We will have many more moments like this, and I look forward to them."

Kara didn't know if what he said was true, but she was touched by his perceptiveness and by the fact that he cared enough to comfort her.

At about that same time, a man walked onto the grounds of the Mt. Pleasant Municipal Airport where a car had been reported abandoned. The man, David Watson, had inquired at the Charleston Police Department as to the whereabouts of Sam Strickland and had been told he was away on vacation. The man had broken into and searched Sam's house, which had produced nothing of value. When his contact in the Charleston Police Department phoned him back and let him know that Sam's car had been found at the airport, the man paid a visit to the facility and interviewed some of the staff.

He gained nothing, that is until he casually asked one of the mechanics who worked in Hanger Three. The man, who sported a wad of tobacco in his cheek and bore a heavy, low country accent, said, "I saw the fellow that got out of the car. A black man, he was. He walked directly to a Beech Craft waiting on the east taxiway and got in. He had only a briefcase and a small bag, so he couldn't have been going far."

After further questions as to any small bags the man might have been carrying, the mechanic remembered something. "Now that you ask, the man pulled something from his pocket and threw it to the ground before he boarded. And the funny thing was he stomped on it, too. I hadn't thought of that again until you asked." He spat on the ground to offer emphasis.

David Watson asked as casually as he could, "Where'd you say that plane was waiting?"

The mechanic pointed, and David Watson walked over to the indicated area and began searching. It didn't take him long to find it. A crushed cell phone. So, Sam Strickland wanted to keep his destination a secret. David Watson walked to the airport office and quickly flashed a badge that indicated he was a security guard at the NSA offices in Washington, DC, but he told them he was an agent for the FAA. The woman working in the airport office was too intimidated and naive to ask to see the badge closely, and she began looking at the logs from the day the man asked about.

She found a Beech Craft that had landed briefly at the airport on the indicated date, and told the man the plane was registered to "Marion Aviation" in Marion, Virginia. The flight plans indicated they were flying to Ft. Meade. David Watson wondered if there was something screwy going on within the NSA, or if the flight plan was filed to screw with anyone who inquired. Ft. Meade is the headquarters of the NSA, 15 miles southwest of Baltimore, Maryland, and being an Army base, only approved flights would be allowed to land there.

David Watson thanked the airport employee and walked quickly from the building. Once in his car, he called New York and reported what he had learned; that a plane had landed here from Marion, Virginia, picked up Sam Strickland, who didn't want his destination known, and had either flown to Ft. Meade, or had intended to keep their true

destination hidden and leave a tasty message to whomever inquired –
that they knew who was after them and that they were prepared for
battle.

The man on the New York end of the line promptly reported his
findings up the chain of command to his employer, who ordered him to
contact a woman in Washington and find out what the Hell was going
on. David Watson smiled to himself, partly because he had found what
he needed, or at least part of it, but mostly because it was likely
someone was screwing with those assholes in New York and
Washington who thought they owned the entire world. 'Cocky
bastards,' he thought to himself, and then he began to wonder who
knew enough and was either brave or leveraged enough to screw with
these people.

He intended to find out, and he wondered if he would choose to keep
helping the assholes in New York and Washington, or if he would turn
and offer aid to whoever was bold enough to do what he suspected
they were doing. They were either very stupid, or had the biggest balls
he had ever heard of. So, he either pitied them or admired them, and
he intended to find out which of his appraisals properly applied.

*****

Ned and Kara walked back into the kitchen and were greeted by the wonderful aroma of a stew. Jimmy was standing at the stove stirring a large pot with a wooden spoon. He had an apron tied around his waist, his holstered .45 on his hip over the apron, and it painted quite a picture. Kara felt as if she had just walked onto the set of on old western movie, and she let out a laugh as she soaked in the scene. Jimmy smiled a big smile and said, "I found your freezer and decided I'd make myself useful and whip up a batch of venison stew. Now that you're back, I'll put some corn bread in the oven and we'll have a country feast in a little while fit for a country king – and queen, too, Kara."

Sam stood from the den table where he was writing out lists, plans and contingency plans, and still trying to isolate and identify the gnawing feeling of the unknown that he and Ned felt in common, although the two of them had yet to discuss it. The three of them finished unloading and stowing the supplies while Jimmy tended to his feast preparation. The sun was sinking low on the horizon, and Ned threw a log on the fire that Jimmy and Sam had kept burning and asked Jimmy, "Do we have time for a cocktail on the back deck?"

Jimmy answered with a grin, "The corn bread has 20 minutes in the oven, then needs to cool for another 10, so Happy Hour it is."

Sam opened a bottle of red wine and poured a glass for Kara, opened a beer for Sam, and poured a whiskey and water for himself and another for Jimmy. As they gathered on the deck, Kara raised her glass and said, "To a long a prosperous future for all." The others granted a hardy "here here" and the sipped on their drinks. As threatening as the world around them was, and as dismal as their futures appeared to be, at that moment on that mountainside in Colorado, they felt a comfort and a unity with each other that made every one of them feel a sense of security, as fleeting as it may be.

Chapter 14

Bedekowski walked slowly into the Oval Office, gripping the gold handle of his wooden cane in his right hand. Secret Service agents closed the door behind him. The President waved acknowledgement to him and said into the phone, "I'll have to get back to you. My appointment is here," and hung up the phone. The President stood and paid deference to Bedekowski, something he was reluctant to do, and something he did to only this one person. He owed Bedekowski his position, his wealth, his everything. Without the man with the money, power, connections and determination, he would be nothing more than a want-to-be working sucker, just like all the other serfs who thought themselves independent Americans.

The President waited until Bedekowski sat, then asked, "To what do I owe this unexpected pleasure?"

Bedekowski gave him a cold look and said, "You owe everything you can imagine and more."

That erased the politician's smile from the President's face. Bedekowski lifted his cane and pointed it at the President, "We have a problem. While you have served me fairly well during the last six years, you have committed more than your share of blunders. Granted, most of them

144

have been verbal offenses when you thought yourself smarter than those around you, smarter than you are. In spite of my repeated instruction, you have gone off script on numerous occasions, and without exception, each time you have done so I have had to pull strings to make the offense fade away. I have created an economic collapse to cover for you, more than one international incident, and a war in the Middle East to distract attention from your blunders."

The President interrupted, "As I recall, you have profited handsomely from each of those situations."

Bedekowski slapped the President's desk with his cane. "Silence! I will always profit from a situation, no matter what it is. This is a capitalistic society, is it not?"

The President replied, "I hope you don't mind if I smile at the irony of that statement, since your primary goal is to destroy capitalism."

Bedekowski didn't slap the desk again, but he was visibly angered and the insubordination of this puppet character, a character he himself was responsible for creating. Caricature was more appropriate, since he had erased the President's laughable college transcripts, silenced his critics on many, many occasions, written the 'autobiography' the President had claimed as his own work, and covered up too many of the man's glaring flaws to count.

He said as calmly as he could muster through clinched teeth, "We have a problem. It seems one of your NSA employees has some critical information that could harm me – could harm our cause. The young lady, a miss Kara Allyson Teals, reported some intercepted communications. She filed a report. Fortunately, we intercepted the report, erased it and minimized the damage. But now the young lady has gone missing. We traced her, found her in a remote location in western Virginia, and sent in two separate teams to clean up the situation. Both teams failed, and the last one encountered a formidable force that eliminated one of their team members and damaged another. That got my attention, since we have what are supposed to be the best people in the World. So we did some investigating, which proved difficult under the circumstances."

Bedekowski paused to catch his breath. He glared at the President again and said, "It seems the young lady ran to the home of one of our former CIA employees. And to make things even more interesting, she then ran to his next door neighbor, who is a former Army intelligence officer, who before holding that distinction was a special black operative. Between the two of them, they are credited with some of the most difficult, most influential missions in the history of the United States. They are great heroes to the success of the American power structure and the American capitalistic system, and did more damage to the cause of communism than any other two people. Ever."

The President sat, staring blankly, knowing only that the situation was bad because it had upset Bedekowski. Bedekowski continued, "These are two of the people I have warned you about, two of the people I have told you to eliminate."

The President worked up the courage to ask, "And just who are these two people?"

Bedekowski answered with gritted teeth, "Mr. Jimmy Taylor, former Army intelligence officer, and Mr. Ned Harrison, former dark CIA operative. These men are our enemies. Grave enemies. They are true believers in the Republic, the constitution, and democracy. They spent their rather distinguished careers fighting for their cause and against ours, and they are the kind of men that are willing to die in order to succeed."

The President smiled, "Well, then, we'll simply call in our soldiers, from Special Forces to HHS and all the other SWAT teams from federal agencies, plant a cover story that they are terrorists and are close to performing a terribly destructive mission, and we'll eliminate our problems."

Bedekowski glared again. "And I had thought you a rather poor student."

Bedekowski pulled a paper from his coat pocket and unfolded it. He looked at it one more time, the hatred spilling from his eyes as he read the names one last time, and tossed it onto the President's desk with electric disdain. He said, "These are the men and their addresses. Take care of this immediately. Consider it your highest priority. In fact, delegate everything else and focus solely on this."

Bedekowski stood and walked to the door. He smacked the door with his cane, and it was opened by a Secret Service agent. Bedekowski didn't acknowledge the agent, or anyone else he encountered on his way back to his waiting car.

As the President picked up the paper and read the names. Now that Bedekowski was gone, the feeling of dread swept over him and his face went pale and cold sweat immediately formed on his brow. These men! He remembered both of them.

He was familiar with their files, he knew their history and their accomplishments, and worse yet, he knew their capabilities. Several communist countries had been trying to locate and eliminate these two men for more than 20 years. And since he had been in office, their own country had been trying to locate and eliminate them and other men of their sort. These men were so good that not only had all those countries, including their own, failed to eliminate them, they had failed to even find them. Then an even more ominous thought occurred to him. All those countries, all those agents, and lately, all those agencies had failed to locate the men, but Bedekowski had found them in a matter of days.

This was bad. Two of the most crafty, skilled men, and their adversary, Bedekowski, were coming to blows, and he was caught in the crossfire. Bedekowski would hold him responsible for handling what several countries and even Bedekowski's private troops couldn't. He had to find the men and take them out, and he had to do it quickly.

The President wiped the sweat from his face. What should he do? He had to call in the most ruthless people he knew – besides Bedekowski. He stood and walked into his private bathroom. He opened the cabinet beneath the sink and put his hand on the palm reader on the front of the safe. He opened the door, found his private directory, and walked back to his desk as he looked up the number. He dialed. The phone rang, and a voice answered, "Chris Johnson."

The President said, "I need you in my office tonight. Where are you?"

Chris Johnson answered, "I just landed in Columbia."

The President replied, "I'll send a plane. Someone will contact you with the details." He hung up the phone without awaiting reply and wiped cold sweat from his face again. He looked at his watch; quarter after one. He opened the bottom right drawer of his desk and grabbed the bottle of the most expensive scotch the taxpayers could pay for, which was the most expensive ever made, and took a long pull.

He put the bottle back in the drawer, closed it and noticed that a drop of sweat had fallen from his chin onto the Presidential Seal on the top left corner of the paper Bedekowski had given him. He didn't bother to ask himself, or even to wonder, how Bedekowski had the Presidential stationary. He also failed to see the irony that Ned Harrison and Jimmy Taylor had given many of their years and a good part of their souls to preserve their country and the freedom of millions of their fellow countrymen. Now the country they had fought so valiantly for had turned on them, considered them a threat, not to the country as it was now, nor even what it had been years prior, but to the new America the President, Bedekowski and many others like them were striving for.

The struggle to change America had been in the works for decades, and they were so close to taking the country to a point of no return that they could taste the victory that would be theirs. They would control the food supplies, the energy sources, and the health care of every person in the country. That was already done. Now they only had to disarm the citizens, and it would be complete. There would be no way for people to resist change, to resist becoming complete subjects of the ruling class. Controlling the food, energy, money and health care gave them leverage, powerful leverage, but once no citizen had weapons, it was no longer leverage but force that could be administered at will.

Any uprising would be quickly extinguished and the people responsible would be shot in public, just as had been done by the Russians, the Chinese, the Cubans and now in the Middle East, although they fought under a different but similar banner. Complete control was the goal, but not only for the U.S., but for the World. It should have been accomplished years ago, but as ruthless the other communist leaders had been, they went weak after too many years of gluttony. As a result, their efforts had failed; but not this time, and not with Bedekowski pulling the strings. There was no possibility of Bedekowski losing his ruthlessness. No chance.

The President caught himself and focused his thoughts on his next tasks, instead of his silent musings about what they were about to accomplish. He took another pull from the whiskey bottle, put it away, picked up the phone and called the majority leader of the Senate, Harold Isom.

After being routed through two screeners, the President's call was picked up by the senator. The President said, "Harold, I need you in my office at seven tonight. Don't put it on your calendar, and don't sign in to the visitors' log. This is a dark meeting."

The senator hesitated and said, "Mr. President, I have a campaign fundraiser tonight," expecting the President to understand, since he himself would skip anything to go raise funds. Getting in office was important, but not as important as staying in office.

The President replied, "Cancel it or send someone else." Before the senator could say anything else, the President slammed down his phone, ending the call.

*****

Chris Johnson arrived in the President's office at 6:45. As they awaited the senator's arrival, Chris and the President discussed campaign strategies; IRS actions, inactions and information they had provided about opposition candidates; and gun control strategies. Harold Isom finally arrived, and the three of them exchanged pleasantries before the President said, "We have a problem, three of them, and we need to eliminate the problems immediately. We need to pay a visit to three people, and we need to use maximum force. We want no post event interviews from these three people ... of any sort, with anyone."

The President stared coldly at both men to make sure they understood his meaning. They did. He continued, "They are two men and one woman. One of the men is former CIA, and the other former Army intelligence. The third person is a woman who worked with NSA until she recently went dark. She stumbled upon some critical communications that leave us exposed at a high level. She sent the information up the chain, and Bedekowski intercepted it and cleaned up the mess. The woman is connected with one or both of the men we are after. We traced her to one of their houses, which are on adjacent property in southwestern Virginia."

The President waited, knowing the two men in front of him were dying to ask who the three problems were, but he, as was his tendency, enjoyed the anticipation and the building drama. He always had a flare for the dramatic performance, and that was almost solely responsible for his present position. So he waited.

Chris Johnson obliged, asking, "So, just who are these two men, dare I ask?"

The president answered, "You dare. Jimmy Taylor, former Army intelligence officer, and Ned Harrison, former CIA operative."

The senator's raised his eyebrows and enlarged his eyes. He said, "I thought, or maybe hoped these men had been eliminated." He shook his head slowly, realizing the gravity of the situation. "I know of these two men, and they each are very capable."

Chris Johnson asked, "How capable?"

The senator answered, "Put it this way, every communist country on the planet has been trying to eliminate these men for years, and so have we. Not only have they escaped detection, but numerous people of various ability levels have tried to take care of them. If they ever found Mr. Harrison or Mr. Taylor, they failed to accomplish their missions. In fact, many of the people who sought the men either failed to find them, or they were never heard from again."

Chris Johnson began to have cold sweats, and beads of moisture gathered on his forehead and upper lip. The president noticed it, even anticipated it, and reached in his drawer. He retrieved the whiskey and slid it across his desk toward Chris, who eagerly took a long swig, wiping his lips with the sleeve of his suit. The President frowned as he retrieved two glasses from the same drawer, setting them on his desk with loud twin thumps.

The senator continued to shake his head slowly, first at Chris' crude behavior, but also at the situation. He asked meekly, "How in the hell do you propose we eliminate these ... problems, and who is insisting we do it?"

154

The president hesitated before saying matter-of-factly, "Who else?

"Now, I propose we get Homeland Security and their domestic strike force to raid the men with superior fire power … enough power that there is nothing left but smoke and ashes, and pay a visit to southwestern Virginia."

He looked at Senator Isom and said, "Make the call to Wallings at DHS. Chris, I want you to oversee the operation. And remember, superior fire power, and nothing left but smoke and ashes. Understood?"

Chris Johnson wiped sweat from his brow again before saying, "Yes, sir."

The president turned to the senator and said, "You give Chris anything he needs to successfully complete this mission, and I mean anything. Understood?"

The senator answered, "Yes, sir, anything he needs. I'll make the call as soon as I get back to my office and a secure phone."

The president chuckled. "'Secure phone', you say. I remember the days." The President stood and said, "I don't want the details of this mentioned to anyone. Chris, you create the cover story, and both of you remember to tell people only what they need to know to complete the mission, and make sure none of it is about the three subjects."

Before Chris could speak, the president walked into his office bathroom and shut the door behind him. He turned to the sink and splashed cold water on his face. After several minutes, he walked back into his office, turned on a TV and watched a news segment on the upcoming elections. When he heard a news personality say that the President's lack of economic success and the disastrous start of the Presidents health care takeover would hurt their candidates in the elections, the president angrily jotted down the name of the news person and, by heart, dialed the personal cell number of the president of NBC, who answered the call before the second ring.

The President shouted into the phone, "Can't your fools stick to the talking points we sent over? I just heard Chris Shellings say that my lack of successes will damage democrats in the upcoming elections. I want this man fired immediately, or you can expect IRS audits for the next 20 years!" He slammed the phone down and turned the channel to another news program.

Chapter 15

After everyone had gone to their bedrooms for the night, Ned jotted notes in a black notebook, which he would later shred and burn. He jotted down possible scenarios and counter moves, one after another until he had exhausted every possibility he could conceive. He reviewed each, scratching out some possibilities and adding others. He continued the process for another two hours. There were a few problems. First, he didn't know who was coming or when, but he did know they would be coming. Second, he didn't know how much firepower they would bring, so he assumed the worst – that it would include conventional military weapons, and probably a collection of Homeland Security SWAT teams. He hoped for the latter – a bunch of weekend warriors who had never faced live combat from anyone who had military or CIA training or experience. They would be a poor match for Jimmy and himself, as well as a police detective, and as a bonus, an NSA employee who might be able to tap into their communications.

But what he did know was who was behind the situation and what motivated them. He also knew their tactics, since he had fought against the very governments these people now in power emulated, who they hoped to become. He had survived many battles with them, and their biggest weaknesses were that they were overly confident in their superior firepower. In addition, centralized control always resulted in poor morale and inefficient operations, and they were very predictable.

Ned suspected that the last thing they could conceive was to be attacked on their own turf, before they were ready to undertake their mission. So, Ned decided that he would claim the element of surprise for himself and his friends. He would be the first to attack. Go straight to the head of the snake – kill the head, and the body dies.

He flipped to a new page in the notebook and began writing. Over the next four hours, he detailed his strategy, the tasks that each member of their group would perform and when, everything he could anticipate. And he also left room for course changes once the battle began, because Ned was well aware that complex plans never went as expected. Never. And the people who survived were the ones that adapted well while under fire. And that had been his well established reputation, which was a direct reflection of his skills and ability to stay calm under pressure.

At 7 a.m., Ned joined the others at the kitchen table where there were large platters of venison sausage, scrambled eggs, hot biscuits and Southern style grits; salted and buttered. With morning greetings, Jimmy filled Ned's cup with hot coffee, and said, "This is banquet style, everybody, so serve yourselves."

Sam said, "I'm surprised you're the last one up. Not what I expected from a man of your background."

Ned replied, "I was up most of the night appraising our situation and formulating a plan of attack."

Sam raised his eyebrows and said, "Attack? Do you mean that literally, or as a figure of speech?"

Everyone at the table was now fully attentive and tuned in to the conversation. Jimmy had a look bordering on glee, and Kara was wide eyed awaiting more information. Sam wore the look of a road-wise cop who had trained himself to listen to information and process it before letting his mind jump to self-made conclusions. Ned said, "After breakfast, we'll go through the details of what I'm thinking, and I want input from each of you. We have a formidable team here. Each of you has unique experiences and skills that can serve us well. Jimmy and I have military and CIA backgrounds. Sam, you understand SWAT team tactics and strategies, which will be valuable because I suspect they will use various SWAT teams to attack with. Kara, you have a background with NSA and might be able to tap into communications of nearly anyone in the World. Knowing what the opposition is thinking, saying and planning comprise an advantage that has won world wars. All of us understand how governments think and function, and that is also an invaluable asset. If we do this right, we will know who is involved, what they say to each other, what their plans are, the strength of their forces, tactics and strategies, and most important, we will know their timing and their direction of attack. I can't think of another time when a team had such an admirable collection of skills and intelligence."

Silence filled the room in the seconds following Ned's words, but was finally broken by Sam's observation. "That is impressive, but the disadvantages we have are size of force, control of the public message, and firepower. The latter is what concerns me the most. SWAT teams, and police forces in general, have been militarized. They will have armored vehicles with cannons, fully automatic machine guns, grenades, including incendiaries, and they will have helicopters. But the most dangerous element of SWAT teams and militarized police forces is that while they have been through a few weeks of training, few of them have been able to practice in live situations. So, they are itching to play their war games. They will shoot first and ask questions later."

Ned smiled and said, "Excellent points, Sam, and I agree that they will be overly anxious to pull the trigger. And we are going to use that to our advantage. We'll discuss the 'how' after we eat, but right now, let's enjoy this fine breakfast Jimmy prepared."

After they finished their meals and cleaned up the kitchen, they gathered in the living area to discuss the details of Ned's plan. Ned handed everyone note pads and pens, and he began, saying, "Kara, we will need you to have computer access to NSA systems. How can we do that so that you won't be detected and your location can't be determined?"

Kara began her answer, and they all jotted notes. Two hours later, they had a plan in place that had been shaped by every member of the group. Ned led them through one more review to conclude the meeting, and said, "This is a solid plan, and I think it's workable. Each of you has added equally valuable input, and what we ended up with is far superior to the outline we started with. The first order of business is to get Kara a computer she can work with, and she and I will drive over to Denver to take care of that. We will pick up laptops for each of us. If anyone needs anything else, let us know and we'll pick it up during our trip."

***

Late that afternoon, Ned and Jimmy finished installing the satellite dish and cables, and tightened the last connection inside the house. Kara sat at a table in front of the large southern window that looked over the layers of mountains and valleys to their south. From discs they had bought in Denver, she installed the Virtual Private Network software and an encryption program. In a few minutes more, Ned and Jimmy strung a cable to Kara's desk, and she plugged it into the side of the laptop. Kara said, "What I'm about to do has the highest risk of detection and traceability of anything I will attempt. The VPN and the encryption software will mask my activity from the average IT person or security expert, but if they are really good, they'll find it. I'm going into my server base and downloading a software I – let's say, modified. Once I install it, it will make it almost impossible for anyone to figure out where I am working from or who I am. In short, it creates new IP addresses, routes and encryption code about 40 times per second. If someone were to detect my presence in their systems, it would appear that 40 different computers from 40 different locations around the World had intruded, and that repeats every second. I got the idea from the Chinese when they hacked into the Pentagon's system a few years ago. The only way they figured out that the Chinese were behind it was one of their IT hackers escaped and defected to the UK. In my position with the NSA, I discovered the communications the Brits were having between diplomatic posts, and they described it well enough for me to figure it out and create my own version of it. So, cross your fingers, I'm into the server bank and downloading the software now."

The three men watched in silence as a green bar appeared in a white box, and in about two minutes, the download was complete and Kara terminated the connection.

"Done," she said, and she pushed a few keys and initiated the software install. "That connection will be the last that 99 percent of IT and security professionals will be able to trace to within a few miles. From now on, even if they detect my e-presence, they will have no idea where it is originating."

Ned nodded his head and said, "As I said earlier, we have quite the team. Kara is clearly the technical expert of the lot of us."

Jimmy muttered a few colorful words, punctuated with "It's FM … fucking magic."

Sam remained silent in his stoical appraisal.

About an hour later, Kara called the group to her. Once they gathered, she said, "OK, I'm into the NSA system and I'm downloading the call data that includes the list of key words, phrases and names we created this morning. Within the first couple of minutes, we've had multiple hits on Chris Johnson, Evan Lee, Bedekowski, and as we suspected, the president himself. I haven't been able to comb through it carefully, but I believe we have another player involved as well."

The group waited, the looks on their faces indicating their curiosity. Kara continued, "The majority leader of the Senate met with the president and Chris Johnson last night. Shortly after that, the senator placed a call to Homeland Security."

Kara clicked a key and the majority leader's voice emanated from the laptop. "Dan! Harold Isom here. How the hell are you?"

Wallings answered with a trace of sarcasm, "Fine, and how can I make your evening more pleasant." Wallings had never liked the grandstanding senator, and knew him to be an expert ass kisser and masterful manipulator who placed his own interests above any one's and any country's, including his native U.S.A. The senator usually volunteered for projects with which he could make himself look good, and then dump all the responsibilities on someone else who did all the dirty work so the senator could claim all the credit. If the senator was calling him, he was quite sure that he was about to bear the responsibility for something while the senator spent his time on political maneuvers.

Senator Isom said, "I've just left a meeting with the president. We have some terror suspects cornered in two adjacent properties in southwest Virginia, and we need your teams to eradicate them post haste. They are ready to conduct a major attack on U.S. soil, and we have to prevent that from happening. This is a eradication mission. We have all the information from them we need, and total destruction is the goal from the top brass. I'll get the dossiers to you by lunch tomorrow."

Wallings replied, "Can't you email the files to me tonight? I can get a jump on this."

The senator paused for a minute, and Ned, Kara, Sam and Jimmy glanced at each other. They could feel the senator's hesitation, and Ned made a mental note.

The senator said, "Tomorrow. Now, I have to scoot to a fundraising event. I'm losing money by the second, so until tomorrow."

The call was terminated. Sam asked, "Why did the Senator want to wait until tomorrow – or today, I should say – to send the files. Is campaign funding the top priority for these politicians even in times of real threat?"

Ned answered before Kara could. He said, "Yes fundraising is the top priority for politicians no matter what is going on in the world, but that's not why the senator put off sending the files."

Sam asked, "Then why?"

Ned and Kara said in unison, "Because there are no dossiers and no files." Ned continued, "The senator has to create the dossiers, and that will take him a few hours. I would love to see how good of a fiction writer the senator is."

Kara said, "If all goes well, the entire world will find out how good the senator is at creating fiction. But that's a minor point. What's important is that we can scratch one thing off our list. Homeland Security has already been activated."

Ned said, "That's right, so now we'll turn our attention to the IRS, the National Forest Service, the other federal agencies and the Virginia State Police." Every one of them smiled at that prospect.

They agreed. Ned retreated with his note pad to the deck outside his bedroom, and Jimmy sat on an old stump near the barn, and the creative writing began. Kara continued her computer work, and Sam wrote his strategy for getting the maximum bang for the buck from the Virginia State Police.

Chapter 16

Ned handed Kara the communication he wanted her to send to Louise Lawrence, head of the criminal investigation unit of the IRS. Kara read through it, and asked, "Are you sure this will work?" Ned answered, "We'll find out together when we read Lawrence's subsequent communications, but there's something I'm worried about. What if she communicated via an alias email, like the IRS and others have been caught doing lately?"

Kara smiled, "No worries, we will intercept all emails, and we will do key word searches to uncover any email or phone call that includes the words we choose."

Ned nodded his head at the depth to which the U.S. government had sunk since 9-11. No one had anything resembling privacy anymore, and the U.S. government was spying on its own people at a level no one could have imagined before that terrible September day in 2001. The government no longer feared the people, but the people feared the government, and that spelled the end of America as a free country.

So, Bin Laden had succeeded in his mission to destroy America. Flying planes into the World Trade Center didn't in itself bring down freedom and civil rights or the Constitution that had made it the most successful country in the World, but his dastardly deed set the gears in motion. Some in power reacted out of ignorance and naiveté, but the people now pulling the strings saw it as an opportunity to destroy civil rights, freedoms, capitalism and democracy itself by taking more and more control under the guise of patriotism and national security. And so they had, and they had expanded their cover story to include the illusion that they were looking out for the good of the people.

The U.S. had deteriorated from its lofty status as a democratic, capitalistic republic to a place where the president and his administration routinely thumbed their noses at the Constitution and the rule of law with no accountability and no consequences. The government had been arming itself so it could control its citizens through intimidation, hopelessness, IRS audits and harassment through various agencies. In the mild cases, if those in power decided you were a threat to them, they could ruin your reputation, wipe you out financially and preordain you to a life of poverty, possibly even imprisonment. And the government had been literally building up an ammunition cache, had formed SWAT teams in many agencies that had no business bearing arms, and seemed to be preparing for a violent assault on its own people. The Department of Education needs SWAT teams? Hardly, but they have them, and 15 years ago that would have seemed too far-fetched for inclusion in a work of fiction.

Ned remembered the conversation he had with a Soviet Union counterpart decades ago. The man had smiled an evil smile and said, "Your republic is doomed to a slow, painful death, and it will happen from within. We are infiltrating your institutions. It may take years – even decades – but true believers will take over your country and you will fall to our communism without the Soviet Union having fired a single shot."

Ned had thought that preposterous at first, but his fears grew as time passed and he saw the myth of socialism take root in America. He saw the same tactics the Soviet communist had used playing out in America, even the same wording that had been used to overtake Russia and Eastern Europe. And to his amazement, the current president had actually used a Soviet theme in his latest election, but the education system of the U.S. had long ago been infiltrated, and enough of the citizens were ignorant of history that they didn't even realize what was happening.

And now it had come to this. Two former patriots who had put their lives on the line for their country for years were now considered enemies, as was Kara, a government worker who stumbled across the wrong information, and a police detective who had pledged his life to protecting citizens. Who used to be highly regarded patriots were now enemies to the State. The people now in power were so aware that what they were doing was against the will of the majority of the people that their grip on power was tenuous, reliant on the control of its citizens, their hopelessness to prevail, their ignorance of what was happening. However unlikely it was that the citizens rise up in huge numbers, their power could be vanquished and they could be prosecuted and jailed, even face legally mandated firing squads should the people rise up in sufficient numbers. Hence, the communist and socialist leaders around the world, throughout history, bore a huge paranoia that their power was much thinner and weaker than so many citizens assumed it to be, and governed with an oppression that was much weaker than it appeared to be.

Ned said, "Read it to me again."

Kara began, "Top Secret, Classified Information. To Director of Criminal Investigations, Internal Revenue Service. The Department of Justice has determined that two terror suspects are residing on adjacent properties in Virginia. The Department believes the suspects have attained large stockpiles of U.S. currency, along with counterfeit documentation regarding the acquisition of such. The Department requests that IRS agents perform a raid on the property and seize all currency, regardless of its nationality or origin, along with all documentation, computer equipment found at the scene. In addition,

the department requests that the IRS agents use the most advance tactics to secure evidence, and that the suspects be considered armed and dangerous. Names of suspects and their location are shown below.

"Please proceed with operation at precisely 4:30 a.m. EST, October 14, 2013 and deliver result reports to Attorney General Edward Helgen within 10 days of mission completion. All other communications should be considered National Security matters and handled accordingly, and are protected from subpoenaed disclosure by the National Security Act of 1944.

"Edward Helgen, Attorney General of the United States."

Ned sat silently for a moment, and said "I think it works. How about you?"

Kara replied, "I think it has just enough bull shit and ass-covering deniability to pass as an official government document, and is unlikely to be questioned."

Ned said, "So, how will we send this email to Lawrence?"

Kara smiled and said, "I am sending it directly from the Attorney General's email. It isn't that I am making it appear as if it is coming from the AG, but I am actually in his email. Anything you want to read?"

Ned replied, "Lots, but let's save that treasure trove for another day. It might come in handy later in the game."

Kara pasted the contents of the message into a newly created outgoing message in the AG's email account and clicked "Send." She looked at Ned and said, "Item two on our task list can be checked. Now onto the Forest Service. Do they also have SWAT teams?"

Ned said, "They do, indeed. I suppose it requires force to keep all those trees growing properly."

Kara asked, "When will you have that message?"

Ned said, "I already have it. It's on the same thumb drive."

Kara asked, "Who should I send it from and to?"

Ned said, "Send it from Secretary Tom Vasquez, U.S. Department of Agriculture, to Under Secretary of Natural Resources and Environment Harold Smith. After that, we move to the Environmental Protection Agency."

Kara replied, "Don't tell me they have SWAT teams, too."

Ned replied, "OK, I won't tell you that, but the Department of Education has SWAT teams, too, as does the Coast Guard, Customs, Immigration, Transportation Security and FEMA, or Federal Emergency

Management Administration, to name a few, and we're going to involve all of them."

Kara shook her head and pasted a message similar to the first into the Compose box of the secretary. She clicked send. She said, "October 14 is three days from now. Can we get all this done by then."

Ned answered, "We have to. I picked that time frame because it seemed a good balance between completing preparations and making it so far out that people have too many opportunities to talk about it. If the wrong people meet at a cocktail party in Washington and one person brings this up, the whole thing could unravel and we'd be right back to square one. And the longer we're dangling out here, the higher the chance of being located, and that can't end well. Hopefully, these agencies will continue their territorial refusal to share information with each other just a little longer."

Kara felt a chill that penetrated to her bones. She visibly shivered from the icy penetration of fear.

*****

The Director of Enforcement for the IRS picked up her phone and dialed an extension. When her assistant answered, she said "Gather the Enforcement Strike Team and have them in the east, third-floor conference room in two hours for mission planning. Attendance is mandatory." She hung up the phone.

That same morning, similar meetings were called at numerous federal agencies, and the wheels were in motion, rolling toward a night that, if it unfolded as Ned hoped, would be the biggest news event in decades. Its magnitude would help minimize the political whitewashing, denying and spinning.

Sam brought in a thumb drive with his letter for the Virginia State Police, and he walked haltingly. He spun a chair around backwards, sat in it with his arms resting over the back of the chair, and said, "I have to tell you that I am very reluctant to send this message ... to involve the Virginia State Police. It isn't the state of Virginia that is after us, who is up to no good. Most of these officers are going to be guys just like me. They work hard, most are from rural areas and believe that America has been the greatest country on earth, and they are likely upset that the Constitution is being trampled upon.

He took a deep breath and continued, "These guys are likely on our side, and I don't feel right about bringing them into this hornets' nest. I just don't feel right about it."

He took a long look at Kara, then at Ned, awaiting their reactions.

Jimmy walked in with his dossier to review with the others, saw the silence of the other three and felt the tension thick in the air. He asked, "What's up? All of you look like you've got burrs in your asses."

Kara answered, "Sam was just telling us he's reluctant to involve the Virginia State Police because most of them are from rural areas, love the country and would be on our side if they were aware of the situation."

Jimmy said, "Oh. Well, I agree with him, and I would feel the same way if we were dragging the armed services into this trap. Most soldiers I know are pissed off that the country has gone to shit, and lots of them were even purged from the military for voicing an opinion or for being Christians, or for supporting an issue or organization that the current politicians disagree with. That's tyranny, and members of the armed services don't like it, and neither do the veterans."

Ned spoke. "We'll leave out state and local police forces, and we aren't involving the military, either. Sam, I'm glad you spoke up. Destroy your message. We'll keep our focus on the federal agencies and the people pulling their strings. And speaking of keeping people out of the crossfire, is your cousin going to steer clear of this, Jimmy?"

Jimmy replied, "I told him to, and he said he would, but I'm not 100 percent confident that he will. He's smarter than he looks. He served two deployments in Iraq, including desert Storm when we actually fought to win ... until we quit. So he knows enough that when the enemy is harming himself to stand aside and get out of their way."

Ned said, "Good."

Jimmy said, "But he'll jump at the chance to fight the Feds if we need him to."

Sam said, "I've been thinking about something. If all these SWAT teams actually show up at the designated date and time, if they all take positions on the property, what if they don't start firing at each other. What if they discover the other forces and instead of firing a single shot, they sit around and bullshit and coffee?"

As the group pondered the possibility, Sam said, "We just might need to light the fuse to make this thing explode, and maybe that's where Jimmy's cousin could help us out. He could set up an explosion in or around the house, or could fire a few shots to get things going."

Jimmy grinned. "That's a great idea, and Huldon is just the person for that. But there's a problem. How do I get in touch with him without exposing our entire plan?"

Kara asked, "Does he email?"

Jimmy answered, "He sure does, and he and his militia buddies figured out they were being monitored a few years ago, and they created their own encryption networks."

Kara said, "We would have to be on the same network with the same encryption software for that to work. Do you know the name of the group?"

Jimmy said, "That's easy … The Virginia Militia."

Kara said, "Give me fifteen minutes and I'll be into their network. I'll need his email address, and I'll need to send him a copy of my encryption software so we can escape detection, unless their IT people are smarter than the Feds."

Jimmy cracked, "That sounds more likely than possible."

*****

Chris Johnson walked into Evan Lee's office unannounced, as was his usual practice. He threw open the door and walked toward the senator's desk, startling the college intern into an upright position, leaving the senator to close his fly. The girl wiped her mouth, muttered something about dropping a pen, and scurried from the office with a reddened face.

Chris Johnson wasn't surprised, but angered. He waited until the office door closed and said sternly to the senator, "An intern? I hope she's not a minor, and I sure hope she doesn't involve her parents when you toss her out like today's trash."

The senator gathered himself and asked, "Is there something I can help you with, Chris?"

Chris re-focused on his reason for coming into the office. "I woke up during the middle of the night bothered by something, and I need to ask you a question."

The senator said, "I'm waiting."

Chris asked, "Senator, what type of gun did you use in Charleston?

The senator stammered, "I'm, I think it was a Smith and Wesson. Why?"

Chris said, "I don't mean brand. Was it semi-automatic or a revolver?"

The senator replied, "Semi-automatic. Why are you asking this?"

Chris Johnson took a breath and asked the question that had kept him awake the night before. "Senator, did you pick up the ejected shell casing?"

The senator had a sinking feeling and the color drained from his face. "No, I didn't pick up the shell casing." He knew the implications.

Chris Johnson said, "I'll check with the Charleston police and see if a shell casing was entered into evidence. The police always look for spent shells, so I expect that your Charleston problem lives on. IF the police found the shell, and IF I can get it, and IF they haven't already started the tracing process, we still have a chance of controlling this. If not, you have a serious problem. If that turns out to be the case, I'll have to involve Bedekowski, and he won't be pleased with any of us, especially you."

The senator was visibly shaken. Sweat formed on Chris Johnson's forehead, knowing that Bedekowski would view Chris' mistake of not thinking about the shell casing as one of the first things on his check list. This might be the last straw for the senator, and possibly for himself. Bedekowski didn't let any misdeed go unpunished, and he had a reputation for doling out severe treatment for the offenders.

Chris walked over to the senator's desk and picked up the phone. He knew such a call would be recorded by the NSA, and he wasn't going to make the call from his own phone. He called his contact in the Charleston police department and asked for the evidence list from the shooting. His contact put him on hold for almost 15 minutes before returning and saying, "Here's the list. Tire track plaster impressions, blood samples from the scene of the crime, a piece of clothing that was ripped off of someone and stuck to a saw palmetto, blood samples from the boat the woman was brought in on, photos of the boat, photos of the scene. Statements from the victim, statements from a Mr. Ned Harrison of Bland, Virginia."

After a few seconds of silence, Chris Johnson asked, "That's it? Nothing more? Did the statements identify a perpetrator?"

The contact said that was everything in the file. He said that the Good Samaritan in the case didn't know the perpetrator, and the woman made up three different names, all of them fictional. She refused to identify her attacker."

Chris Said, "I owe you one."

The contact said, "You always owe me, and you never pay your tab." Chris hung up the phone without offering a response.

Chris Johnson dialed another number. When a deep male voice answered, Chris said, "I need you to go down to Charleston with a metal detector and find a spent nine millimeter shell casing. I'll text you directions the place." Chris hung up the phone without allowing the other person a chance to respond.

Chris walked toward the door of the senator's office. He stopped short a couple of feet, and turned to the senator. "Evan, when you become president, IF you stay out of jail, it is customary to reward the people who helped you into office with positions in the administration."

He paused and said, "I want you to break that tradition. I don't want to be a part of your administration, because I'll end up a fulltime maid cleaning up your messes all over the world. I'll let you know when you can do me favors to repay all of my work keeping you out of trouble all these years. There'll be many favors I'll call in, and every one of them will make me a wealthier man. The tables will be turned."

Chris Johnson opened the door, quickly walked through it and slammed it behind him without giving the senator the opportunity to respond. The call he had just made was productive. The police hadn't found the shell casing, and that was good. It was still the missing piece of the puzzle that could link the senator to the crime, but at least the police didn't have it. And as a bonus, he now knew the name of the witness and where he lived. He had another phone call to make, and he needed a new prepaid phone to make it from. He walked into his office, opened the bottom drawer of his desk and pulled out one of several pre-paid phones that he had had his staff purchase for him.

Aside from the many messes the senator had created, political campaigns were very messy operations and confidential conversations were a requirement. Deniability was essential in politics, and pre-paid phones were one of the tools required by the job. Chris Johnson turned to the safe in his credenza and spun the dial. He opened the safe, retrieved an address book and looked up a number. He punched the number into his phone, but did not push the "call" button.

Chris Johnson left his office and walked out onto the capital grounds and sat on a wooden bench beneath a large oak tree. He touched the "call" button on the pre-paid cell phone, and listened as it rang three times before a deep, quiet voice spoke. Chris Johnson said, "I have an assignment for you. Ned Harrison, Bland, Virginia. Usual terms, immediate action."

Chris Johnson pushed the "end" button on the phone, stood and began walking back toward the capital building. As he passed by a trashcan, he dropped the phone in it without breaking stride. He smiled to himself. Within 24 hours, another of the senator's loose ends would be wrapped up. Chris Johnson wondered what would pop up next from this episode. It seemed to be the problem that kept reappearing.

Chapter 17

As Ned and Kara, Jimmy and Sam served their dinner plates and sat at the large wooden table, Ned stared out the expansive glass rear of the house overlooking the rolling Colorado hills. Things looked so peaceful out there it would be easy to forget that they held a loose grip on the tail of a monster that could end their lives and affect many others for decades to come. He didn't wish it wasn't so or regret that he and his friends were involved in it. He accepted it as his – and their – duty, their lot in life. It just was. No use wasting energy or time on wishing a problem away. The time was best spent of finding a solution, or manufacturing one, as they were presently attempting.

Kara broke the silence. "Ned, do you think our plan will work?"

Ned answered. "Well, we have involved Homeland Security, the Coast Guard, the IRS, National Forest Service, Department of Education and EPA. They all have SWAT teams, and we have laid out the bait to draw them into a conflict with each other. As with any plan, there is no way to anticipate every possibility or accurately predict an outcome. All operations are fluid and complex. Things can unexpectedly go wrong, and things that we didn't expect can break our way. So, I don't know if the plan will work, but I think it is a solid course of action. By this time tomorrow, we'll have a better feel for where things are headed."

Kara took a sip of red wine and stared at the glass as she carefully placed it back on the table. She said, "This afternoon I compiled a list of media contacts and their numbers and email addresses. I have all the key people from the major networks and news outlets, as well as several popular bloggers. Once the shooting starts, I think we should alert all of them so there is no way for the Feds to claim that this was a training exercise or find some other way to sweep it under the rug. The more coverage we have, the safer we'll be."

Ned, Sam and Jimmy enthusiastically agreed. Ned said, "Kara, can you sketch a script we can use? We can divide and conquer so that we call each contact as quickly as possible."

Kara said, "Sure, and we can use the same script to send emails to every news network and outlet, much the way the companies send mass emails with news releases. I'll break the list into four and get them to everyone tonight."

Jimmy raised his glass of beer and said, "Here's to the best damn special ops team that I've ever worked with."

The next morning, Kara called to the others and urgently asked them to join her at her computer. As they gathered around, Kara clicked on the "play" icon of a news video. An image of senator Evan Lee filled the screen, and the sound of his voice cracked through the scratchy sounding speakers of the laptop. The senator said, "It is my humble pleasure to announce to the citizens of the great state of South Carolina, and the great country of the United States of America, that I am entering the race for the office of President of the United States. After listening to the urging of my constituents, the support of my wife … come up here, Betsy … Betsy has been the best wife on earth. Not only has she been my confidant, my best source of support and the better half of our union, but she is also the smartest person I know. Thank you, Betsy, for all you do and all you are."

The senator kissed his smiling wife on the cheek, which was unnaturally frozen in a pleasant expression. He turned back to the podium, and she shrank from his thoughts and eased back into the shadows of the rear of the stage. Anyone who kept their focus on her noticed that she quietly left the stage, leaving the senator as the only one in the spotlight, which was the way he liked it.

The senator continued addressing the audience, mostly the one on TV. "I intend, with your support, to lead this country back from its errant venture into mediocrity and back to the ways of success and freedom for every citizen. In other words, I intend to re-awaken the American Dream, where people have pride in what they do, and I will clear a path for everyone to reach his highest level of success without the burden of government interference, without the drag of over taxation, without the terrible burden of dependence on government agencies who don't care about them. We became a great country by being self reliant while being quick to offer a helping hand to our fellow citizens.

"We have accepted the false premise that government has something free to give us and will always be there to bail us out no matter our level of effort. As a result, we have lost our pride, and too many people in power have destroyed our belief in ourselves and in our fellow man. The very characteristics that made us the greatest country in the history of the World have been replaced by a false sense of security that our government will reach into its infinite coffer and keep us from harm and suffering. We have learned, have we not, that the government's coffer is our pockets, and while taking from those of us work to give to those who won't has killed our incentive to strive for greatness, and eroded our self worth day by day?"

Kara paused the video, slid the indicator in the bar at the bottom of the page and forwarded the video to the post-announcement comment by news commentators. The black-haired news host said, "You heard the senator announce his run for president, and you heard his comments that could be considered a pivot to the middle from his usual positions of wealth equality and social justice, government expansion and regulation."

Kara stopped the video and sat silent. Jimmy said, "In other words, he is bullshitting to try and conceal his track record and appear as if he is something other than another leftist."

Jimmy's frankness and matter-of-fact presentation broke the somber reality of the room and made the group, to a person, break out into spontaneous laughter. After it died down, Sam said, "Ned, it looks like the stakes were just raised. We are now up against a sitting president and his supporters, and power of the agencies and forces that they continue to rain down on us, and possibly an incoming president who we know to be a cold blooded murderer."

Ned silently rubbed his chin as he stared at the image on the computer screen. After a few seconds, he spoke. "I am not surprised. I expected this development and accounted for it, as I believe all of you did. We continue on as we were."

Sam said, "True enough, but it has transitioned from suspicion to reality. And the reality is that we can't allow a murderer to become president."

Everyone in the group turned to look at Sam, who wore an expression of confidence. Kara asked, "Sam, you look as if you hold the magic bullet. Do you know something we don't?"

Sam stood and without a hint of a smile, said, "Wait here." He turned and walked from the room. He returned a couple of minutes later and sat, looking seriously at the group from one person to the next, filling the room with anticipation. Then he spoke. "Kara, you mentioned a magic bullet, and that's an interesting choice of words. The answer is that no, I don't have a magic bullet." He paused, reached into his shirt pocket and said, "But I have the next best thing." He pulled a plastic bag from his pocket and let it unfurl, revealing a brass, cylindrical object. He said, "I have the shell casing from the gun the senator used to kill the woman in Charleston."

The group was silent for a few seconds. Jimmy broke the silence with, "I'll be damned." Kara stared blankly, and Ned was thinking through scenarios of how they could best use the casing to their advantage. Ned finally broke the silence.

"We have to play this carefully. If we let it be known that we have the casing, the senator will claim his gun was stolen and he didn't realize it. Then we have accomplished little."

Kara said, "But suspicion can be enough to derail a political campaign, don't you think?"

Ned said, "True, it could, but there's no guarantee. Think of all the politicians who have overcome scandals and gone on to successful campaigns. Ted Kennedy, Bill Clinton, the mayor of Washington D.C. who was on film smoking crack. Suspicion is good, but we need more. What we need is the senator's gun, and we need to get it before we release this information. Sam, do you have any suggestions?"

Sam answered, "It's clear … we have to steal it. And I will be the one that does it."

After thirty minutes of debating the risks and rewards of various plans, they all agreed to call their pilot and fly Sam to Columbia, South Carolina. Kara asked, "Sam, tell me again what will happen if you are caught?"

Sam answered, "I will show my police ID and say I am on official police business investigating a murder. If that doesn't work, I try to run for it. If that fails, I take the fall and refuse to talk. Ned will send his choice of attorneys, and I will remain silent and let you folks handle the fight."

Kara shook her head. "It seems so risky. I mean, we have Ned and Jimmy here, both who have worked black operations for years. Why do you want to do this?"

Sam answered, "Because I have investigated burglaries, murders and other crimes for almost three decades. I know how to break and enter without being detected, and how to cover my tracks. And besides, I have police credentials. If local cops show up, they will be more likely to offer leeway to a fellow officer than someone who claims to be a federal agent with no badge. Anyway, I will most likely outrank anyone who responds to a break-in, and police officers have been taught to be reluctant to hassle any officer of superior rank. It's been pounded into their heads since the first day of their careers."

Kara nodded her head at that. It seemed as plausible as anything else they had come up with. The debate over, they looked up the senator's schedule on the capital events calendar, and learned that he would be out of town campaigning starting the next day. Ned made the call to the pilot, and arranged transportation on the other end, renting Sam a car in a fictitious name. Ned then went to work creating a fake ID and credit card for Sam with the equipment he kept in the gun storage room in his basement, which was much like the one in his Virginia house. An hour later, he came back upstairs with the items in hand. The group gathered around the table and reviewed their plan.

Ned said, "Sam, here is a new ID and credit card so you can rent a car without being detected by our friendly Feds. But remember that the name on the care rental contract differs from badge, so you don't want to provide the paperwork or even have it in the car with you as you carry out your mission. "

Sam acknowledged.

Ned would drive Sam to the airfield 35 miles away as soon as darkness arrived. Sam had his story straight in case he was caught, and he agreed that he would take the fall alone without exposing any information. He would entrust Ned, Jimmy and Kara with the information control and dissemination. He would remain silent, no matter what.

The pilot met them at the airfield 15 minutes ahead of schedule. He taxied over to the fueling area. Ned shook hands with the pilot, and re-introduced him to Sam, which was more a courtesy than a necessity. They had flown with the same pilot a few days ago.

Ned paid for the $3,800 of fuel in cash, as was his usual practice at the field. He didn't want an electronic transaction to be created, which could be a powerful lead for anyone who was looking for him. Within seconds of the plane taking off on its southeasterly route to South Carolina, Ned drove away from the airfield, taking a circuitous route back to his house, checking the rearview mirror for anyone following him. He had chosen darkness for their travel to make things a little more challenging for drones or satellites that could be observing him. They could still detect them with infrared or night vision technology if so equipped, but this would eliminate any detection vehicles that lack the proper technology, or people on the ground that could easily observe him in the daylight. The stakes were high, and he didn't intend to make it easy for anyone.

*****

 In Bland, Virginia, the man looked at his map, trying to find the address that Chris Johnson had given him. At a loss, he pulled into a small country gas station and walked in. There were several locals sitting at a round card table in the back corner of the store. Although they had been involved in a raucous discussion when the stranger walked in, they fell silent as the man approached the back of the room. All eyes were on the stranger, and the eyes were filled with suspicion. Not only because they distrusted all strangers, but because this man was dressed as if he was a city slicker and he had a cold look to him.

The man asked, "I'm looking for 2322 West Mountain Road. I think it's in the middle of nowhere. Can you tell me where it is?"

The group was silent until the largest man who had the look of leader of the group spoke. "Boy, you found the middle of nowhere. As for the address you look for, never heard of it."

The stranger was suspicious of the men and looked from one to the other, searching for the weak link. Then he threw caution to the wind and said, "Looking for Ned Harrison. You know where he is?"

The group kept their faces of stone, but the stranger detected recognition in the leader's expression. The leader spoke, "Never heard of him, neither."

The stranger looked again from one man to the other. When he focused his appraising stare on the last man, the man said in a thick mountain drawl, "You heard what the man said. Is they anything else you wanted?"

The stranger knew he would get no help from this group, not voluntarily. He would wait until the store closed or until the rest of the group left the leader, who was apparently the store proprietor, alone. Then he could use his persuasive techniques to get the information he needed. Those techniques usually involved the use of a very sharp knife, like the one he carried in his pocket.

The stranger returned to his car and sped off. Once down the road about a mile, he turned around and drove with his lights off. He found a spot on the edge of a side road that overlooked the store, and he waited. After an hour or so, the fourth of the five men in the store got into his old, beaten up, yellow Chevrolet truck and drove off, passing thirty feet from where the stranger was parked. The stranger feared he had been seen, but the yellow truck didn't slow down.

The stranger waited ten minutes and drove back to the store with his lights off. He parked to the side of the building. When he walked in the front door of the store, the proprietor didn't look the least bit surprised to see him. The proprietor said, "Ain't we already talked about this?"

The stranger decided that the knife wasn't enough for this situation, and pulled the nine-millimeter pistol from his right coat pocket. The proprietor didn't bat an eye. He reached down beneath the counter, and before the stranger could react, pulled up a double barrel shotgun and pointed it at the stranger's chest. The stranger quickly appraised whether he should dart right or left, but before he could make a decision, the proprietor said, "You best make peace with your maker before you pull the trigger on that hog leg. You might get me, but you won't get the man behind you before he makes a tunnel out of your head."

The stranger heard the two clicks of a hammer being cocked on another twelve gauge, double-barrel shotgun just a few feet behind him.

The proprietor spoke again. "Now just drop that hog leg, peaceful like, and put your hands over your head."

The stranger complied. He would find an opportunity to take out these two country bumpkins, but this wasn't the time. He would get the drop on them sooner or later, or might even have to talk his way out of it with the local sheriff.

The instant he raised his hands, he was tackled from behind, his arms were jerked violently upward, and two large cable ties were ratcheted around his wrists. Before he could react, his feet were also locked with cable ties, and he was roughly rolled over.

He looked up to see the two large barrels of the shotgun the proprietor held, and the smiling face of a man missing a few teeth. "I guess you figured you'd come in here and roll over on us country folk. You ain't the first city boy to sell us short. Been happening for two hundred years. You forget that we perfected our own law enforcement around here during prohibition. We ain't to be fucked with, we're to be reckoned with. Best you learn that real quick, if you ain't in the last two minutes."

The proprietor smiled a wicked smile and said to the second man who had secured the cable ties, "Search him, and look out for other guns and knives. Then lock him in the cooler and stand guard about ten feet outside the freezer door."

The second man said, "Alright. What you gonna do?"

The proprietor said, "I'm gonna call Huldon. He'll want to have a talk with this city boy."

The stranger felt beads of sweat break out on his forehead and upper lip.

He thought, these hicks aren't even going to call the police, they are going to render their own justice, and that can't be good. These hicks are crusty and seasoned and likely don't appreciate me coming in asking about one of their neighbors. They probably take greater offense to me pulling a gun on the proprietor. This isn't good.

The man who put the cable ties on him jerked the 250 pound stranger up like he was a rag doll. The stranger's sweat immediately turned profuse as he realized how strong the mountain man was.

More thoughts ran through the stranger's mind: Fuck Chris Johnson! He was an asshole anyway, and now had gotten him into this mess. If he ever got out of this, he was going to take care of Johnson, and it would be the last anyone would ever hear from him. Asshole politician!

*****

Five hours later, Kara opened her email, just as she did every morning. There was a message from Huldon, and she felt nauseous as she read it.

She called frantically, "Jimmy, Ned, come and look at this. Now!"

Both men ran into the room to find Kara pale and breathing rapidly, covering her mouth as if she may vomit. She pointed to the computer screen. Ned and Jimmy walked over to it and Jimmy read aloud, "Jimmy, though you'd want to know we were visited last night by a man said that someone by the name of Chris Johnson hired him to visit Ned and leave a bullet in his head. He admitted this after pulling a gun on one of our men, and after a few hours of persuasion that we gave him. You won't have to worry about the man anymore; he's gone on to have a face-to-face with his maker. He attacked one of us with a knife, and we had to help him on his way to judgment day with a .45 slug."

Jimmy stood silent for a moment, then said, "The stranger should have known better than to try and strong arm a group of locals, at night, and with gun in hand.

Once you pull a weapon on a mountain man, especially a group of them who are all in the Virginia Militia, you better shoot first and often."

Ned said, "He should have known better, but he probably thought he could roll over some ignorant locals without a challenge. I almost said 'live and learn,' but I'm afraid that doesn't apply in this situation."

Kara stood and said with emotion, "That's not funny!" before running to the bathroom and throwing up. Jimmy looked at Ned and said,

"Sorry about that. I thought she would be prepared for the violence that's about to go down, but I guess not."

Ned said, "Don't hold it against her. One of the great things about her is that she believes that everyone can be redeemed no matter how bad they are. She hasn't seen the things we have, and hasn't come to grips with the fact that some people are just pure evil. And to survive evil, it often means that evil people have to be eliminated to rid us of the evil they manifest. That's the eternal irony people like us have faced since the beginning of time. We have to walk the line carefully to keep ourselves from becoming the same as them. I hope we can continue to do it."

Jimmy said, "Amen. You should you go check on Kara."

Ned said, "I should. See you in a bit." Ned walked to the bathroom to which Kara had retreated and gently knocked on the door. He opened it slowly to find Kara bent over the sink washing bile from her mouth and tears from her face. She blurted between sobs, "This is so ugly. I just wish it would go away!"

Ned gently took her in his arms and held her close, saying, "I know, Kara, I know." He held her there until she exhausted her emotions and fell silently into his chest. She said, "I wish we could turn back the clock to the time when we were innocent and in love."

Ned was surprised. He had never known she had loved him. He had let it pass years ago. He wondered if he would be able to let it pass again. He secretly hoped he couldn't.

*****

Sam waited until 3 a.m. He had been watching the senator's home for more than two hours, and the last of the lights had been turned off long ago. Sam slid on his latex gloves, exited his rental car and walked silently through the edge of the two yards that were between him and the senator's home. A black car matching the description Ned had provided was parked in the carport. Sam had the door jimmy kit he had purchased at a local auto parts store.

Sam pried at the top left corner of the doorframe with the plastic wedge from the kit and inserted the inflatable balloon. He hand pumped the balloon until there was a two-inch gap between the doorframe and the body of the car. He took the three-foot steel rod with the 90 degree bend in the last few inches and slid it into the vehicle, felt around for the lock/unlock button and applied pressure. He heard a click from the door lock, and he removed the rod and laid it carefully on the ground.

Sam took a breath and opened the door. As he expected, the alarm sounded. Sam quickly sat in the car and opened the glove box. There it was, the black Smith and Wesson Ned had described. He grabbed the gun and removed the magazine. He racked the gun to eject the bullet in the chamber and slid the magazine and gun into the pocket of his black coat.

Sam picked up the parts of the door jimmy and jogged back to his car. He tossed the door jimmy kit into nearby shrubs, jumped in his car and drove slowly away.

He had driven about four blocks when blue lights lit up behind him. He slid the gun under the seat, pulled over to the side of the road and took a deep breath in preparation for the encounter he was about to have. He rolled down his window as the officer approached his car. The officer had his right hand on his gun, as was standard procedure. Sam kept his hands on the steering wheel in plain view of the officer.

The officer stopped near the back door of the car. Sam said, "Good evening, officer."

The officer stepped a little closer to Sam and shined a bright light in Sam's face. The officer spoke. "Sir, could I see your license and registration?"

Sam said, "My license and badge are in my jacket pocket. The car is a rental, and the paperwork is in the glove box."

The officer said, "Badge, you say? Could I please see it?"

Sam reached slowly into his jacket, removing his leather badge wallet. He held the wallet up in plain sight, opened it, removed his license from his wallet and handed the license and the badge wallet to the officer.

The officer read Sam's name and rank out loud, and said, "You're a long way out of your jurisdiction, detective. What, may I ask, are you doing out so late so far from home?"

Sam replied, "I'm not here on official business. Let's just say I'm here on a social matter I would rather keep quiet, if you know what I mean."

The officer smiled, and asked, "Have you been drinking tonight, detective?"

Sam answered, No, officer, I have not. Did I commit a traffic violation? Between us, I was thinking more about my … social visit … than I was my driving, and I apologize for that."

The officer handed Sam his wallet and badge and said, "No violation, detective. We've had a problem with drunk driving in this area, as well as late night gang-related activity including burglaries and shootings.

We are trying to raise awareness that we are out in force. Naturally, seeing an out of state tag and this being a college town, I suspected a student on his way home from a bar. I'll let you be on your way. But detective ..."

Sam looked up again and said, "Yes, officer?"

The detective said, "You be careful with your ... social visits. Those can be as deadly as a gang shooting, if you mess with the wrong types of people, such as married ones. Angry husbands take things personally."

Sam didn't smile, only said, "Good advice, officer. I'll keep that in mind. You have a good night, and be safe out there."

The officer gave Sam a curt salute, turned and walked back to his car. He turned off his blue lights, did a U turn and sped off. Sam drove off, too, and noticed in his rear view mirror that the officer turned his blue lights back on and took a sharp right turn down the road Sam had come from, the road the senator lived on. The officer was likely responding to a call of a car alarm going off. Sam accelerated and headed directly to the Columbia Municipal airport where his plane and pilot awaited him.

Once there, he pulled to the front of the terminal, walked quickly to the drop box and put the keys into the box, then jogged toward his plane.

Sam knocked loudly on the door of the plane, and the pilot opened it with a cup of coffee in his hand.

Sam climbed into the plane, made his way to the co-pilot's seat, buckled in and said, "Let's get moving. Immediately."

The pilot started the first engine, then the second and taxied to the end of the runway. He didn't bother contacting the control tower. No one would arrive to work in the tower for another hour and a half. The pilot pushed the throttles forward and the plane increased speed down the runway. Sam didn't take a deep breath until the wheels left the ground. Once they were airborne, Sam felt the gun and magazine zipped into his jacket pocket. He thought back to when the blue lights lit up behind him as he left the senator's neighborhood. Sam smiled as he thought how stupid, or arrogant, the senator had been for failing to dispose of the gun in the nearest river after the shooting, and that he had left it in the car he had been driving when he shot the woman. What had the man been thinking? Then Sam reminded himself that the senator was a well-connected politician who had become accustomed to a charmed, protected life beyond the reach of the law, as many high-powered politicians had. But the senator had made several grave mistakes during and since the episode in Charleston, and Sam intended to do what he could to make sure the senator faced justice.

Sam leaned back in his cockpit seat. He couldn't sleep with the adrenalin running through his veins, even if he didn't have to remain alert to fulfill his duty as co-pilot. Knowing the adrenalin rush would soon fade, leaving him exhausted, he turned to the pilot and asked, "Mind if I have a cup of your coffee?"

The pilot answered, "Be my guest. Beware, though, it's high-test. Only fellow pilots brew it as strong."

Sam picked up the thermos that rested between their seats. The pilot handed him a metal cup, and Sam filled it. The pilot was right … the brew was the strongest he had ever tasted. Reminded him of his stints on the night shift when he first began his career as a detective, and those weren't all bad memories. He thought to himself, too bad I can't call Ned and give him an update. Ironic how the vulnerabilities of modern technology had made them revert to the times before cell phones, giving credence to the old adage, "As much as things change, they stay the same." Although he wanted to communicate his results immediately, he would have to wait until he returned to the airfield in Colorado and tell Ned in person.

*****

As Sam's plane was on its final approach in Colorado, Senator Evan Lee's wife called him on his cell phone. He ran from the bathroom of his Iowa hotel room to the bedside table. He looked at the caller ID and saw that his wife was on the line. "Hello, honey, how are you?"

She responded, "I'm fine, everything here is fine, in spite of the excitement we had here last night."

The senator instantly became anxious. "What happened?"

She said, "No harm done, it appears, but someone broke into your car last night. It doesn't appear that anything was taken or damaged, but the alarm sounded. When the police arrived, the only thing they found was that the glove box door was open.

"I told them you didn't have anything in there of value that I knew of. They suspect that someone broke in to steal the car or to look for laptops or other things of value, but it seems there was nothing taken."

As she spoke the senator racked his brain doing a mental inventory of the car. He had his laptop with him, his watch on and he was talking on his phone. His briefcase was on the desk of his hotel room. He couldn't think of any reason someone would break into his car. He said to his wife, "It must have been a random crime executed by a local gang banger looking for a quick buck. No harm, no foul, I suppose."

She said, "That's what I told the police officers. Nice young men, they were. I had to force them to take a cup of coffee and a slice of my mother's pound cake."

The senator felt instant sympathy for the officers, and made a mental note to thank them personally. His wife made the worst cup of coffee he had ever tasted, rivaled only by his mother-in-law's bone dry pound cake. The officers deserved a medal for suffering through the worst food and drink they could have encountered. But he didn't say that to his wife.

They exchanged a few more mundane bits of information, said their pleasantries and wished each other a good day. He hung up the phone, relieved that the 22-year old blonde prostitute in his bed had remained asleep through the conversation, and he hadn't had to come up with a cover story.

He poked the woman on the ass with his index finger to wake her. She murmured, "Is that your dick, or are you holding a gun on me?"

The blood rushed from the senator's face, leaving him pale and in a cold sweat. She rolled over and looked up at him. "Damn! You drink that much champagne last night? You look like death warmed over?"

The senator swallowed hard and caught his breath. Gun! The prostitute had said the word gun, which reminded him of his own gun. Where was his pistol? He flowed through a collection of mental images of the scene in Charleston.

He had shot the woman, hustled back to his car and driven away. What had he done with the gun? Had he thrown it out the window? Had he later tossed it into a trashcan? Everything that day was fuzzy, but he couldn't remember disposing of the weapon, that day or later. What had he done with it? Had he put it back in the glove box?

The senator said to the hooker, "Get out. Now!"

The woman protested, but the senator ignored her as he dialed Chris Johnson's number and paced the room. As the phone began to ring, Chris saw the woman moving slowly, looking around the room and casually gathering her clothing. The senator, in a highly intense mental state of panic, grabbed the woman by the arm, rushed her to the door, opened it and shoved her violently into the hallway holding her panties, dress and one shoe. She screamed as he slammed the door in her face.

Chris Johnson answered the phone. The senator blurted, "We have a problem! I think I left my gun in my glove box, and someone broke into my car last night. They have the gun!"

Chris was thrown off guard, but not surprised by the phone call; he had received so many similar ones from the senator. He said, "Calm down. Where are you … and is anyone with you? And what fucking gun are you talking about?"

The senator yelled, "THE gun! The one I shot the woman with in Charleston."

Chris Johnson realized what the senator was saying. He said, "Don't say another word. Where are you? Oh, that's right, you're in Iowa. Stay in your room. Don't talk to anyone. Don't go anywhere. Don't do anything. I'll get on a plane and meet you there."

The senator protested, "But I'm scheduled to give a speech in two hours, and my staff is expecting me at breakfast in 30 minutes. Someone has the gun!"

Chris Johnson yelled, "Shut the fuck up, senator! I'll contact your staff. I will tell them that you are very ill with food poisoning. I'll tell them to cancel everything.

"Now don't talk to anyone, and don't leave your room. And even if the hotel is burning down, do not talk on the phone and do not send any emails. Do you understand, senator?"

The senator let out a loud sob, just beyond the verge of being out of control. He took a deep breath and managed to say the words, "I got it. I will stay here until you arrive."

Chris Johnson hung up his phone. Holy shit! It was entirely possible that someone had the shell casing, the slug from the woman, and the senator's gun. Whoever was playing this game had better realize the stakes and the players. If those people were found, their time on earth would be over. So, why would they risk shaking the hornet's nest? Who on earth would literally risk their lives? It had to be someone who could enjoy a tremendous gain from the senator's demise. Maybe his opponents in the upcoming primaries? No, the entire field was rigged, so it had to be someone from the opposing party who thought their path to the White House would be clear without the senator in the race. They had the most to gain, so it had to be them.

Chris began punching the numbers of the private cell phone of governor Rob Roberts of Florida. The governor answered, and Chris Johnson blurted, "What the hell do you think you're doing? We have an arrangement!"

The governor said, Chris, is this you?"

Chris Johnson said, "You know damn well it's me. Now what the fuck do you think you're doing breaking into his car and stealing his gun?

You think you can get away with blackmailing the senator, Senator LEE, the next president?"

The governor gasped, tried to gather himself and said, "We do have an arrangement that I have honored to the T. Now, why would I want to break into the senator's car and steal his … gun, did you say?"

Chris Johnson shouted, "I know it was you! You have the most to gain?"

The governor fired back with a sharp edge in his voice, "I didn't do anything to your fumbling senator, but it sounds as if he certainly did something of horrible magnitude.

"I have nothing to gain, because I know the election is a charade. So, let's not pretend I stood to gain anything. However, the senator has a track record of ruining people for his own gain. Maybe it was someone who had nothing else to lose; you ever think of that? I told you to watch out backing people into corners and putting them in desperate situations. A person poses the most danger when they think they have nothing more to lose. Now, don't ever call me again, you son of a bitch! And my advice to you is to get as far away from the senator as possible, because one day he's going down, and he's going to take down everyone around him when he blows. You mark my words."

The phone went dead. Chris Johnson sat at his desk panting. What the hell was happening? The governor was lying. He had to be. Chris Johnson slammed his cell phone into the trashcan beneath his desk, sending parts and shards of plastic flying in all directions. Then, after several breaths and a million thoughts flashed through his brain, Chris Johnson said aloud, "Fuck! Maybe the governor was right."

Chris Johnson's assistant broke his daze by saying, "Mr. Johnson, is there something I can do for you?"

Chris looked up to see his assistant standing just inside his office door, one hand over her chest and the other at her mouth to figuratively cover her shock and fear, and guard her heart from the wrath that was likely to follow her intrusion.

Her presence seemed to shake Chris Johnson from his rage. He sat stunned for a moment, wondering how much she had heard, then caught himself and blurted, "Call the pilot! I need to go to Iowa immediately!"

His assistant muttered, "Sir, the senator has the plane in Iowa, and the pilot is with him."

Chris quickly transitioned back into his state of confusion and rage. He slammed his hand down on his desk and shouted, "Then get another one! Now, you dumb fuck! Prove to me you have more than just a great rack and skilled lips! Get me a fucking plane, and get it now. I am headed to the municipal airport right now, and I better have wings when I get there!"

He threw his chair back and began walking rapidly toward her, toward the door. In tears and in fear, she ran out of his office and down the hall to the office of another assistant who was also her friend. As Chris entered the hall and saw her retreating, he yelled, "I better have that fucking plane when I get to the airport!"

As Chris Johnson drove toward the airport, his assistant, after arranging air transportation for him, walked into her lawyer's office a block from the office. Her friend who was with her handed her another tissue to wipe away her tears. After a short wait, she was shown to her attorney's private office, where Chris Johnson's assistant told the story of this morning's events, including what she had overheard. The lawyer's face went pale. He punched a button on his phone and said, "Could you come in here, please, and bring Mr. Sands with you? Tell him it is gravely urgent."

When the law firm's scribe and the chief partner entered the office, the attorney told Chris Johnson's assistant, "We are recording this statement and will consider this to be an official deposition. Please tell the story again. Mr. Sands here, our firm's founder, and our firm scribe, Ms. Smith, will serve as witnesses. Being a legal statement, everything said here is protected as we are your legal representation.

"Except for your friend, who is present at your request to provide moral support, everyone in this room is immune to subpoena powers regarding this discussion. It is our advice that your friend leave the room, but you have waived that advice. Regardless of legal standing, we urge that everything said here remain confidential. Should this information be leaked or released, people could be in danger, both legally and possibly otherwise. I want to be very clear about that. Does everyone understand and agree? If so, please review and sign the confidentiality agreement I have put before each of you. If you decline this agreement, we urge you to leave the room." The lawyer kept his gaze squarely on Chris Johnson's assistant's friend. The middle aged woman, who looked as if she could be the mother figure of the two, read the agreement and curtly signed it. She looked to be a little offended, but the lawyer didn't waiver.

The lawyer continued, "Now, please state your full name and address, your position on Senator Evan's staff, and tell us, with every detail, what you witnessed today."

An hour later, the account of the events of the morning altercation with Chris Johnson was part of the official legal record of the state of South Carolina, and in addition to Chris Johnson's assistant, four more people knew the entire account of the morning events, as well as the entire phone conversations Chris Johnson had with the governor and with the senator. At least the words Chris Johnson had said.

*****

Jimmy was sitting with Kara at her desk when they heard Ned's vehicle amble up the gravel drive and straight into the barn. Thirty seconds later, Ned and Sam entered the room to find Kara and Jimmy staring at them.

Ned said, "You two look like the cats that found the store of nip."

Jimmy and Kara laughed. She said, "Actually, it's no laughing matter, but there is good news. First, Sam is back, and we can't wait to hear about his trip. But no matter how successful it was, we have a special surprise for you."

Ned said, "I'll let Sam tell about his venture. Or maybe adventure is more apropos."

Ned and Sam pulled up two chairs facing Jimmy and Kara. Sam told his story in detail only a detective would notice and recall. He left out

214

nothing, finishing it with a dramatic climax of putting a latex glove on his hand and slowly pulling the senator's gun from his pocket, where it had remained untouched since he put it there the night before. He said, "Jackpot, as long as this is the same gun. It's the right caliber and it matches the description Ned gave us, so I would say the odds are in our favor, although it defies all odds that even the most amateurish murderer would keep the murder weapon."

Jimmy said, "We can do a ballistics test easily enough, but just wait until you hear what Kara has for us. Kara, let it rip."

Kara said, "Well, I've been mining NSA call and email data using the key words lists we all composed. This morning I picked up three calls that are pretty significant.

"First, there was this one from Senator Lee." Kara turned to her laptop and clicked on a "play" button. The senator's voice filled the air, and Ned, Kara, Jimmy and Sam listened to the entire call the senator made to Chris Johnson.

When the call terminated, Ned let out a whistle. Sam said, "That's still circumstantial evidence, but damning, nonetheless."

Jimmy laughed and said, "No offense, Sam, but I say that call carries enough weight to squash a tick on a hound's ass. But wait; Kara has more."

Kara played the call Chris Johnson placed to the governor of Florida, leaving Ned and Sam stunned. Sam said, "I knew politicians were emotional, stupid beings, but these men should know better. Unbelievable! Kara, you should save these recordings in about a dozen different places. These calls, the senator's gun and the shell casing are the kind of evidence people kill to get, and I mean that literally."

Before Kara could respond and tell him she was way ahead of him, Ned said, "You said there were three calls. What is the third?"

As Kara queued up the last call, she said, "This call wasn't from either the senator or Chris Johnson, but their names were mentioned. Since there can be an untold number of calls that mention well-know names at any time, I was lucky to have found this one. But with a combination of very effective mining software and pure luck, I stumbled on this."

She turned and clicked on "play."

A female voice filled the room. "Sara, this is Veronica. You remember me telling you about my friend who works in Senator Lee's office, Chris Johnson's assistant? Well, wait until you hear this. She overheard two phone conversations this morning about a gun that was stolen from the senator. And that's not all; the senator was in a panic because apparently the senator shot someone with the gun. There was also a call where Chris Johnson accused the governor of Florida of setting up the senator. Something big is happening, and we are in the inside loop. My friend is going to email me a copy of her deposition as soon as she gets it from her lawyer's office in a couple of hours. Say, what did you say your reporter friend's name is?"

The voice on the other end of the phone interjected a few comments, but the only one of note was near the end of the conversation when she warned the caller, "This is dangerous! These are ruthless people, and I am afraid for you. You better take a vacation and stay below the radar until this blows over. And you better tell your friend to watch her ass. She's in a bad position. But the reporter friend, he's an asshole and I wouldn't give him anything that he might benefit from if my life depended on it. You remember he said he would call me after that night? He never did. Asshole!"

Ned rubbed his chin and said, "The governor of Florida, election charade, arrangement, this is all huge information if we can play it to the public at the right time, the right way. And an inside snoop looking for her fifteen minutes of fame with information that could cost her dearly, and could cost us, too. We have to discuss how we play this.

We have more ammunition than I ever imagined, and we need to make sure that we aren't victims of the shrapnel. And we need to make sure that scorned woman doesn't release information we need to use as leverage."

Jimmy said, "One damn thing's for sure, it sure is snowballing. It's what you planned, Ned, but even bigger than we had in mind. This could change the course of the world for decades. But for the scorned woman, I couldn't profess to know how to deal with that."

Kara said, "I know how to deal with that, gentlemen. I know how."

Jimmy said, "How, pray tell."

Kara grinned and said, "This is Kara Jones, reporter for the New York Times. I understand you have some rather juicy information, and I would like to talk to you about that." She paused, sighed and muffled a sob. She continued, "I am so sorry. Please forgive me. I recently broke up with my boyfriend and the wound is still raw. Some men are so inconsiderate. Please forgive me." She leaned back in her chair and smiled.

Jimmy said, "Women! They eat their own and feel not a hint of remorse. Of all the adversaries I've faced in the world, including the ones that shot at me, stabbed me, and threw grenades at my feet, women have caused me more pain and have created more fear in me than any of the world's armies."

Kara said with a grin, "Maybe that's why you are single, Jimmy. Maybe you think of women as adversaries rather than assets you should have in good favor."

Jimmy said, "Staying in their good favor is the problem."

Kara, laughing, said "The problem is you've been setting unattainable goals for yourself. It's impossible for you to stay in good favor, because you are as likely to get in trouble by not saying or doing something a woman wanted as you are from saying or doing something ill received. What you need to know is how to regain your favorable status."

Jimmy asked, "So, what's the secret formula for regaining favor?"

Kara laughed again and said, "And that, my friend, is the Holy Grail."

Ned said, "That's enough about the war of the sexes. Jimmy, she isn't going to give you the Holy Grail because women themselves don't know what it is, they only know when you've achieved it. And 'it' is a moving target. Anyway, you might fall out of favor with Kara if you continue."

Ned turned to Kara and said, "That's a great plan. You are now a reporter for the Times. Can you intercept the email of the deposition so the woman doesn't receive it?"

Kara said, "It's on my list."

Ned said, "Excellent. You should call the woman we just listened to."

Kara said, "Will do, and I'll make her my best friend in the process." She winked at Jimmy.

Jimmy shook his head. "Eat their own!"

Sam added, "Men make better sport for them. Ask my ex-wife."

Kara shook her head in pity at the men. "Three grown, single men; pitiful lot you are. Only one worth saving is Ned." She winked at Ned.

Jimmy said to Ned, "Ned, my friend, you're both the luckiest sumbitch alive and the most cursed. A woman sets her sights on you, you have no choice but to face the fate that awaits."

Ned looked at Kara, who wore a devilish grin. Ned said to everyone, "Let's focus on the task at hand, shall we?" With the eye only Kara could see, he winked at her, mirroring her earlier expression. He thought to himself how surprising and amazing it was that the power of attraction could exist, let alone prevail, amidst the pressure and strain they were all under. Come to think of it, it wasn't surprising considering Kara, whose beauty, strength and allure were also very powerful.

Chapter 18

The governor of Florida placed a call to New York, careful to use a prepaid cell phone in a location where no one could overhear his side of the conversation. A gruff voice with a deep Brooklyn accent answered, "Yes?"

The governor identified himself and said, "I need to talk to Bedekowski, and I need to talk to him ASAP. It is about his arrogant lap boy, Chris Johnson."

The voice said, "No names, please. I will have him call you back."

The governor waited 15 minutes as he sat on a bench in the city park. When his phone rang, he answered it immediately, mimicking the voice he had heard in New York.

"Yes?"

The voice on the other end said, "You called me? You mentioned names. You know the rules."

The governor said, "Right. Your errand boy called me this morning accusing me of digging up dirt on your favorite candidate. Not only that, but the things he said implied the senator is about to be exposed in a major scandal. I ask that you reel him and instruct him to lose my number, and to treat me with respect next time he addresses me. I advise you to find out what is going on with the senator and put some distance between the two of you. If not this time, sooner or later, the senator will do something so stupid that it brings him down along with everyone within range of the fallout."

Bedekowski said, "I don't need your advice, but your information is duly noted." Bedekowski hung up the phone. He called one of his assistants into his office. As the man entered the room, Bedekowski said, "Close the door and have a seat."

The man, wearing a black suit and intentionally looking all the part of a common mobster, obliged. After he sat, Bedekowski said, "Get on the plane immediately and visit our people at NSA and have them send me recordings of all calls the governor of Florida has made in the last 12 hours. Do the same with Chris Johnson's calls, and most important, with Senator Lee's calls. Here's the critical part: Make sure they erase all records of the calls in the NSA systems. I want it to be just as if the calls never happened."

Bedekowski wrote down the phone numbers of the parties involved. He tore of the top page of his note pad and handed it to the mobster imitator. To close the meeting, Bedekowski said, "This is the last time I'll tell you to lose the mobster look. For God's sake, you're a Naval

Academy graduate and veteran of Naval intelligence. You have no background or roots that make you a hood, and I want you to look like an IBM executive when you bring me the NSA recordings this afternoon."

The man slapped his heals together, snapped a sharp salute, spun on his heels and walked out of the office. Bedekowski made a mental note to punish the man for his behavior and appearance. This was a tight organization with no room for rebels. The work was too important, and they were so close to their goals. He thought to himself, one more occurrence like that and the man's friends and family will be filing a missing persons' report.

Within three hours, the man was sitting in the offices of one of their people in NSA headquarters. The woman who occupied the office was downloading recordings of the calls in question onto a thumb drive. She ejected the drive and handed it to the man. He said, nodding toward the computer screen, "Now erase the records."

She did as she was directed. She always did as she was directed. She wasn't stupid, although the man treated her like she was. She erased the records. The man stood up and walked out of the room without another word. She thought to herself, what an asshole. He really thinks I'm stupid.

She turned back to her computer screen and pulled up the recordings she had saved on her hard drive. She said aloud, "You think I'm stupid, but I'm smart enough to have saved the files of the calls in question. She copied them onto a thumb drive of her own, ejected the drive and leaned back in her chair. Under her desk, she hiked up her dress, pulled the waistband of her pantyhose and slid the thumb drive into her panties. She moved her pantyhose back in place and straightened her dress. She could feel the thumb drive resting against her pelvic bone.

When she got home that evening, she would go into her basement, unlock the hidden steel lockbox she kept hidden in the floor joists behind a heat duct. She would drop the thumb drive in and replace the lock box. That box contained almost twenty thumb drives. She mentally referred to the box as her insurance policy and her supplemental retirement fund. In three more years, she would retire from NSA with full benefits.

Once she did so, she planned to write a book using the files on the thumb drives as her reference material. Then she would offer the book to the highest bidder, be it a publisher or some of the powerful politicians of whom she had recordings. Boy, was this going to be a juicy book. A best seller ... easily. She rubbed her pelvic bone so she could feel the shape of the thumb drive. Just knowing it was there got her excited. She had something in mind for her husband that night. She always felt that way after the rush she got from smuggling out juicy information.

An hour later, Kara called Ned, Sam and Jimmy into the room. Jimmy wore an apron. He had been in the kitchen cooking their next meal, and looked the part of the country chef. The apron symbolized the chef skills, and the .45 holstered on his hip portrayed the country.

When they all sat down, Kara said, "I used to work down the hall from a woman at NSA. One afternoon about a year and a half back, I was walking by her office. I was in my stocking feet since my shoes I wore to work were killing me. Apparently I made no sound when I walked. When I got to her door, I could see her with her back to me. As I passed by, I saw her pull up her dress. Naturally, that got my attention, so like at car crash, I had to watch. The woman removed a thumb drive from her computer and slid it inside her panties, then pulled her dress back down. I turned and quietly walked away so she wouldn't know I had seen her.

"Being in IT, I can get into any computer in the NSA system, and some others. So, that night after everyone had gone home, I walked down the hall to the desk of my least favorite person in NSA, a woman who had gone out of her way to drop snide comments about me and never missed a chance to slide a knife in my ribs if the opportunity ever presented itself. She kept a list of passwords in her top desk drawer, and I knew where to look. I logged onto her computer, and then used our IT back door to get into the computer used by the woman who put the thumb drive in her panties.

Through some IT magic I won't bore you with, I looked at every file the panty woman had ever saved on an external drive – like a thumb drive – and what I found was very interesting. It appears this woman was gathering damaging information on many of the NSA brass, as well as some movers and shakers in the senate, house and even the White House. I'm not sure what she planned to do with the information, but she has a reason I'm sure the people in the files won't like."

Ned whistled and said, "Blackmail, writing a tell-all book, something along those lines?"

Jimmy piped in, "Maybe she's selling the information to the Russians or the Chinese."

Sam listened quietly and intently.

Kara said, "Like you, Jimmy, I also suspected espionage, so I checked her bank accounts, her spending habits, her home and cars to see if I could find evidence of having extra money. There was nothing there. No cash deposits.

Plenty of transactions at grocery stores and clothing stores, which are often purchases made with cash if someone has income they want to keep under the radar. No phone calls out of the ordinary, and none with anyone who sounded foreign. Her home was a modest one and her cars were American run-of-the-mill Fords and Chevys. I saw nothing that indicated an extra money stream."

Sam interrupted, "Pardon my asking, but how did you get a warrant to search her phone and banking records?"

Kara laughed. "I worked with the NSA, and the FISA court has given us blanket permission to listen to anything we want and to see any email, electronic banking transaction, tax forms, IRS statements, W2s, you name it. If it exists in electronic form, and nearly everything does, NSA can see it and has a record of it. We also can, and do, keep records of locations of cell phones, and can access toll records and police license tag scanners, and can drop in on any municipality's video monitoring systems, so we not only know who you are, what you do, but also where you are."

Sam was shaking his head. "That's an invitation for abuse."

Kara replied, "It certainly is, and it is often abused by people in power, and sometimes by people who don't have power but have access to the data. There have been several incidents where someone snooped

228

on their ex, their boss, their adversaries, and on and on. It's a terrible thing we've created, and spooky, too."

Ned said, "This serves as a reminder to all of us to keep your cell phones off, even though we are all using pre-paid phones. And stay off the Internet unless it's through the network Kara set up for us. I don't have a landline here or cable TV, so we don't have to worry about those avenues. There are very few toll roads in Colorado, but I don't use the EasyTag system, preferring cash transactions in the rare occasions when I've ended up on a toll road unintentionally. They can still find my toll passage if they search by tag number, but I make them take that one additional step.

"There are still traffic cameras and police car cameras, some of which have plate recognition software that record every plate and its location with date and time stamp, as Kara mentioned. Not to mention satellites and drones, but those require direct orders to look for you. If someone wants to find you and they have the power or access to the data, they can find you unless you hole up in a cave and never communicate with the outside world. If you are really lucky, live totally off the grid or use false identities, false vehicle and property registrations and use really good disguises, you might evade authorities, maybe even for a long time, but it takes diligence, knowledge and lots of cash."

Jimmy said, "Well, we've both avoided detection for long periods of time, but technology has made that much more difficult in the last few years. I mean, we don't have our official names on any property, voting records, banking documents, phone bills, etc. And I have several sets of ID, as I'm sure you do, Ned. But if someone wants us badly enough, our lives become much more difficult and likely shorter."

Ned said, "And I suspect that we are about to stir the hornets' nest to a degree that we will be in high demand. We had best remain diligent, and always assume the presence of a drone, bug, trace or camera of one sort or another."

Kara said, "I have a problem. First, I don't have alternative ID.

Kara continued, "And I also have a question: What is our escape plan if all goes to hell? I mean, let's face it. To one degree or another, this entire operation is going to create a new kind of hell for us. What are we going to do then?"

Ned and Jimmy looked at each other. Ned spoke first. "Jimmy and I were talking about that last night. We've discussed some options. First, we will create additional fake IDs for each of us. But part of the first option we discussed was that we separate just as the carnage begins and escape during the smoke and confusion of developing chaos."

Jimmy said, "But neither of you – that we know of – has training and experience to evade governments that want you." Neither Kara nor Sam objected.

Ned said, "Then we discussed hiding out here, which we can probably do for a few months if we are careful. I have adequate supplies to hold us over for weeks.

"Then we discussed the four of us escaping together, either by private plane or sailboat, and taking up residence in the Caribbean or South America."

Sam said, "I think the four of us staying together is too risky. Assuming they put the pieces together and figure out that we are all together, the APB descriptions would be too easy. 'Two white males in their mid-forties traveling with a middle-aged black man and a younger red-headed woman.' That's too easy for a civilian to remember, and too easy to spot. Like it or not, we're a pretty unusual group."

Kara unconsciously grabbed her hair and began running her fingers through its length. When she was five years old she came home from kindergarten crying because some other girls had teased her about her hair color. Her father told her that the girls had been jealous because every girl wished to be among the top three percent of people on earth that had red hair. "Auburn hair," she had corrected him. He said,

"You're right, you're among the top three percent of the luckiest humans on earth that have auburn hair. When you see those mean girls tomorrow, or when someone later in life makes a negative comment about your hair, just say to yourself, 'I'm lucky. I'm in the top three percent. Everyone wishes they had my hair, and they are jealous that they don't.'"

Kara had had pride in her hair from that day forward, and the thought of coloring it to evade detection made her edgy. Her edge was reflected in her comment to Sam when she said, "Auburn hair, thank you very much."

"Sam said, "My apologies. I meant no offense."

Kara smiled and said, "None taken. You aren't actually black in color, after all, and I hope you aren't offended if I refer to you as such."

Ned said, "Regardless of hair color or skin tone, Sam has a valid point about traveling together, so we might better plan to split up and travel separately. I still think we should pick a common area so we can get to each other if we have to run for it, but we might be better off avoiding public exposure when we're all together."

Ned paused for a few seconds and said, "Let's change the subject for a moment. Something had bothered me for a few days but I couldn't put my finger on it. Last night it came to me, and I thought of something that could really help us, but there's one complication that I'll tell you about in a minute."

Jimmy said, "OK, Ned, let's have it."

Ned said, "I've been thinking about the person who has been pulling the political purse strings for a decade, the power behind the throne, if you will. Before I retired, I had clearance that allowed me to access some classified information that very few have been privy to. Before the NSA existed and all the modern-day technology was developed, I heard about this man who had recently emigrated to the U.S. from Eastern Europe. I heard he was insane, like a character from a James Bond movie, and a very wealthy man. He professed to be devoted to Marxism. So I did some digging. What I learned was that the rumors were true, but he wasn't actually devoted to Marxism, but was intent on using the premise of Marxism to create a one world totalitarian government. Sound familiar? But anyway, I decided I had best keep an eye on this guy, and over the years, I have.

"One day I was digging through some information and found transaction documentation of this guy transferring money to several American bank accounts every month. I got curious, so I found out whose accounts they were. They belonged to several high-powered politicians ... a few senators, several congressmen, three Supreme Court Justices who are still on the bench, and the man who was president at the time.

"I've kept track of the transactions since then, and his payroll includes about a third of the U.S. senators and congressmen, five present Supreme Court justices and the current president and vice president. And the best part, I found numerous bank accounts the man used. I still have the transaction records ... and I have all the account numbers."

Kara's eyes had been wide since Ned started telling about the political payoffs, but her jaw dropped when he mentioned the transaction records and the account numbers. She said, "You know what this means?"

Jimmy said, "Tell us, Kara."

She said, "Not only do we have all this evidence of corruption that goes all the way to the top, but we have access to the accounts ... and we can take all the money."

Jimmy laughed out loud, Sam smiled and Ned said, "There are PINs and the accounts are separated by several layers. It's a complicated scheme that will be difficult to explain to the public, so the leverage of the evidence is marginal. But you're right, Kara, we can take the money."

Ned said, "We can take the money and move it to other accounts. We'll want a good bit of it in cash so it can't be taken back with a few clicks on a keyboard. We could spread it around, we could hide it; we could cash it out and keep it, that's all pretty much irrelevant. But we will take it, and then we have ultimate leverage."

After a moment's pause, Jimmy asked, "What's the one complication you mentioned?"

Ned looked flatly at Jimmy and said, "The information is in the vault in my house in Virginia. I have to go get it before all hell breaks loose."

Kara audibly gasped.

Ned, always thinking of the next move, said to Jimmy, "First, contact Huldon and call him off. We don't want him to put holes in us. And second, I am going to get it, and I should leave … within the hour. I'll line up the pilot. Work with Kara to get a message to Huldon. I'm going to start packing."

Jimmy said flatly and without hesitation, "I'm going with you. I'll get my gear together and be ready in ten minutes."

Ned began to protest, saying the risk was too high and Jimmy needed to stay here and help look out for Kara.

Jimmy silenced him with the wave of his hand and said, "We motivated numerous agencies to send their SWAT teams to your house tomorrow. They typically conduct their raids before dawn, so we have a little more than 16 hours to get to Virginia, sneak into your house, get the data and get out before Hell descends … if they take the bait."

Kara interrupted. "They have taken the bait. That was next on my discussion agenda, and I apologize that I was distracted by this latest development. I've been monitoring communications traffic. Every single agency has organized a raid on Ned's house."

She looked at Ned. "And I'll note that your messages were taken literally. Eleven of the 12 agencies are planning raids from the points of the compass, and another is conducting an air raid by dropping the agents in by helicopter. And as you hoped, they are setting up command posts at each compass point, with the airborne group command post set up at an airfield 12 miles from the house. Just as you hoped, with the command posts and raids coming from different compass points, the chances of them discovering each other beforehand are reduced."

Ned looked at Jimmy. "Well, we've created our own ambush. The first thing we'll have to do is determine where the command posts are set up and where they have people stationed. We can't get caught before we even get to the house, and we have to get out alive. We better get moving.

Ned turned to Sam and said, "You and Kara come with me. I want to show you a few things."

*****

Bedekowski's phone rang and he picked it up with his usual gruffness. The voice on the other end said, "I have some information for you. You'll like it, but it will cost you big."

Bedekowski sat silent for at least thirty seconds before saying, "What is this information?"

The voice on the other end said, "I can deliver it. It will cost you one million dollars, cash, on delivery."

Bedekowski recognized the voice. It was one of his NSA contacts, but he wouldn't use any names on the phone.

Bedekowski said, "Bring it to my office."

The voice asked, "You have the cash?"

Bedekowski said, "You know I do." He had no intention to pay one million dollars to anyone. No one was worth that amount of money, especially a government worker who wanted to peddle information that had been illegally acquired … twice.

The voice on the other end said, "I will meet you on a bench on the east side of Central Park in one hour. Be on time, have the cash in a black athletic bag, and be alone." The man was a rookie when it came to clandestine operations of any kind, but he had read enough spy novels to know that he should remain in a public place at a time when many people would be around. And he knew Bedekowski would try to cheat him out of his money.

Bedekowski said, "You'll have to give me a hint of what we're dealing with before I risk that kind of money."

The voice on the other end said, "It involves the location of a certain female NSA employee you've been looking for. Do you want to know where she is or not?"

Bedekowski's heart rate increased. "I will see you in one hour, but there are dozens of benches on the east side of Central Park. Which bench?"

The voice said, "Just pick one and sit down on it. I'll find you. And you better have the cash."

The voice hung up the phone. Bedekowski called one of the goons into his office. He said, "get a car ready immediately and a take me to

Central Park. We have thirty minutes to get there. I will meet a man there, and I'll give him a bag of cash."

The goon said, "Yes sir. Anything else?"

Bedekowski said, "Have a crew ready to intercept the man before he reaches the street with the bag. Retrieve the bag and dispose of the body. That will be all."

The message was clear. The goon noticed that a cold sweat had broken out on his forehead, and he couldn't decide if it was the result of excitement or fear. He turned and walked from Bedekowski's office.

Bedekoswki smiled, pleased with himself for planting the seeds at NSA. Now those seeds had sprouted into the location of one auburn haired woman who was missing from NSA. He walked to his living quarters and retrieved a black athletic bag from his closet. He walked to the safe and considered how much to put in the bag. He decided on a half million, but thought the better of it. He continued counting bundles of bills until the amount totaled one million. He decided the man would likely count the money, and he didn't want to jeopardize the information. He wanted that information, and he wanted that auburn-haired NSA woman dead. She knew too much. Way too much. Anyway, the man would never make it out of the park with his money, and he would get the information for free.

Bedekowski stood and walked to his office door. He walked straight to his private elevator where one of his goons stood guard. The goon pushed the "G" button, and the elevator began its descent.

***

Sam and Kara stood and followed Ned through a thick, triple locked steel door and down a flight of dark stairs into a basement. Ned hit a light switch to reveal a completely stocked basement that contained enough food stocks and water containers to last weeks. They followed Ned across the room to a set of pantry shelves. Ned moved a stack of cans, removed a panel you wouldn't see if you weren't looking for it, and put his palm flat against the bio reader. There was an electronic beep, and the entire stack of shelves pivoted backward into a large, dark concrete chamber.

Ned pushed several buttons on the touchscreen control panel, and had Sam, then Kara, place their hands on the screen. He punched several more buttons, turned and said, "You both are programmed into the system and will be able to unlock the vault door."

Ned walked in and motion detectors turned on lights. Sam and Kara looked around to see a completely stocked weapons vault that also had food, water, clothing, radio and satellite telephone equipment and a

large monitor on the far wall. On it were images from cameras

240

placed around his property. Sam opened all the weapons cabinets and showed them the variety of weaponry and survival equipment. Then he showed them the food, and last, he opened a large drawer that contained flashlights and headlamps of various sorts. He pointed out the backpacks that hung on the wall ready to grab and run with, and then he showed them the vault door hidden behind the wall.

He opened it and walked in. Motion detectors lit up the 10'x10' room. At the other end of the room was another steel vault. Ned told them the 4-digit combination, opened it and showed them a long corridor that led beyond their sight.

Ned said, "This is your escape route if anything goes bad. It's part of an old silver mine. I had it reinforced with concrete and steel throughout its length to the same specs that our government uses to protect leaders from nuclear attacks. It's two miles long and leads to the other side of Grouse Mountain.

"At the other end, there is a series of vault doors like this one, and last, there's a garage-size room that contains an armored jeep that is full of gas with the batteries maintained. If all goes bad, here's your salvation. And there's one more thing."

He led them back into the first vault and opened one of the backpacks. He said, "Down in the bottom of each pack is 1000 one-hundred dollar bills. It's bulky and heavy, but it's essential if you have to survive or travel off the grid.

"Sam, I'm putting you in charge of the escape and survival should it become necessary. Give Kara whatever support she needs on the electronic end. She'll have her hands full with all that's about to happen and the surveillance, media manipulation and banking transactions she'll handle."

Sam nodded in agreement and looked around the room soaking it all in. Ned looked at Kara and said, "Come here."

Ned opened a drawer and took out a black, hardback notebook. He opened it and said, "Here is a list of banks and contacts in the Caymans, Switzerland, the Bahamas, Brazil and East Germany." Ned picked up a highlighter and marked two banks from each country. He said, "When Jimmy and I get the account numbers to you, contact these bankers on one of the unused pre-pay phones and tell them you are calling for '4749833.' Tell them 4749833 asked you to transfer money from the accounts to secure accounts in their banks. They will understand you are working with me and they won't ask questions. They will give you no flak as long as you give them this number." He wrote it on the top of the page with the highlighted names.

Ned looked at Kara and smiled. He said, "Short of imminent death or extreme pain, money is the greatest motivator of all, and when we have all their money, they'll be motivated to do whatever we tell them to do."

Ned grabbed two of the smaller packs that hung on the wall. He opened them and checked the chambers of the two .45s that were inside each pack. For good measure, he thumbed through the $100,000 that was in each pack.

He checked the batteries on the radios and cell phones in the packs. He turned to the gun cabinet and selected two sets of night vision goggles and a radio-jamming unit. He put a set of goggles in each pack and carried the jamming unit in a briefcase. Satisfied, he put one of the packs over each shoulder and slung the strap of the jamming unit over his right shoulder. He locked all the vault doors, leading Kara and Sam back to the den where Kara's computer was.

Ten minutes later, Ned and Sam left in the old pickup truck on their way to the airfield. The pilot would have the plane warmed up and ready for the flight to Virginia.

*****

Bedekowski selected a bench on the east side of Central Park and sat. He was excited at the prospect at taking care of the NSA woman who had accessed his data. He wondered what else she knew. The NSA could get any information on anyone, and it wasn't limited by the law. Even if someone discovered the vast amount of data NSA collected on U.S. citizens without a specific warrant, and even if they brought a case to court, and even if they found a lawyer with balls enough to take the case, and if they got a judge that he didn't already own in one way or another, in the end the NSA would claim that national security was at risk. Everyone involved would run from the case and it would go away.

So the woman knew as much as she was willing and capable of accessing. Bedekowski didn't know what the woman had uncovered, but it was enough to make her go into hiding. And there had been no trace of her for weeks. As long as she remained on the loose, she was a danger to him and everything he had worked for. He had dedicated his life to creating a one-world government, of which he would run, of course. To do so, he had to either weaken the United States to the point that she could no longer defend herself, or he had to overtake the bastions of power that controlled how far into Marxism he could take the country. Either way, the citizens of the country would be too weak

to rise up and defend the direction of the country, or to escape, although that wasn't the threat it had been when the Soviet Block and other countries had slid into communism.

The U.S. was the last domino to fall. Every other country was already under the control of communists of one degree or another, or hidden by one label or another. Where would U.S. citizens escape to? All he had left to do was to disarm the citizens – and he was close to achieving that – and to secure the last of the remaining power by nationalizing the oil and gas companies. Then, he would have it all. This was better than any James Bond movie ever created. He would control everything across the world. He already controlled food and money supplies. He already controlled health care and access to it, and he had sufficiently trained politicians to use all the tools of the government to dissuade or destroy any opposition. It was all in place. Another year and everything would be done. The U.S. would be a total police state, and he would be top cop.

But he had to get rid of this auburn-haired NSA woman, and he had to make her demise a public spectacle. She had to die, and she had to die tonight.

Chapter 19

It was late afternoon as the plane flew past the east side of Ned's Virginia property. They were at 5,000 feet to try to remain undetected, and were leaning to the windows with binoculars scanning the area for command posts and personnel.

Ned said, "There's the east command post in that grassy meadow ... right on the side of the highway across from my property. I see their meeting tent and radio gear. They won't be able to take heavy equipment because of the terrain and they will have a tough hike to the house from there. They will have to traverse two very steep mountains that are fraught with cliffs and rocks, plus several small streams and one large one. They have a long night ahead."

Jimmy said, "I see it, and I see a group of five readying gear. They'll probably start their hike soon while there's still an hour of daylight."

Ned added, "I see them. Good luck, boys. I hope you're in tip top shape."

The plane flew well past the property and turned, making a pass over the western border of the property. The scene was similar, as it was on the southern border. The north side was different.

Two miles east of Ned's driveway was a command post in a field a couple hundred yards off the road. What made this group different was the heavy equipment. Parked next to the command tent were two Hummers and an armored vehicle with a turret atop it.

Ned said, "That vehicle that looks like a tank is an armored assault vehicle. The turret gun is a .50 cal machine gun, and the apparatus beside it is a grenade launcher. The vehicles are impregnable by anything less than a .50 cal, but they are weak on the bottom and rear. IEDs took out many of them in Iraq, and rocket propelled grenades took out more. Anyone with a RPG launcher could hide until the vehicles passed, fire off the RPG and take out everyone on board."

Ned considered the whole of the forces, and said, "Jimmy, I think we should go in from the southeast. It's a tougher route, but we can use that to our advantage. It's a couple miles of rough terrain, and we'll have to avoid that team we saw packing up to enter the forest, but we have an ace on that side."

Jimmy said, "And that ace is?"

Ned smiled and said, "One thing I never told you about is the mine shaft I tied into. I discovered it when I was digging my escape tunnel. I continued on with the tunnel as planned and built the exit four hundred yards from the house in that little cliff we scouted out. I covered over the mineshaft, but I kept thinking about it. One day I tied off a rope at the intersection of the tunnel and the shaft and followed the shaft. The rope ran out long before the shaft did, so I kept retracing my steps and getting more rope. It took almost a week, but I finally made it to the end of the shaft. It was old and ragged, so over the course of the next year I reinforced it from start to finish. I put two sets of steel vault doors at each end, and wired it for lights that feed off a generator that is installed at the exit end. When you open the interior vault doors, on either end, the generator starts and the lights come on until you manually turn them off. Taking fuel to the generator is a bitch, so I run the generator only occasionally to keep it in proper working order, but it works."

Jimmy smiled and said, "I remember that mineshaft. I know the area like the back of my hand. Remember that I grew up in these mountains. I stumbled upon that mineshaft when I was about 10 years old, and I used it as a secret fort to play in, and as a shelter when out in the woods camping or hunting and the weather turned bad. I could find it then, and I can find it now. But no one else will."

Ned said, "From the east road it's about two miles to the shaft, then another mile to the house. In the dark, the hike to the mine will take about two hours, and another 45 minutes to the house."

Jimmy said, "So, assuming these SWAT forces will do their thing at about four a.m., and giving us a half hour at the house and another thirty minutes to spare, we need to start our hike by 9:30."

Ned considered the calculations, nodded and said, "I agree. That will have us off the property and a little more by the time the shooting starts, and I prefer to be well away before bullets start flying. When these toy soldiers get excited and lead is flying, they are likely to shoot at anything that moves."

Jimmy smiled and said, "That's what we're counting on."

The plane landed and taxied into a hanger at the east side of the field. The pilot turned to NED and asked, "You want a ride to the property?"

Ned said, "That's too risky. But it would be great if you could drop us off at the Knoll River Bridge about a mile from the land. That's a safe distance away and will give us a good place to gear up. Jimmy, you OK with that?"

Jimmy said, "That's good. That'll add about 45 minutes to our walk, so we need to back up our start time to 8:45, and we'll need to be careful crossing the east road."

The pilot stopped at the end of the bridge over the Knoll River as the sun sank behind the mountains to the West. Ned and Jimmy jumped out and walked quickly into the heavily wooded forest. They walked a half-mile to a flat area about 50 yards above the river. Ned sat on a fallen tree trunk and said, "Let's review our plan again and talk about contingencies."

Ten minutes later, the plan reviewed and their stories rehearsed should they be caught, they stood, donned their packs and set off toward Ned's mine.

*****

At NSA headquarters, the woman ran name searches through NSA files. When she was in the coffee shop on the first floor this morning – one of her favorite hangouts and richest sources of company gossip – she overheard a conversation between two women at the table behind her. One of the women asked the other, "Did you hear that Kara hasn't shown up for work in two weeks? She's missing. No word to her boss or coworkers, she just stopped showing up. They've been to her house and alerted the local police, who also went to her house. No one was home and her car was gone. Yesterday they found her car in Blacksburg at an access point for the Appalachian Trail. They said her car had been broken into and ransacked, but they thought that was done by a bunch of locals since they hit three other cars in the same parking area. But there was no sign of Kara. No one knows where she is."

The other woman asked if that was typical for Kara, and the woman replied, "She hasn't ever been away from work more than a week, and she has never left without notice. I have a bad feeling about this."

The other woman asked, "Do they think she was kidnapped or just burned herself out and left?"

"I've heard all types of theories, but Jenny, you know the lady in the office next to mine, she said she thinks Kara was sleeping with someone in the office – one of her superiors – and it went bad so she disappeared. You know that Robert Johnson *is* on *vacation*.

"I don't think the rumor of a love gone bad is true. I think she's off having a tryst with Robert right now. He always had the hots for Kara."

It was only office gossip, and none of it was remotely true, but people were talking about juicy office malfeasance, and the woman at the computer screen couldn't wait to get back to her desk. This was the kind of information that would be great in her book. After all, no story is complete without a lovers tryst and quarrel, and boss and subordinate affairs were specifically forbidden and could lead to nasty lawsuits.

So the woman searched Kara's name, including the phone files. She didn't have clearance to access the information, but that bitch across the hall did, and her after-hours snooping over the years had reaped lots of great information, including the bitch's access code. The beauty was that if the access was detected, she would say that the woman had asked her to query the call files and email records, and since the bitch outranked her, the story would hold water and the bitch would be the one in trouble.

So she ordered the search and clicked "enter." What appeared on the screen not only surprised her, it scared her. It was an email string between someone high in the government. She didn't recognize the names, but the emails were marked "Top Secret," so it had to be someone of high rank who was likely using fake names. The original message discussed NSA security breaches, and in the aftermath of the Snowden incident, people all the way to the Oval Office were paranoid about leaks like never before. Then the message specifically mentioned Kara, and that she was missing. And someone in the White House was aware that Kara had been seen in a car in Virginia with some ex-CIA guy that was considered a risk to the White House.

She didn't recognize the name, but to start her next search she typed in "Ned Harrison." But she was confused when the search came back with no bank records, property records, IRS files, military service or anything else. She re-checked the name and performed the search again.

Nothing. Then she searched the phone files, and there were five calls placed early that very morning that mentioned Ned Harrison. Two were calls to one phone number with a Washington area code.

One call was to a different number in the same area code, and yet another to a number in New York. The two remaining calls were between New York and South Carolina.

She searched the numbers to see to whom they belonged, and that's when sweat broke out on her upper lip, which was something that had never before happened to her. One of the Washington numbers was a senator's office, and not just any senator, but the highest-ranking senator in Washington. Things got even worse when she looked up the other Washington number. It was listed as WHPL – White House Private Line, and only one office had numbers listed that way – the Oval Office. Holy shit!

She looked up the New York number, and found out the number was listed to Organic Change for American Workers. She researched the organization, and when she saw the name of the founder and CEO, Nicholas Bedekowski, she went pale. She knew who he was. Rumors had flown around Washington for years about him, and he was reputed to be the most powerful and ruthless man in the world. He was said to be the power behind the last three presidents, and when he said jump, people jumped … or else.

After taking a few deep breaths, she worked up the nerve to listen to the calls where Ned Harrison's name had been mentioned. In the first call she listened to, the one between New York and the Oval Office, she heard the New York voice tell the president himself that there had been a security breech. A woman at NSA had made unauthorized access to classified data and that the woman was associated with Ned Harrison. Then the man said that the woman at NSA was responsible, and he identified her as Kara. The man, whom she assumed to be Bedekowski, told the president that he was to drop whatever he was doing and order that Ned Harrison and Kara be found and eliminated immediately. He told the president to use any means necessary, and that witnesses were not acceptable. He said that the two of them were reported to be hiding out at the home of a Jimmy Rogers in some bumfuck place in western Virginia. The man read off an address.

The woman pushed back from her desk, grabbed her trashcan and threw up twice. Several minutes passed before she could sit up straight.

She breathed a few more deep breaths, opened her drawer and got a thumb drive from the back, right corner of her drawer. She hesitated, then inserted the drive into her computer and downloaded the call and email files. She rolled back from her desk slightly, hiked her dress and slid the thumb drive into the front of her panties. She thought to herself that this practice of downloading files to another drive would soon be shut down in the aftermath of the largest NSA security breach in the organization's brief history, but as with most things involving the federal government, it would take government agencies months, maybe even years, before they shut down all access paths to critical information. By the time they did so, she would have all she needed to write a best-selling blockbuster that would make her famous ... and rich. She reached her hand down and pressed against the thumb drive, smiling at her new bounty of information. This was the best yet, and it guaranteed that her book would be a success ... if it didn't get her killed first. The risk turned her on, as did the foreign object she was pressing against her intimate parts. She thought to herself that her husband would be a happy man tonight. She might even leave the office early.

*****

An hour later, Kara ran her searches of NSA data. As an afterthought, she ran a search for Sam, Jimmy, Ned and herself. That's how she found the calls in the NSA banks. When she listened, she felt a chill run through her. She called Sam to the computer and let him listen.

Sam frowned, muttered something about "deep shit" and then jumped up and said, "We've got to let Ned and Jimmy know about this. They are walking into a massive booby trap. If the risks weren't high enough with all these weekend warrior SWAT teams descending on the place, now they'll have professional forces descending on them. And according to the call to the president, no means will be spared. That means that Special Forces teams will likely be used. "

Kara said, "It could be worse than that. The president could order an armed drone or a plane-originated missile strike."

Sam asked, "In the continental U.S.? Can they even do that?"

Kara said flatly, "By law, that's debatable. But they will do it anyway, and they'll cite a presidential memorandum the current president quietly put into place. They'll label Ned and Jimmy terrorists and say it was done in the interest of national security. Even if it's not legal, and I don't believe it is, who will do anything about it? The biggest flaw in the American system is that the attorney general is appointed by the president, and the current AG won't challenge the president, and no politician in congress will stand up, as they've shown each time the president ignores or breaks the law. So, yes, I think they'll do it, and it won't be the first time. It won't be the last, either.

"As for contacting Ned and Jimmy, they won't have their phones on and won't do anything that will give away where they are. We have no way to contact them."

Sam rubbed his chin. He looked up and asked, "What about Jimmy's cousin? Can you call him and see if he can make contact?"

Kara said, "No, but I can send him an email. Not sure what good it will do or if he can even find them, but I'll do it right now."

Kara turned and typed a brief message. When she finished, Sam said, "We need to be on our toes and ready to evacuate at any moment. I'll station myself at the camera monitors."

Sam walked quickly to the upstairs monitor room. He had barely settled into his seat when Kara showed up at the door to the room. She said, "Sam, I heard a buzzing noise. I hate to say this and I hope I'm wrong, but I think it might have been a drone." She was pale.

Sam jumped up ran to the den desk and picked up a pair of binoculars. He ran to a window and crouched below the sill scanning the sky. Five minutes later he heard a buzzing sound to the west. He searched with is binoculars until he found it. He said, "Shit! It's a drone all right, and it appears to be circling over the house. Can you access the computer network from the tunnel?

Kara said, "No, but I can from the first vault … the one that has the second bank of monitors."

Sam said, "Gather your equipment and any files or storage devices. Let's get down into the vault now. We will hole up there. If someone shows up, we'll run into the tunnel."

Kara went pale again, then began frantically gathering up files, thumb drives and her computer. They ran into the tunnel. Sam looked at his watch after he closed and locked the vault doors behind them. Five after four, Mountain Time; after six in Virginia. It was game time in two states, and four people, Kara and himself being two of them, were now in the fight for their lives ... literally.

Sam opened the vault doors as Ned had instructed. As he did so, he reviewed in his head every step Ned had described and demonstrated. Kara began hooking up her laptop. Sam began looking through the gun cabinets and the backpacks, assessing what they would need should they have to escape into the tunnel. He selected two of the packs, put a holstered .45 pistol on his hip and selected a 12-gage pump shotgun and shells, as well as a bolt action .50 caliber sniper rifle. "You never know," he said to himself as he checked the rifle's magazine. As he worked he thought through the different scenarios they might face, although this would likely be unlike any situation he had ever faced. Kara's voice brought him back to real time. She said, "Sam, you better come look at this."

Thomas Lide

Sam turned and looked at Kara. She pointed to a screen showing the gate at the bottom of the road that led to Ned's Colorado house. Sam looked to see three Hummers parked at the gate. They watched as two men in SWAT gear got out of one of the vehicles and walked to the gate to assess it. One of them walked back to a vehicle and retrieved bolt cutters.

After ten minutes trying to open the gate, the men walked back the one of the vehicles. Sam and Kara watched as one of the SWAT team members made a phone call. For the next hour, Sam and Kara watched as the men waited. Then an army truck pulling a flatbed stopped on the road in front of the gate. A man jumped out of the truck, walked back to the trailer and began unfastening the chains that held the bulldozer on the trailer. Five minutes later, the bulldozer rammed the gate the first time. It took two more attempts before the gate swung open, but it did open. The bulldozer backed up and stopped beside the Hummers. A SWAT leader said something to his men, and the men chambered rounds in their pistols, then their rifles. They were locked and loaded, and they would be at the house in a few minutes.

Sam said in a calm but authoritative voice, "OK, shut everything down and put it into my pack." He grabbed his pack and set it on the floor next to Kara. She shut down the laptop and put it, the files and thumb

259

drives into the pack as Sam had said. He pulled a .45 out of her pack and asked, "Have you ever handled a pistol?"

Kara said, "You men are always underestimating women. As I told Jimmy, I grew up hunting and shooting with my father. I am not only familiar with several types of weapons, but I'm an excellent shot with pistols and rifles. Shotguns, too."

Sam said, "My apologies." He checked the chamber and handed her the weapon butt first. Kara checked the chamber and buckled the holster to her hip. She slid the pistol from the holster and racked a round into the chamber.

Sam said, "There's another pistol just like it in your pack, as well as 100 rounds of ammunition."

Kara counted the pockets on her holster belt and said, "Plus the eight magazines on each of our belts."

Sam picked up the shotgun and the heavy .50 caliber rifle, sliding the latter's strap over his shoulder. Kara stepped over to the rifle cabinet, scanned the arsenal and selected a .30 x .30 Winchester rifle. She said, "Not the best range in the world, but I grew up shooting one of these. I want a weapon I'm familiar with." She looked up at Sam and said, "Well, what are we waiting for?"

Sam smiled, opened the vault door to the tunnel and they walked through. Sam closed the door behind them. He reviewed Ned's instructions, remembering how solemnly Ned had described the last step. Ned had said, "If you are absolutely certain you are under attack, you have absolutely no doubt that your life is on the line, the last thing I want you to do after you enter the tunnel to escape is to push these three buttons in this sequence. This one once, then this one twice, then the third one four times.

Sam had asked, "What do the buttons do?"

Ned had said, "They arm a series of booby traps. The initial ones are to discourage people from coming any further into the house. Those aren't lethal. The first is a shot of tear gas. The second level is propelled nets that are hidden in the ceilings. The third is flash-bang grenades, and the closer they get to the vault, they become progressively more lethal. Sam pointed at one of the monitor screens and said, "There are two Claymores behind those screens. The first one goes off if the door to the vault is forced open. The second is timed to go off one minute later to take care of anyone who wasn't killed in the first wave. Everything here has three levels of safeties, and nothing will be triggered unless these three buttons are pushed in proper sequence."

Sam had asked Ned, "What if I arm it and you come home later?

Ned said, "There is a nail over each door. The nails aren't structural, and if the traps are armed, the nails protrude an inch and a half. There is also a buzzer that sounds as soon as you open a door or window. If you enter the house and the traps are armed, all the lights in the house flash until the unit had been disarmed. If the traps are armed, I'll know it. I will have thirty seconds to disarm the traps by punching the same sequence in the security panel by the front door."

Sam cleared his mind of the memory of the conversation to be fully in the present. He carefully went through the sequence. Once the traps were armed, Sam turned to Kara and said, "I don't know what these SWAT teams have in mind, but I would rather hear about it later than see it up close."

Kara said, "Lead the way." They began walking at a brisk pace. They were well down the tunnel when the SWAT teams began using their battering ram on the main door of the house. The men were perplexed that the wood door didn't give way, so they rammed it again. On their fifth try, a piece of the oak wood broke loose and one of the team members said, "Damn! There's steel behind the wood. He did a closer inspection and ordered one of his subordinates to bring him a crow bar.

Before the man could return, the leader of the team charged with rushing in from the back of the house walked up and said, "We can't get in. The doors are steel and the windows are bulletproof glass with steel wire sandwiched in the panes. The window frames are steel and the walls are rock covering poured concrete. This place is a damn bunker.

The mission leader swore, pushed the transmit button on his headset and said, "Bring up the bulldozer." He looked at the man who had told him about the steel doors and impenetrable windows, "We'll get in!"

Fifteen minutes later they did. They noticed the buzzer but didn't slow down. As soon as they stepped into the house, they were taken aback when the lights began to flash and loudspeakers barked, "Warning. The premise is armed with lethal traps. Do not proceed. Exit the premises immediately."

When the tear gas hit them, they kept moving, protected by their SWAT gear gas masks. The propelled nets entangled half of the men. The team leader, following up in the rear, cussed his men, told them to cut their way loose, and ordered the others to continue. One of the men protested, citing the audible warnings. All the leader could think was that there was no way he was going back to the station saying they didn't complete the mission because of a few scare tactics. "Move forward and secure the premises. That's an order!"

Flash-bang grenades exploded four seconds later. The leader wet his pants. He thought to himself that this was way beyond the training the Colorado State Police had given them. Then the men figured out that they had been harmless grenades and the leader mustered his courage and ordered the men forward. Four minutes later, the men discovered the vault. It took them an hour to break down the door. When it broke free the men rushed into the vault ready to shoot anything that moved. Four seconds later the first claymore exploded, killing six of the 12 men.

Almost a minute later, the leader entered the room alone to prove to the remaining men that they had to move forward and that he deserved his status as leader.

The second claymore exploded a second after he stopped in the middle of the room and shouted to his men, "It's safe. Come in here and secure this mess."

The two men who were posted on each side of the door were wounded. The team leader suffered a worse fate, a gruesome albeit short death by total body destruction. The remaining men quickly retreated. Most began to climb into their Hummers, but two didn't wait for anything else to happen. They ran full speed down the hill toward the gate. Twenty seconds later the vehicles blazed past them, not stopping to pick them up.

Two hours later, the Chief of the State Police skidded to a stop on the side of the road. A tall man, he straightened himself from his car, stood up and put his hat on, looking solemnly at the remaining men.

He walked up to a group of men sitting on the side of the flatbed trailer. He said, "Who's in charge here?"

One of the men spoke up reluctantly. "Captain Hagood was our mission leader, but he is a casualty, sir. The rest of us are all corporals, sir. We have no leader."

The Chief shook his head and said, "I always knew that Hagood was a loose cannon and would get himself – or more likely some of his men – killed if he ever had to engage a lethal enemy."

The corporal said, "He did both, sir. Out of two SWAT teams, we are the only four men left."

The chief swore, pulled the hat from his head and slapped it against his leg. He asked, "How many people are up there in that house?"

The corporal said, "Alive? None. Eight dead, sir." The chief swore again and said, "I mean perps, son."

The corporal said, "We … we didn't see any, sir."

The chief said, "What the hell? Don't tell me your men killed each other."

The corporal said, "No … no sir. The place was booby-trapped. Elaborate stuff with flashing lights, buzzers, audio warnings, tear gas, propelled nets, and finally, deep in the house there were series Claymores, sir."

The chief stood taller. "Claymores?"

"Yes, sir. Two of them, the second one delayed. Whoever lives in that house knows his stuff. Only place I've seen a place booby trapped like that was Afghanistan. I warned the captain. Three times, sir. I begged him to retreat and call for backup and a bomb squad, but he wouldn't listen."

The chief said, "No, son, I expect he didn't listen. That son of a bitch never would listen, and I recommended that he not be awarded SWAT team status. Has the bomb squad been called?"

"Yes, sir. They said they'll be here by noon tomorrow."

The chief shouted to a state trooper who leaned against his car a few yards away. "Take these men's statements, but get them some coffee first. Get their statements and let them go home and get some sleep."

The corporal said, "Thank you, sir, but I don't think we'll be getting any sleep any time soon."

The chief slowly nodded his head and said, "No, son, I don't expect you will."

The chief shouted for everyone to gather around. When everyone was close by, the chief said, "As much a clusterfuck as this mission was, and no matter how ill advised it was, we are under strict orders that it remain top secret and confidential. Get this heavy equipment out of here. Get your gear and gather a quarter mile up the drive, out of sight of the public. Prop this gate back in place, and not a word of this to anyone. Not your wives or girlfriends, not your pals at the bar, and certainly not the press. Is that clear?"

Several of the men muttered "yes, sir" and they gathered their gear and did as they were told. The corporal who had served as spokesperson to the chief said to the man standing beside him, "Once this is over, I'm retiring from the force. I don't know what kind of shit someone brought us into, but the police shouldn't be busting into people's houses no matter what they are accused of. Citizens are, after all, accused and not necessarily guilty of anything."

The man beside him muttered agreement, and they walked 400 yards up the dirt drive toward Ned's house.

*****

Chris Johnson and senator Evan Lee sat down across the desk from Bedekowski in his New York office. For ten seconds, Bedekowski was silent. He wore a look of disgust as he shifted his gaze between senator Lee and Johnson, as if trying to decide which of the men he found most distasteful. The he broke his silence.

"You two have no idea the can of shit you two have opened, do you?"

Senator Lee looked at Chris Johnson with a look of disgusted pity, his instincts directing him to shift blame for whatever Bedekowski was pissed off about.

Bedekowski noticed and said, "Lee, don't even try that shit with me. You are the initial cause of this shit. You're the one that can't keep his dick in his pants. You are the one that shot that woman. You are the one that failed to retrieve the shell casings from the scene. You did all that. Now for you, Johnson, you are guilty for doing sloppy cleanup work. How long did it take you to think of the shell casings? A week? More? And you still don't know who has them, do you?"

Senator Lee knew he was in deep shit, but he was glad that the heat was on Chris Johnson for a moment. To show agreement with

Bedekowski and in an attempt to regain favor, he said to Chris Johnson, "I'm disappointed in you, Chris."

Bedekowski slammed his palm onto his marble desk, making a cold slapping sound. He shouted, "Shut the fuck up, you worthless piece of shit!" He returned his gaze to Chris Johnson and said, "Some hick-town police detective in South Carolina or some redneck kingdom or another has outsmarted both of you. He outwitted both of you!"

Chris Johnson asked meekly, "The detective has the shells? Why haven't they brought charges against the senator?"

Bedekowski slapped his hand on his desk again and shouted, "Because he's smarter than either of you two ass wipes."

Bedekowski looked coldly at Chris Johnson and said, "The only possibility is that the detective has the shells. And we would go take care of the matter, but the detective has disappeared. He left a few days ago without a word to anyone. We can't find the shells because we can't find the detective. Yet."

He let the room fall silent for a moment. Then he looked at the senator and said, "You're done! Tomorrow you'll call a press conference and withdraw from the presidential race."

The senator lost his cool at that point. He stood and shouted. "I'm not withdrawing from the race! I'll go to the press and expose this whole load of shit you run. I'll take you down!"

Bedekowski said coolly, "Sit down and shut up. I own the press, you idiot."

The senator began to stammer. Chris Johnson, as he always did, looked for a solution and said, "What if we find the detective and destroy the evidence?"

Bedekowski turned his gaze to him and said, "You aren't capable, and you had your chance to clean up for this piece of political shit sitting beside you. Anyway, I have the matter in hand. I located the chief, and as a bonus, he's with someone else that stole some data from the NSA."

Bedekowski looked at his watch and said, "In fact, a SWAT team should be cuffing them about now. They'll soon be on a plane to nowhere. They'll be dropped into the Atlantic Ocean after a few pleasurable hours at the hands of our best … interrogators, if you will. Now get out of here. I have bigger fish in the frying pan tonight, and tomorrow morning, you two will no longer be my problem. Senator, I better see you on CNN withdrawing by ten o'clock. If not, I'll leak a story that you

are responsible for the death of a woman on South Carolina, in addition to numerous indiscretions, and just so you know, I have photos and phone and email records of each of them. Now get out!"

The two men stood to leave. Bedekowski said, "Not you, Mr. Johnson. I'll have another word with you."

Chris sat, and the senator walked quickly toward the door, his face bright red with anger and embarrassment. Once the door closed behind the senator, Bedekowski said to Chris Johnson, "I admit that you had a very tall task keeping that shit bird out of the news for all the stupid shit he's done, but it was the only job you had, and you failed. You let a critical piece of evidence escape you, and the only thing that saves you from being fish food is that I learned about all this before we were locked into the presidential race with that blowhard. We have time to recover and insert another candidate. I have to admit that we're probably better off for it, but you failed, and I can't have that. Now, if you want to keep from taking a dive from an airplane from 30,000 feet, I don't ever want to see you on the news or read your name in the paper. You're fired, and you should feel grateful that you'll wake to see another day. Now get out."

Chris Johnson didn't protest, he simply stood and walked out of the office. He knew what usually happened to people who let Bedekowski down, and he comforted himself that he must have done enough right for the man to escape with his life. As he rode the elevator down, he smiled to himself and thought that Bedekowski was going soft. Maybe the man wasn't untouchable, after all. Maybe there was a way to outsmart the man and knock him from his throne. That was it! He would find a way to expose and take down Bedekowski. He certainly had enough evidence stored away in his safe deposit box in the Bahamian bank.

He felt as light as air when he walked through the doors onto the New York sidewalk. Two steps toward the curb to hail a taxi, two men descended on Chris Johnson, one from each side. They wore suits and were neatly groomed, and they were big and strong. Chris tried to pull free, but he was no match for either of the men, much less both of them. Before he could protest, they pushed him into the back of a black SUV and the vehicle roared off.

The next morning, Senator Evan Lee addressed the press from a podium in the South Carolina State House. Wearing a sad, regretful expression, he said,

"This morning, it has come to light that my trusted assistant, the man I relied on to handle things from mundane to those of critical importance, has met with misfortune. Chris Johnson was found this morning in a park in New York. Suicide is suspected, and we extend our sympathy to his family, and to everyone who knew him. Many of us were fortunate to have spent time with him, and he made our lives better.

"Due to these circumstances, and its reminder that time with our families is more important than any job or office, I am withdrawing from the presidential race."

The room was filled with audible gasps, and reporters began to shout questions. The Senator silenced them by waiving his hand and saying loudly into the microphone,

"Furthermore, so that I can spend more time with my lovely wife, who stands devotedly by my side," the senator paused and pulled his wife closer to him, "I am resigning my post as senator representing the great state of South Carolina. Of course, I will offer my support to the person who succeeds me, but starting now, I will be spending my time with my lovely wife."

The senator hugged his wife. A few who were paying close attention to the woman noticed that she seemed to suppress a cringe. The senator turned and led his wife from the stage without taking a single question.

Bedekowski would have been watching the press conference and would have laughed at the senator's ability to bullshit with the best of them, but Bedekowski was dealing with something much, much more important. Something dire.

Chapter 20

Ned and Jimmy crouched in the rhododendron thicket that lined the road. They watched for several minutes. The only traffic appeared to be locals, and they saw no police or military vehicles. The listened and watched the sky for drones, but heard none. Drone use was relatively new in the U.S. so no usage standards or patterns had been established. But running drones wasn't free, and federal agencies were always penny pinching on fuel costs, ironic in light of the incredibly wasteful things government agencies routinely spent other people's money on.

Ned and Jimmy discussed drones, and suspected that if they were used in this raid, it would be around "Go" time early in the morning rather than hours before the raid. They watched as the taillights from a passing pickup truck faded around the bend. Ned looked over at Jimmy and said, "Let's go."

 Ned went first. Once he disappeared into the underbrush, Jimmy followed. They regrouped fifty yards into the forest. Ned said, "OK, Jimmy, lead us to the Promised Land."

With Jimmy in the lead, they started through the forest, winding around trees and rhododendron thickets, over and around boulders, and into the shadows of the canopy. There was a quarter moon overhead and a few stars, lending them enough light to move comfortably, but both men were painfully aware that the light also made them more visible. They climbed the mountainside, which got increasingly steep as they ascended. Both men were breathing heavily, although both were in great physical condition.

Every few minutes, they stopped and silently observed their surroundings. Each time it took thirty seconds or so for their breathing to slow enough that they could hear all the sounds of the forest. They didn't speak during their recoveries, only breathed, and to the extent that they could, listened and looked at their surroundings.

About a mile in, they crested the first mountain of the two they would climb. They stopped at the top, hidden between three large boulders that had fallen from the rock precipice above them. They were protected on all sides.

Jimmy said, "I used to hunt from here. I had visual of most of both sides of the mountain. And when Huldon and I and several other guys played army or hide and seek to most kids, I would come here. They never found me. I always called it Jimmy's perch, like a hawk always perches at the highest point around.

Ned looked around and said, "Great spot."

Jimmy pointed at a recess at the bottom of the rock precipice and said, "You see that shadow at the bottom of the rock? I used to crawl under that when the weather was bad or if the guys came too close during our games." Jimmy smiled and said, "If you hear a drone while we're here, dive under. It's plenty big enough for both of us, with room to spare."

Ned said, "Duly noted, soldier. Should we press on?"

Jimmy said, "We should. Stay close behind me and take the same path I take. There are several small cliffs and drop-offs on this side of the mountain, and footing when going down hill can be sketchy."

Ned smiled and said, "This is your home field and I'll heed your instructions." Ned looked at his watch. "We're on schedule, but we have no time to spare. The hair on the back of my neck will be standing on end until we're out of here with the account numbers."

They got to their feet and walked to the edge of the peak, carefully starting down the hill. A mile away on the peak of the mountain they were approaching, a young Homeland Security SWAT team member clicked his transmit button and said into his headset. "Base, unit four reporting. I had visual on two people on the mountain east of me. Could you acknowledge?"

After a few seconds, a reply came. "Roger, unit four. You have confirmed visual on two individuals. Stand by."

Twenty seconds passed before unit four's radio crackled. "Unit four, this is base. Your visual is confirmed. Be aware that units one and two are in route to your location, approaching from the east. Those are friendlies on their way to you. After they arrive, proceed to target at three hundred hours."

When the first radio transmission was made and crackled across the airwaves, Ned signaled for Jimmy to hold up. Ned listened intently to the transmissions on his hand-held scanner/radio and said to Jimmy, "We have one bogie stationed on the top of the next mountain and two more approaching from our rear."

Jimmy said, "On the peak of the next mountain? That's about three hundred yards beyond the entrance to the mineshaft. That's cutting it close, especially if he has night vision."

Ned said, "I guarantee you they have night vision.

Jimmy thought for a minute. "One of our options is to squeeze out of the sandwich to the north or the south. But, if we do that, we will be in a direct line of two of the command posts, and that will put us in their approach paths. We're surrounded, or effectively so. I think our best option is to continue on course to the mineshaft. Even if the bogie at the peak sees us coming, we're a pretty long way from him and we'll have trees and rocks to obscure his view of us. And we might get lucky enough that he thinks we are the two men on his team, even if he sees us."

Ned said, "Agreed. We better get moving. I don't know how familiar with these mountains the guys behind us are, but I guarantee you they're a good bit younger than either of us, so we must assume they can travel fast."

Ned removed the binoculars from his pack and did a scan of the area behind them. Seeing nothing, he stowed the glasses and said, "Let's move."

*****

In the cold Colorado night, the men gathered on the road to Ned's house shivered as they drank their coffee. After what seemed like an eternity, several vehicles pulled off the road, opened the gate and drove up to where the men were gathered.

The vehicles roared to a stop and a man in Army Special Forces jumped out and approached the men and said, "Who's in charge here?"

The corporal chuckled as he said, "Our leader is a casualty, as are the next two in command. It's only us corporals left, sir. And who are you?"

The soldier abruptly said, "Lt. Major Abe Crissler, U.S. Army Special Forces Commander. I am now in charge of this operation, and I am commissioning you men as support staff for an official Special Forces operation critical to the security of the United States."

The corporal said, "Excuse me, sir, but none of us are military. We're state police. But who is this you are after and why are you after them?"

The Lt. Major was unaccustomed to anyone questioning him, and he answered curtly. "The two individuals are threats to national security, and it is our mission to neutralize the threat."

The corporal, having enough wartime for the night said, "You mean kill them. Are they U.S. citizens, Lt. Major, or foreign nationals?"

The Lt. Major approached the corporal and put his face so close to the corporal that their noses almost touched. With seething anger, the Lt. Major said, "They are threats to national security, no matter where they come from."

The corporal leaned even closer to the Lt' Major and said, "That means they are U.S. citizens, and we have a Constitution that guarantees any U.S citizen a fair trial. You kill citizens on American soil, and you are breaking laws and making a mockery of the Constitution. What you're doing, no matter your bullshit excuse, is tyranny. I'll have no part of it."

The corporal turned and began walking down the road. One by one, the remaining members of his team followed him in spite of the curse-laden tirade the Lt. Major directed at them. On his way down the hill, the corporal stripped his gear away and tossed it on the ground. He did the same with his uniform, save his t-shirt, his pants and boots. He was done with this shit. Forever.

*****

Ned and Jimmy continued to pick their way down the steep mountainside, altering their course to avoid cliffs and deadfall trees. They tried to be a quiet as they could be, but an experienced local hunter would have heard them from afar. As they paused at the base of the two mountains looking for the best way to cross the stream that marked the valley floor, Jimmy muttered something about the perils of crossing streams at night. Ned cut him off by a sharp hand signal to be silent.

At the same time, Ned and Jimmy heard the football-sized rock tumble down toward them from the mountain behind them. The two SWAT team members were closing the distance between them faster than Ned or Jimmy hoped. They guessed that six hundred yards separated them. They had to move, and they had to move faster … and quietly. Jimmy motioned forward and took three large steps atop rocks that stood above the stream's surface. Ned copied his movements, and scrambled up the opposite bank behind Jimmy.

Jimmy's pace was noticeably faster than before, and Ned pressed to keep up. They were climbing now, and the ascent angle was severe. Jimmy and Ned were breathing hard and had worked up a good lather as they fought gravity for elevation gain.

They tried to ignore the pounding they felt … and heard … as their hearts pumped massive volumes of blood through their bodies, and they each told themselves that they were always in shape and had the advantage over their younger pursuers of local knowledge and confidence in their abilities to navigate the mountains in the dark, and to avoid their enemies. They each had long histories of all such activities.

Thirty minutes later, Jimmy paused and leaned against a truck-size boulder breathing deeply, sucking oxygen into his lungs to replace the carbon dioxide their strenuous activity created. Jimmy took three more steps and stopped by Jimmy's side. Neither man talked for a good twenty seconds. They were breathing too hard to get any words out.

Each man was lost in his thoughts about what lie ahead, tonight and afterward.

Their internal thoughts were pierced by the crackling of the radio. "Units one and two, this is unit four. Please verify your location."

After a few seconds, the reply came. "Unit four, this is units one and two. We are at the streamside at the base of the two mountains readying to cross. Over."

There was silence before unit four asked them to repeat their location. They did, and a few seconds lapsed before unit four spoke again. "Roger, units one and two. Base, this is unit four. I have two bogies four hundred yards to my east, traveling westerly. Request orders for counter measures."

Ned and Jimmy quickly moved to the downhill side of the boulder. They heard a series of transmissions confirming locations and accounting for all dispersed units. The hair literally stood on the backs of Jimmy and Ned's necks when the base unit gave the order. "Units one, two and four, we have unidentified bogies approximately four hundred yards east of unit four's station. Orders are to proceed and acquire visuals on the bogies. The bogies are to be considered armed and dangerous, and are to be treated as enemy combatants. Respond to base once visual contact is established."

Jimmy and Ned looked at each other in the starlight. Ned asked Jimmy, "Can we make the mine entrance without getting our heads shot off?"

Jimmy smiled his sly grin and said, "Follow me, soldier. As you said, this is my home field, and I'll be damned if I'll let some toy soldiers take us out. You best lock and load and expect engagement. Stay low and move tree to tree, rock to rock. We have to move quickly, but we need to maintain stealth as well as we can. These guys are a tender box of men itching for a chance to fire their weapons. I don't intend to give them an easy target. Let's go."

They dashed from tree to tree and boulder to boulder for the next ten minutes. Ned was indeed in good shape, but Jimmy was moving with a grace that defied his bulk and the rough terrain. Ned doubted the units behind them could move any faster, but he was well aware that they were being squeezed by two enemies.

Ned caught up to Jimmy as he crouched behind a large boulder. After catching their breaths, Jimmy said, "The mineshaft entrance is 60 yards above us. See that deep shadow the shape of a bus? That's it."

Ned looked around the edge of the boulder, saw the shadow and said, "It's steep between here and the mine entrance, and there is less cover. That last few yards looks very steep."

Jimmy said, "It is steep. In fact, it's a twenty foot cliff and we have to climb it."

Ned said, "We'll be vulnerable to anyone behind us."

Their conversation was interrupted by a radio transmission. "Base, this is units one and two. We have visual on the bogies. They are armed, and are perched on the downhill side of a boulder four hundred fifty yards east of the mountain peak. Request orders."

Ned and Jimmy glanced at each other, then down hill to see if they could make out their pursuers. They couldn't. Jimmy said, "Let's go," and bolted around the boulder. Ned dashed behind him and the scrambled up the hillside. The radio cracked again. "Base, this is units one and two. We have interrupted visual and will change location to reacquire the targets."

The next transmission was ominous. "Base, this is unit four. I have visual. Request instructions."

Base replied. "Units one, two and four, permission to fire at will."

The first round hit the rock a foot to the right of Jimmy's head as he began climbing the rock cliff to the mineshaft. He dropped to the ground and scrambled to the base of a tree three yards to the left. Ned scrambled to his side as three more rounds sent dirt and rock fragments flying. Ned said, "The rock face is no good. We're sitting ducks there. We have to find an alternate path."

Jimmy said, "We'll go around the left side of the cliff. Follow me. I think we'll be OK if we make it the first ten yards. After that, we will be sheltered by boulders and trees. It's a tougher route and will take longer, but it's our best option." Without another word, Jimmy scrambled off on all fours, bullets flying all around him. Ned didn't hesitate.

Just before Jimmy reached shelter, Ned took off, hoping that by the time the shooters changed their aim from Jimmy to him, he would reach the shadowy area Jimmy scrambled into. But that was too much to hope for.

*****

In Colorado, one pissed off SWAT team member, or as of this morning, former SWAT team member, pulled over at an old gas station, one that was run by a third generation of owners. Not much had changed at the gas station, which also served as a general store, coffee shop, bar and host site of a poker game every Thursday night. In fact, nothing about the place had changed since he had first walked into the old building when he was five years old. Including the pay phone on the outside wall of the building.

The man dialed 411 and asked the operator for the number of the Colorado Springs Herald. She gave it to him, and when the phone was answered by a nightshift attendant, he asked for the reporter by name. He picked Jeff Henry because Jeff had for years written articles on policemen who abused their powers, and lately there had been more and more examples, mostly from federal forces that had decided to flex their muscles. He told the attendant that this was an emergency, and that a big event was taking place as they talked.

The attendant put him on hold. Five minutes later, she patched the two together, staying on the extension to hear the call. She wasn't missing this for the world. It could be something juicy she could share with her friends before the news hit the wires, and that always made her feel important. She was known in three counties as the best source of gossip there was.

Twenty minutes later, Jeff Henry skidded to a stop at the end of Ned's Colorado driveway with a camera crew in tow. The crew followed him as he ran up the driveway, the cameras running. They caught the tail end of the replacement SWAT team's meeting. They were so wrapped up in their tasks that they almost didn't see the camera crew. The leader approached Jeff Henry and said, "Get the hell out of here immediately."

Jeff Henry, always quick on his feet, replied, "I was sent by the governor to film this event to use for SWAT training across the state, maybe even sell it to the Feds. He insisted that I tell you, how did he say it, that 'he is the best of the best, and the film of his raid would be textbook, because all of your raids are textbook examples. Oh, and he said to tell you that he sends his best to you and your family."

The leader was disarmed by the governor's flattery, and he would make damn sure the raid was textbook. He told Jeff Henry, "OK, well you stay in the rear, and tell those damn camera folks that no lighting will be permitted. I'll tell you exactly where to position yourselves, and you will stay there until I tell you to move. Is that clear?"

Jeff Henry turned to his camera crew and they all nodded 'yes.' Jeff Henry said, "No problem. We're ready and will follow your orders to the "t," although he knew damn well he and his crew would do what the story dictated, not what some dick with a pinecone stuck up his ass said.

The leader told them to follow him, which they did. They filmed as the first two agents swung into the house behind their weapons. When they gave the all clear and told the leader about the tunnel door, the leader directed his men to blow the door. An explosives specialist rigged up plastic explosives around the perimeter of the vault door, and everyone retreated to the safety of the trees. The camera crew filmed as Jeff Henry narrated what was happening. They captured on film the orders to blow the door, and they captured the explosion, which nearly destroyed the entire structure.

The explosives expert hadn't been all that good at his task, and he rigged so much explosive that every door and window were blown out of the house, but the roof also lifted six feet in the air, and fell to pieces back on top of what remained of the house. They also captured it on camera as the resulting flames roared through the house, and they captured it on camera as they discovered the three men who had been killed by flying debris. They also filmed segments of the structure burning to the ground, which only took about 45 minutes due to the massive explosion.

As the sun rose, the camera crew went into the smoldering remains with two SWAT team members, and filmed as they dug their way down to the vault door. Once enough debris had been cleared, the cameraman got a great shot of the vault door, which stood securely in place. It was warped from the heat and was charred black, but it still secured the tunnel.

Jeff Henry pulled his crew back to the edge of the clearing near the house. He looked into the camera and filmed his closing to what would be a spectacular story on today's news. He said, "And this, folks," he turned and pointed to the smoldering remains of the house and the camera panned over the smoking embers, "This is what happens when government runs amok. This is what happens when power goes unchecked and when the Constitution is shredded by those in power."

He looked straight into the camera and said, "The irony is that the members of the SWAT team told me that had no idea what the residents of this house had done, or even if they had broken any laws. And they don't even know if they were home. But two things are certain. They completely destroyed a citizen's property, a citizen who has not been found guilty of a crime, and hasn't even been charged with a crime. And the second thing that should every person viewing this news cast is – your house could be next."

The cameraman saw the SWAT team leader walking briskly toward them. He shut down the camera, removed the memory card and stuffed it down his pants. He handed the camera to his assistant and looked at Jeff, who told him, "Run for it. I'll meet you back at the station as soon as I can get there. When you arrive, make as many copies of that as you can in case they raid us looking for it, and email it to the home office. I'll stall general turd here as long as I can."

The cameraman took off running and didn't slow until he reached the car. He jumped in and sped to the station as fast as he could drive. Jeff met him there thirty minutes later with the SWAT team leader in tow. They walked up to the cameraman where he sat. Jeff said, "General Lee here demands that we hand over the memory card from the camera, and he wants it now."

The cameraman put up a mock argument, even swearing at the leader until finally handing over the card, which he had erased and replaced with video another reporter had done as a joke to one of his co-workers. The video opened with the fellow shooting birds at the camera, and closed with a full on moon shot of the man's bare ass. When the leader left and the cameraman told Jeff what he had done, they broke into laughter. After a minute or two, they recovered their wits and Jeff said, "Let's get into the editing room and get this thing on the air before the noon news. And I mean every noon newscast in the country."

They had finished editing by 10 o'clock, and had secured management approval to run it by 10:30. The first airing took place fifteen minutes later by eastern sister station near the end of their noon news show. They preceded the film with a bright red "Breaking News" banner. By noon Mountain time, the film had made national news. A conservative news station ran it first. Twenty minutes later, the mainstream stations reluctantly began to include segments in their newscast since viewers were changing channels in droves as they heard about the news from other sources.

Jeff Henry was right; the event was national news. His station manager approached him and said, "Jeff, run home and get a shower and some clean clothes and get back here as soon as you can. The cable news stations are already requesting interviews with you. You're going to be a busy man for a few days."

As Jeff began to walk out of the office, his manager said, "Hey Jeff. Good work. You're famous."

Jeff smiled and kept walking. As he strode toward the parking lot, he began to wonder why it hadn't occurred to him to find out whose house the SWAT team destroyed. Instead of going straight home, he drove to the county administration building. He walked in and talked up the female attendant, trying to earn favor, which he didn't find to be very difficult. The gray-haired woman didn't see many people during the course of a normal day, and most of them were hard-core ranchers tending to normal business, and people who had met hard times and were delinquent on their tax bills.

After sweet-talking her for a few minutes, he handed her a piece of paper with the destroyed house's address written on it and asked to see the tax records. She said, "It's public record. Follow me."

She led him down the hall to a large room filled with gray metal filing cabinets. She attempted to explain the coding system so he could find the file, and he began searching. After twenty unsuccessful minutes of searching, he walked back to her desk. With all the softness he could muster, he said, "I can't find the file. I've looked and looked and I just can't find it. Could you please help me?"

The woman smiled and stood from her desk. "Come with me, honey." She led him back into the room and took the address from him. After ten minutes, she said, "That's funny. I can't find it either. In my 31 years here, I've never seen this." She put her finger to her chin and thought, then smiled and said, "Let's go look in the state tax files. I can access them on my computer."

After fifteen minutes of the computer search conducted with Jeff looking over her shoulder at the computer screen, she said, "You must have the address wrong. There is no tax record for this property. It's as if it doesn't exist."

Jeff thought for a moment and quietly muttered, "Or the owner doesn't exist. Something's fishy here. I got this address from the top of a SWAT team member's paperwork. I saw it listed on his map."

The woman said, "Let me see it again."

After a few minutes, she said, "You know, I thought this string of numbers was the plat number and I was trying to find it there. But now that I think about it, I wonder if these could be those location numbers from that satellite system. I saw something like this a few years ago, and now that I think about it, we ran into a similar situation a while back. Maybe you could go to the fire department and they could tell you."

He did. They confirmed that the numbers were indeed GPS numbers that pinpointed the location. He asked the fire chief, "Is this common?"

The chief said, "No, it's not. The only government people I know of that use these are the Feds."

That's when it hit Jeff. He had noticed that the SWAT leader that took charge was wearing a uniform that was different than the local SWAT team members. Were the Feds behind this raid? If they were, why? And who owned the house they had just obliterated?

*****

Ned was three steps into his dash for the shadows on the Virginia mountainside when he felt a jolt and a burn on the right side of his waste. He also was showered by the dirt and rock fragments from the impact of the bullet that passed through him and imbedded itself in the earth. He kept running, and bullets kept hitting the earth on both sides of him. He dove the last few yards into the shadows, and as soon as he hit the ground, he scrambled on all fours until he felt Jimmy grab him by the top of his pack and jerk him behind a boulder.

Ned said, "I'm hit."

Jimmy asked, "Where?"

Ned pulled his shirt up and they both looked at the wound. It was bleeding, not profusely, but enough that that area was covered and they couldn't accurately appraise the wound. Jimmy pulled his pack off and dug into a First Aid kit. He unfolded a large gauze pad and wiped the wound. He said, "It took a chunk of your waste about as wide as a dime and about four inches long, but it's shallow. You were nicked."

Jimmy pulled a roll of tape from the kit and several more gauze pads. He covered the wound with antibiotic cream and taped the gauze over the wound applying as much pressure as he could. He taped all the way around Ned's body to maintain the pressure and said, "This is going to hurt like hell in a little while. But you're OK and we should get moving."

Their radio crackled and they heard, "Unit four, this is units one and two. We believe we hit one of the bogies, and we are pressing forward. We will drive them toward you. Be alert."

Ned and Jimmy looked at each other. Ned said, "I hope we'll have better cover the rest of the way. We better get moving before the guys behind us catch up."

Jimmy crawled up a steep slope in at the base of a large boulder to the left of the main cliff face. Ned followed a few yards behind, deferring to the man who knew the terrain even better than he did. They were careful to move in unison, and they moved quickly. They were crawling through moist ground at the base of the rock in a depression created by millenniums of water erosion when rainwater ran down the face of the rock and carried away the soil. They continued this for another thirty yards.

Jimmy stopped and turned to Ned. "I think we're home free now. We're at the edge of the mineshaft."

Jimmy crawled up and into the darkness of the mineshaft. Ned followed. When Ned got to the entrance to the mine, he looked back. He couldn't see out. The entrance to the mine was hidden from view by the rock face that jutted above the cliff. It was as if this place had been designed as a secret hideaway. The rock stood tall in front of them, and the ground sunk away from it to the mineshaft. Unless someone stumbled to within six feet of this place, they would never find the shaft, which was about nine feet in diameter. Ned crouched down and led Jimmy fifteen yards into the dark mineshaft. It was so dark Jimmy walked into him as he was crouched over working on the combination lock that secured the vault door.

As Jimmy's eyes adjusted more to the darker environment, he could see that the vault door looked just like the round vault found in banks. After a couple of minutes, Ned pulled back on the door and opened it a couple of feet. They slipped through the door, and Ned pulled it closed behind them. The eight rods made a metal rubbing on metal sound as they traveled one foot into the thick steel ring that surrounded the door, with a deep clank when they reached the end of their runs.

Ned felt along the wall of the shaft until he was ten yards in with Jimmy close behind. It was completely dark in the shaft and they could see nothing at all. Ned stopped, and Jimmy heard the sound of a switch being flipped. The mineshaft was lit up in a dim LED light.

Ned said, "These are the emergency lights. They run off of that battery bank right there, which is charged by a hydro turbine generator that is turned by a spring that crosses the shaft floor fifty yards in. The batteries will last about two hours, then a generator kicks in."

Jimmy asked, "Are these lights powered by the generator in the barn by your house?"

Ned said, "Yes."

Jimmy said, "I know the generator is quiet, and that you added additional mufflers and sound dampening material so it wouldn't pollute the quiet of the mountain nights, but can you hear it outside the barn?"

Ned said, "If you are within a few feet, yes, you can hear the generator."

Jimmy said, "If I were going to raid your house, one of the safe approach points would be along the side of the barn. We should assume there will be someone there that would hear the generator."

Ned said, "I agree. Let's make sure to be off the property before the generator activates. That could tip someone off that something is being powered by the generator, and they might eliminate all possibilities and figure out there is a tunnel."

Jimmy said, "When I was a kid, I got lost in here and thought I was a goner for sure. It took me 23 hours to get out, and I was damn lucky to have survived. I took a wrong turn, and I only stumbled back into the main shaft. I burned out my flashlight batteries. I ended up tearing off strips of my shirt and draping them over a shard of a structural timber. I finally got the wood to catch fire and I found out that creosote soaked timbers burn well, although they create awful smoke. That poor light saved me. If I had had no light source, there is no way I could have escaped. My folks would still be wondering what happened to me."

Ned said, "We each have flashlights in our packs that should last us, but it would still make for significantly more difficult travel navigating by two small beams of light. Let's get moving." He groaned as he turned his body, aggravating his wound.

A hundred yards farther in there was another vault door, which Ned said was a "just in case" door if someone discovered the shaft entrance and somehow got the outer door open. Ned opened it by spinning the combination dial back and forth until he was satisfied he had entered the right combination. He grasped the locking lever and retracted the steel rods out of the outer frame and pulled the heavy door open. He considered leaving it unlocked to aid a hasty retreat, but he thought of the people chasing them and how close behind they had been. They had been close enough to see them and to get off some shots at them. His bleeding side bore the evidence.

The mineshaft was rough, making for rugged travel. The air was musty and cool, and occasionally at branch junctions, there would be a subtle movement of air as it passed through the labyrinth of passageways toward unseen and unmarked vents. Ned's wound was beginning to throb with each heartbeat. He looked at it under one of the lights. It was still oozing blood, but it was covered and there was nothing more they could do right now. He tried to push it from his mind. This wound was nothing compared to what would happen to them if they were really shot up, or if they got trapped in the mine.

After what seemed like an eternity, they came to another steel door. Ned spun the combination and opened it. They walked another ten feet and the tunnel seemed to be stymied by a wood wall. Ned walked up to the wall, slid a bolt and pushed on the panel until it opened. He stepped through and Jimmy followed him into the initial escape tunnel that led to Ned's house, 60 yards away.

Jimmy said, "Ah! So this is where you ran into the mine. I wondered about it, and didn't realize the old mine came this far."

Ned said, "It was a stroke of pure luck. As I was finishing out my escape tunnel, I was scraping off loose dirt and stone from the walls before

I sprayed them with a layer of concrete to add strength and reduce the smell of damp soil. I scraped this area, and dirt and gravel kept falling until I broke through and wind came rushing out. I poked through enough to figure out it was an abandoned mine, so I did some serious investigating of old mines in the area and who owned them. The company was long gone, but I located an old man who had worked for it decades ago. He had maps of the mine, and he gave me one. That map helped me find the mineshaft entrance we came through tonight. I hiked around the mountains for weeks before I discovered it. I guess I would have saved lots of time if I had only asked you."

Jimmy shook his head and said, "Yes, you would have, but I had no idea the mine came this far and was this shallow anywhere. Those old miners used to follow a vein until it ran out, no matter which direction it took them. I guess they didn't realize how close they were to breaking through on this end."

Ned pushed the door closed and turned toward the house. They got to the vault door that led them into Ned's house. Ned slowly opened the door and stepped into the storage room. He clicked another lever and pushed on the back of a shelving unit, and entered the downstairs storage room. Jimmy was close behind him. Ned led them to the stairwell. They proceeded slowly and quietly, making sure to remain undetected. They climbed another flight of stairs, all the while in crouched positions.

They entered Ned's bedroom, then his closet, closing the closet door behind them so the motion-activated vault light wouldn't be visible to anyone outside the house. After another trick shelving unit and vault door, they stepped into Ned's cedar-lined weapons vault. They stood up straight and pulled the door closed behind them. Ned walked over to one of the steel gun cabinets. He opened one of the smaller compartments, reached in and pulled out a smaller steel box. He opened the box and flipped through a black, hardback notebook until he found what he was looking for.

Ned said, "This is it." He closed the notebook and the box and tucked it into his pack. They eased back into the closet, locked the vault and began their crouched trek back to the lower level. They were halfway down the second stairwell when they heard three rapid-fire rifle shots. Someone had fired the first volley, their weapon set on three-shot bursts. It was only a few seconds before return fire started, and the noise got louder and louder as the battle expanded all around them. Ned's radio came to life with a cacophony of panicked voices, several of them yelling, "We are under heavy attack and are returning fire. Request air support stat!"

Thomas Lide

Ned and Jimmy looked at each other. They listened for the sounds of bullets shattering windows and splatting against the interior walls of the house, but there were no such sounds.

Jimmy said, "I'll be damned. Your plan seems to be working. They aren't shooting at us, they're shooting at each other."

Ned smiled. Their plan had come together … so far … as far as they could tell. He wished he could contact Kara and tell her to call the media, but he couldn't. She couldn't have placed any calls right now anyway. She was fighting a battle of her own, every bit as intense as this one.

Ned and Jimmy sped up their pace. They made it into the first tunnel. They could no longer hear the sound of gunfire since they were underground. As Ned approached the door to the mineshaft, out on the dark mountainside a DHS SWAT team member turned to look at the man beside him, who was looking over the top of the boulder they were posted behind. There was rifle fire from all directions, and the situation was rapidly deteriorating into chaos.

He couldn't tell who was firing at them, if they were indeed targets, nor could he tell where the gunshots were coming from. Everywhere, it seemed. He began to form the words to the peering man, "Get down.

Before the sound left his throat, a rifle bullet hit the peering man in the base of the neck. The man dropped, blood spraying as if from a hose.

The DHS SWAT team member panicked. He pushed the transmit button of his radio and said, "Base, this is Alpha team. We are under heavy fire. Repeat, we are under heavy fire and need air support stat."

The person manning the base unit turned to the commanding officer on site and gave him a questioning look, awaiting orders. The commanding officer said, "Tell him we need coordinates of the incoming fire."

The radio operator asked the panicked Alpha team member. "Everywhere!"

The commanding officer grabbed the microphone and said, "We can't blow up 'everywhere.' We need coordinates."

The Alpha member hesitated. He eased his head around the side of the boulder to take a look. When he did, a burst of bullets splattered the rock beside him. Before he ducked back behind the boulder, he saw the muzzle flash and the path of the tracers as they arched toward him. He had just taken fire from a SWAT team that belonged to the U.S. Forest Service, who were themselves under heavy fire from a DOE SWAT team to the east whose members were three weeks out of training and were shooting at anything they saw, and even things they didn't see but feared *could* be in the area. The Forrest Service team was hunkered down two hundred yards on the opposite side of the house, offering the illusion that the fire had come from the roof of Ned's house.

He pushed his transmit button and said into the radio, "The house. The fire is coming from snipers on the roof of the house."

"Roger that, soldier. Fire coming from the roof of the house. We will provide air support."

The commanding officer barked commands to the man at the computer screen, who was looking at images the drone was sending back to them. In reply, the man said, "I don't see any hostiles on the roof of the house, sir."

The commanding officer said, "They must be hidden away high in the house, and it only looked like the fire was coming from the roof. Again, I order you to fire on the house."

The man at the screen sighed, designated the center of the roof of the house as the target, and clicked on the "fire" button. With no delay, the Hellfire missile the drone carried ignited, and in just over two seconds penetrated the roof of the house. It also penetrated the floor of the second level and imbedded itself in the oak floor of the main level of the house. Then it exploded, sending boards and shards of wood, rock, steel and glass over a circumference of three hundred yards. What was left of the house was engulfed in flames that would not be extinguished until all sources of fuel were expended.

The explosion occurred as Ned and Jimmy were entering the mineshaft. It blew both of them into the shaft. When each of them regained their feet, they checked themselves for wounds, but found none. Their worst symptoms seemed to be ringing in their ears. They locked the vault door at the junction of the mineshaft and began to run through the old mine.

Back at the house, the fire was intense and the flame reached 50 feet taller than any of the surrounding trees. The light from the flames could be seen for miles. But it was the sound from the blast that awakened the Blacksburg Times reporter. He ran to his window and looked out. He couldn't see the flames from his window; they were too far away. But he could see the sky glowing to his west. He thought to himself that the old mill must have blown up, or maybe the storage yard of the propane gas company had ignited. He picked up his cell phone and called the one videographer that worked for the paper. When the sleeping man answered the phone, the reporter said, "Get your gear. There's been a massive explosion. I'll pick you up in ten minutes." He scrambled into his clothes and ran toward his car.

Ned and Jimmy were about halfway through the mineshaft, making very good time and highly motivated to get out as soon as possible. Back at the house, the flames were so intense that the barn had combusted from the radiant heat. It took fifteen minutes for the fire to burn enough of the structure to melt the wiring that connected the generator to the battery bank.

The generator wasn't yet running, but when the wires melted, they contacted each other and shorted the circuitry, blowing a breaker. With that, the lights in the tunnel went out.

Ned and Jimmy dug into their packs and retrieved their flashlights, powerful LED models with adjustable lenses and long life. Each unit would burn for 24 hours with brand new batteries. Their batteries were unused but six months old, which cut their battery life down to 19 hours. If everything went right, that would be more than enough reserve power for them to get out of the tunnel. If everything went right. But it never does.

*****

A Secret Service agent woke the President at 5:30 a.m. ET, a half hour earlier than normal. He said, "Mr. President, there are news reports that we think you should see."

The President rolled into a sitting position and said, "Turn on the TV and let's see what is going on."

The Secret Service agent did as he was told, putting the TV on CNN. The lead anchor, Bear Williams, was interviewing a local reporter, who was standing on the side of the road with a SWAT team command center in the background, the sky lit by a yellow-orange glow. The reporter was saying, "Yes, Bear, its mass confusion here. We circled the site of the explosion, which you can see in the background resulted in a massive fire. We are at the site of a Department of Homeland Security command post. But what's interesting is that we saw other command posts, one from the U.S. Forest Service, one from Immigration, Department of Education, the IRS and a couple of others we couldn't identify.

"No one will give us any answers, but it appears as if there has been a raid that involved multiple federal agencies. What's even more strange about that is that we haven't found a central command center, and no one who will acknowledge the existence of one. We aren't sure what is behind this or how massive the raid was, but the one thing we know for sure is that whatever they raided is engulfed in a massive fire that we are told has spread to the forest."

The CNN announcer said, "Thank you to Jim Hest from our local affiliate in Blacksburg, Virginia. As you just heard, there was a massive raid involving numerous federal agencies. No one is claiming responsibility or leadership. Our Washington reporters are trying to reach the appropriate department spokesmen now, and we will report back as soon as we learn more. Let's just hope this isn't another Branch Davidians' situation where the government went in too heavy handed."

The lead announcer's partner, a sharp, beautiful woman in her early thirties who was as ambitious as she was pretty, said, "Let's hope not. But what we do know is that there were numerous agencies involved with their SWAT teams. Frankly, Bear, I wasn't aware that the Department of Education and the IRS had SWAT teams, nor the Forest Service, and I wonder about the necessity of such. And if this turns out to be similar to the tragedy in Waco, Texas that took place under the watch of Janet Reno, it is Branch Davidians on steroids."

The station broke for commercials, and the President said to the Secret Service officer, "I'll be in my office in ten minutes. Tell Margaret to get the Attorney General and the head of Homeland Security on the phone. Now! And get the vice president and press secretary in my office immediately."

After the agent left the room, the President walked into the bathroom and splashed water on his face. As he slipped into a suit, he muttered to himself, "What the hell have these people done now? Don't they know there's an election in 14 months? Can't they just lie low until after the elections. I thought I had drilled into everyone's head to save controversial actions until immediately after election cycles."

When the President entered his office, his press secretary was sitting on the sofa, along with is chief of staff. The vice president was sitting in a chair used by visitors to the Oval Office. The president sat in his chair and looked at the faces of each person. The vice president said, "The attorney general and the head of DHS are on the line, Mr. President."

The President barked at the attorney general on the phone. "Melvin! What the hell is going on in Virginia?"

The attorney general hesitated before saying, "We had our FBI Terrorist SWAT unit perform a raid this morning on a suspected terrorist. There is mass confusion at the scene right now, sir, and we have been unable to raise our command post."

The President said to the head of DHS, "Beth, what is your role in this?"

She also stumbled on her words as she said, "Sir, we ... we conducted a raid on a suspected terrorist, and apparently, we encountered heavy resistance from a suspect who was clearly armed to the teeth."

After a few seconds of silence, the President asked, "Who was in charge of this operation?"

Beth of DHS said, "We were in charge of our own unit only, sir."

The president said, "Melvin, so this was your operation?"

The attorney general said, "Well, we were also in charge of our own unit only, and weren't aware of other agency involvement."

The president slapped his hand down on his desk. He said, "I can only hope that my fear isn't true. What I fear is that you people raided the same place at the same time, but weren't coordinated."

The attorney general was the first to attempt to cover his ass. He said, "I gave no orders for this mission, and am only now learning of this operation in the news."

The president said, anger dripping from his voice, "That's my line, and you do not have permission to use it. You find out who gave the orders, and you find out why. Call me back within the hour with a straight answer. Leave the bullshit answers to me. Same for you, Margaret!"

The president pushed the button on the phone to disconnect the call. He looked at his vice president and said, "If this situation is what I think it is, it's bad. Real bad, and it might cost you any chance you had of winning the election. I realize that you were Plan B, but if you're out, our party doesn't have a candidate, now that Lee has dropped out of the race. Bedekowski will have to do some scrambling."

That vice president jumped to attention. He had been secretly happy that Lee had dropped out and left him a clear path to the most powerful position in the world. With trepidation, he asked, "What do you think the situation is, Mr. President?"

The president looked him squarely in the eye and said, "A government clusterfuck of unprecedented proportion. We can't bury it because the news is already all over it. They know we had multiple agencies involved, and if the attorney general and the head of DHS don't know who was in charge, then it's likely that no one was in charge. It could be the worst case of one hand not knowing what the other was doing, and it likely cost lives."

The vice president, still holding out hope that he could occupy the chair the president was now in, asked, "What are the chances that happened? That several federal agencies raided the same place at the same time, not knowing what the other was up to?"

312

The president shook his head slowly. He said, "Damn likely, I'd say. Most of these damn people are in their positions because they were big contributors or otherwise owned debts politicians had to make good on. Let's face it: Few political appointees are qualified for their jobs. Anyway, you know these agencies are so territorial they won't talk to each other. Frankly, I'm surprised this sort of shit doesn't happen every day."

The chief of staff spoke up. "Excuse me, Mr. President, but I think this sort of thing does happen every day. We certainly can't rule out incompetence, coincidence and poor leadership. But there's one thing we might consider."

The President waited a breath before saying, "Get to the point!"

The chief of staff said, "The only thing worse than a coincidental clusterfuck, as you put it, is that it was orchestrated."

The president rubbed his cheek, then his forehead, and said, "God help us if that's the case. If that's true, we're up against someone with the smarts, the will and the ability to pull off something of this magnitude. There aren't many people with that combination of assets."

The press secretary, whose head was always in he role of press secretary, said, "Worse than being true, God help us if the media gets wind of it."

Ninety-three minutes later, the attorney general and the head of DHS sat in the two chairs in front of the President's desk. The President walked into the Oval Office seven minutes later, sat down, disdainfully put his foot on the desk that had seen decades of Oval Office history, something the president disdained, and said curtly, "What's your story?"

The attorney general said, "There's still some confusion sir."

The president said, "Melvin, don't bullshit me. I'm the best bull shitter on the planet, which means I'm better at it than you are. Out with it."

The attorney general hesitantly said, "Well, sir, it appears that the orders to conduct a raid came from me. But I said, "appears." I swear to you, sir, that I didn't write, approve or even have knowledge of the operation. It's as if someone came into my office and sent the email order from my computer."

The president didn't believe a word of it. He shook his head and said, "Bullshit! Beth, what do you have to say for yourself?"

She was even more hesitant. She said, "Well, sir, I hate to be repetitive, but I have the same situation. I didn't send any email orders for this operation, but someone did ... from my email account."

The President looked from one to the other, trying to decide who he would replace them with, which is exactly what he intended to do, BEFORE the public got wind of this. That's when Beth said, "But there's more, sir. From what I can determine so far, there were five other agencies that conducted raids this morning. I've talked to the agency heads at IRS, Forrest Service, Immigration, Education and the Federal Reserve and they all say the same thing. We don't know what's going on, but it all appears to have been orchestrated."

The president shook his head again said, "Come on! If we tried for a thousand years we couldn't coordinate multiple federal agencies and get them to do the same thing at the same time. No way! We've been trying to do that for decades, and no one has ever come close. Are you going to stick with that story? Are you?"

The attorney general began to say, "Sir, we will investigate this matter and punish those responsible ..."

The President shouted, "Shut the fuck up! The American public is sick of hearing you say that. I'm sick of hearing you say that. We all know your modus operandi … you say you'll investigate, you never do and you just try and stall long enough that everyone will forget. Your bullshit won't work this time. You're fired. Both of you. Now get out."

The attorney general said, "Sir, we always say we'll start an investigation and do not follow through because that's what you ordered us to do. And I have it in writing from you."

The president shouted, "Get out of my office!"

The head of DHS sat motionless in stunned silence. The AG, on the other hand, was furious, and grew a wicked and belligerent grin. The president waited for three whole seconds before he stood, knocking his chair down behind him, and shouted, "Get the fuck out!"

The Secret Service agent outside the door to the office opened the door and walked into the room to escort the two fired political appointees out of the office. They followed him in silence. The former head of DHS had a tear running down her right cheek.

The attorney general was mad. He thought to himself, "How dare that son of a bitch fire *me*! The president seems to be forgetting that I hold enough incriminating evidence to have the him indicted for two dozen federal offenses, including election fraud, stealing taxpayer money, accepting bribes from unions, lobbyists and political donors, and using the IRS to punish and dissuade political opponents or critics, as well as killing citizens inside the U.S. with drones and assassins. Not only that, but he had given the AG written orders to charge companies and people with crimes only to hassle them and extort fines.

The President fired *me*? Of all people, he fired the one person who holds all the cards that could ruin his presidency and land him in jail? If I have learned one thing during my tenure in Washington politics, it is how to exact revenge on political enemies. Hell, the president was my best teacher. Well, now it was time for the student to best the teacher.

The attorney general left the White House with a wicked grin on his face. He was going straight home to gather up all the evidence. He only had to decide to whom he wanted to give the opportunity break the news, to be the star of the news shows for weeks. He thought of the beautiful new anchor at CNN, the blonde who was co-hosting that very morning. He had always wanted to get in her pants, and maybe this bombshell would be his opportunity. He would contact her from his house in Bethesda.

Chapter 21

Kara and Sam reached the end of their tunnel beneath the mountains of central Colorado. After Sam opened a vault door following Ned's instructions, the two of them stepped into an open chamber the size of a four-car garage. Just as Ned had told them, there was a light green 4-wheel drive Toyota Land Cruiser of early-seventies vintage. As Sam got into the driver's seat, Kara opened the rear door and put their two packs and her laptop into the cargo area. Sam turned the key and the engine turned over without hesitation. After about five seconds, it fired to life. Sam got out of the truck, opened the partially closed hood and unhooked the solar battery-charger wires from the battery posts. He walked over to the large, heavy steel garage door that was more a very large blast door that what could be found in old military facilities built in the Cold War era.

It took the both of them pushing to swing the door out enough for Sam to pull the vehicle forward and clear the door. He put the vehicle in park, and the two of them pushed the door closed. Sam locked the door and turned to find Kara standing in front of the vehicle scanning the area. She turned to Sam and said, "I see no sign of anyone around, and I see nothing to suggest that anyone has been here in some time, although there are plenty of deer tracks around, and then there's this."

Kara pointed with her right boot to the large paw print in the soft soil. Sam bent over for a closer look, then straightened up and looked all around them. He said, "The big cat is around. No wonder no one has been around here."

Kara said, "'Cat' is being kind. Other people call the animal that made this print a mountain lion. Let's get out of here."

The 250-pound cat watched from the shadows 60 feet up a 300-foot rock cliff. This was the cat's hunting ground. It had evaded hunters for years, and dissuaded them from coming around by attacking two of them a few years ago, killing one of the men. Local hunters steered well clear of the area ever since.

It watched as Kara and Sam walked quickly to the Land Cruiser and got in. Sam shifted the vehicle into gear and started down the rough road that had at one time been a service road to the tunnel, which must have been an old mine. The vehicle rocked and rolled from side to side with the terrain. They were making slow progress.

Sam said, "I wonder how far we have to go to reach a road. This is slow going, and I want to get out of here as fast as we can."

Kara said, "Slow, indeed, but this is a hell of a lot better than walking through that dark old tunnel. That was creepy. I never want to go into a tunnel again as long as I live. If the lights had gone out, if our flashlights had failed, we would have died a slow, agonizing death as we starved." She visibly shivered.

Sam said, "I was thinking it was better than walking to the road with that big cat lurking. The tunnel was creepy, but I don't like being in the vicinity of another creature that's higher on the food chain than we are. He kept his eyes on the mine road, straining to keep the vehicle going in the right direction. Kara shivered again at what Sam said about the cat.

It took them almost an hour. Sam figured they had traveled 8 or 9 miles over the rough terrain. When they finally reached a road, it was a small track barely wide enough for two vehicles to pass, but it was paved. Sam said, "Ned said the dirt road would terminate on a rural road, and he meant rural. He said to go right, and that it was 20 miles to an intersection, and another 25 miles to a little town. This place is more isolated than any I've ever seen."

Kara said, "I'm sure that's why Ned chose this place. He likes people, but he prefers to select the people he spends time with. He says he is 'eliminating the chaff,' that time is too precious to waste it on disingenuous people. I'm gaining an appreciation for that."

The fastest they could travel on the small road was 45 miles per hour. The next road was slightly bigger and faster, but it seemed like a very long drive. They were on a mission to put distance between them and whoever raided Ned's house, and to get to a place where Kara could contact her chosen people in the media.

Finally, they began to see houses that were closer together than ten miles. There were a few trucks on the road, and traffic became relatively thicker as they neared Buena Vista, Colorado. After a couple of traffic lights, they came to a small strip center that housed a vet's office, a hardware store, feed and seed store and a small diner. Outside the diner was a payphone, and in the window of the diner was a small sign that read "Free Wi-Fi."

Sam went into the diner and ordered two coffees. He sat at a booth by the window, and watched as Kara talked on the phone to six different media contacts. She jotted notes in a notebook as she talked.

When she finished with her calls, she walked rapidly to the diner and joined Sam. She was absorbed in her tasks, and barely noticed the coffee awaiting her. She booted up her laptop, logged onto the Wi-Fi and initiated the VPN network, and launched the scrambling program that would mask the location and identity. She sent to the news contacts copies of the email that each agency head had sent to their staffs ordering SWAT raids on Ned's Virginia house.

As soon as she completed the task, she looked up at Sam and said, "Multiple federal agencies did send their SWAT teams to Ned's house last night, and it did turn into a clusterfuck, just as Ned expected. What we didn't anticipate is that the national media has already caught wind of the situation. A local reporter saw an explosion during the night, and as he investigated, he and his camera crew stumbled upon command posts for SWAT teams from several different agencies. As Ned had hoped, each of the separate agencies set up at different points along the perimeter of the property and remained unaware of the others. The reporter ran a segment on his local TV affiliate this morning, and it was picked up by the national news. And here's the best part."

She paused and smiled, gathered her breath and said, "One of the reporters told me that the White House issued a statement saying that the President ordered a raid on a known terrorist suspect. I countered that by telling them who owned the house that they raided, and that he was a decorated former CIA agent and an American citizen who was not accused of any crime, but was a man who had stumbled across information damaging to the president.

Thomas Lide

"I told them that, and explained that the White House considered him a political opponent that needed to be silenced. I hope that was the right move, and I hope Ned won't be angry or endangered further by the world knowing who he is and where he lives."

Sam rubbed his chin, considering the information, and said, "I suspect that the higher profile he has right now, the safer he'll be. It is more difficult to attack a man standing in the spotlight for everyone to see. Sometimes there is safety in being in plain sight, at least when the enemy wants to remain undetected. All politicians want to stay clear of obvious culpability, and it sounds like this situation is one they don't want to be associated with publicly."

Kara said, "I agree. We just need to make sure the media runs with this, and that we are able to help them connect the dots … the way we want them to be connected. We need to start feeding them information that will be the catalyst of a huge news explosion, one that shines the light of public scrutiny on them so brightly that the politicians and puppet masters won't survive. The emails will help fan the flames, and we'll keep throwing fuel on the fire until it blows up and has a life of its own. We also need to leak some of the NSA telephone calls and emails. If we pick and choose correctly, we can drive this thing home."

323

Her expression changed as her mind switched from a strategic mode to one focused on the next task. She said, "Ned needs to get here soon with the account numbers. We need to move the money so that we control it before the spotlight is focused brightly on the bad guys and they go scurrying off somewhere with their cash in hand. If the story breaks as we hope it will and we don't have their money, then we won't have wasted our time, but we won't cripple them enough that they can't quickly buy their way back into power. We need those account numbers. What I can do now is begin selecting the right nuggets from the NSA databank to feed to the press."

*****

Ned led as they made their way through the dark, musty mine shaft. To keep his mind occupied, Jimmy had begun counting the old timber support structures of the tunnel, which cast dramatic shadows on the rough rock roof and walls of the tunnel as their flashlights shown their powerful LED beams on them. They had just passed the 93rd structure and he was looking up at it as they rounded a slight bend in the shaft and he tripped over a stray rock that had fallen from the wall to his right. He staggered forward with extra long strides in an attempt to catch his feet up with his upper body, which was bent forward from the trip. The rock had stopped the progress of his feet, but not that of his upper body.

He staggered three steps when he lost control and fell into the back of Ned's legs at knee level. It was if he were on a football field and had tackled Ned from behind, his shoulder making full impact with Ned's right leg. The impact buckled Ned and drove him into the rock floor, the whole of Jimmy's weight on him.

Ned had heard the scuffling as Jimmy tripped and struggled to regain control, but had no time to react. Ned's knees burned of pain as they met the rock floor, and he tumbled forward. He caught his upper body with his forearms, sparing him a full face plant, but pain shot up his legs from his knees, and the flashlight in his right hand crashed full force into the rock floor, shattering its lens and most of the LED bulbs, rendering the light inoperable.

Jimmy struggled to his feet, apologized and asked Ned if he was OK. Ned rolled onto his back and felt his knees. His jeans had holes ripped in each knee. He flexed his legs to check for structural damage, and asked Jimmy to shine the light on him so he could inspect the carnage. Jimmy gathered himself and illuminated Ned. Ned removed his hands from his knees, revealing two bloodied joints and hands.

Ned wiped his hands on his thighs and said, "Help me up."

The two men overlapped their right arms, taking firm hold on the other's wrist, and Jimmy pulled him to a standing position. Ned involuntarily groaned, pain shooting up from his knees, but more so from the wound in his side.

Ned flexed his legs and said, "Other than skinned and a little bruised, I think my knees are OK. It's my side that hurts most."

Jimmy re-aimed his light and looked at the bullet wound in Ned's side. He said, "It has opened up again. I need to see if I can bandage you better to slow the bleeding. It's leaking pretty badly right now."

Ned held the light as Jimmy dug through their packs. He gathered all the gauze they had, and tied together the two elastic bandages that were in the first aid kits, and re-bandaged Ned as Best he could. Ned grimaced as Jimmy applied heavy pressure to the elastic that he wrapped around Ned's mid-section. Having done the best he could with limited supplies, Jimmy said, "That slowed the bleeding from a flow to an ooze, and I'm afraid that is all I can do for now, unless you want me to stitch the wound."

Ned broke into a cold sweat at the mere thought of having stitches put in his side with no pain relief, and declined the offer.

Jimmy asked, "You want me to take your pack? Do you want me to lead?"

Ned said, "I've lived through worse … much worse. I'm fine to lead. I'll make it. Let's hurry and get out of here. I don't see time as our ally."

Ned looked at his watch. He said, "It's taking longer than I would like. Sunrise is in 50 minutes. We're cutting it close. I was hoping to be across the road and long gone before first light, but that might not be possible. Let's get the hell out of here."

Ned turned and began walking quickly through the mineshaft, Jimmy close behind being careful with is footing. He was watching Ned. He could only see a dark silhouette against the bright beam of the flashlight Ned was holding, but he could see that Ned was favoring his side, and he was limping on his right leg. Both men were painfully aware that they were walking at a slower pace, although the effort was exponentially more difficult for Ned than it had been five minutes earlier.

Twenty minutes passed with the two men making their way through the mineshaft. Ned was doing his best to ignore the pain for the first ten minutes.

After he stumbled slightly over the rough floor, he made a decision. Rather than trying to deny the pain, he decided to accept it, to embrace it, and to use it to generate anger and energy, which he used to push himself. Jimmy noticed an increase in Ned's speed and less of a lean to his wounded side. Jimmy wondered what had changed, and made a mental note to ask Ned about it later.

Twenty-two minutes after Jimmy's fall and Ned's new wounds, Ned said, "Look!"

Jimmy focused on the beam of light, and could just make out a vault door 40 yards ahead.

Jimmy said, "We've reached the end of the mine, and not a minute too soon, in my opinion. I've never been fond of tunnels and mines."

Ned said, "Neither have I, but tonight I am sure glad that we have this tunnel. There is little chance we could have made it all the way to the house and back this far had we been out in the open with all those armed men out there equipped with night vision. Drones, too, with heat detection cameras, I suspect."

Both men instantly wished they hadn't gone down that avenue of thought. They were at the exit of the mine, and that was certainly a positive milestone, but now that they were leaving the claustrophobic mineshaft, they were also leaving the protection and security it offered. Now they would be out in the open ... with all those men armed with rifles and night vision ... and the drones.

Jimmy held the light for Ned as he spun the vault combination dial. After entering the numbers, he put his left hand on the lever to slide the bolts out of the surrounding steel frame. He paused and drew his pistol with his right hand and turned to Jimmy, who focused the light downward, leaving them illuminated slightly by indirect light, which lent an eerie mood.

Ned said, "Best draw your weapon and be ready for an ambush. For all we know, there is a squadron outside waiting for us to step out and serve as target practice for a bunch of people who've never pulled the trigger when aiming toward a living person, but they will feel safe doing so since they will share the responsibility for killing us with all the other shooters."

Jimmy said, "I already have my rifle in my hand, locked and loaded. Yours is right there where we left it when we entered the tunnel."

Ned said, "That's a better plan." He holstered his pistol and picked up his rifle, which was illuminated as Jimmy focused the flashlight beam on it. Ned slid the rack back an inch to make sure a round was chambered.

Ned said, "You push the door open and I'll move out past you, barrel first and ready to fire."

Jimmy said, "OK, but be ready to retreat quickly."

Ned said, "You can count on that. Make sure I have room to back up if I draw fire."

Ned positioned himself and Jimmy braced to push the door halfway open. Ned raised is weapon into firing position, looked over at Jimmy and said, "Turn your light off and let's let our eyes adjust to the darkness. I'll wait about fifteen seconds before I count down from ten. At zero, push the door."

They waited. After what seemed like an eternity, their minds racing with thoughts of what awaited them outside the mine, Ned began counting. Ten, nine, eight, seven, six, five, four, three, two, one, go!"

Chapter 22

As the news began to gain momentum, the president said to his chief of staff and his press secretary, "We have to put the brakes on this thing before it careens out of control. Get on the phone with the heads of each major news outlet and tell them this is a matter of national security, and to cool their jets before they endanger the entire country."

The president called the vice president into his office, filled him in and said, "The three of you divide and conquer and put the heat on these news organizations. Coerce them, pressure them or threaten them, I don't care. We have dossiers on each of them, so review them and pick out your leverage. I don't care how far you have to go to accomplish this, but stop this thing before it gets worse and we get questions we don't want to answer."

The president put his vice president in charge. The vice president had his own political ambitions, and he not only had no trust in the president, who was a genuine pathological liar who would lie about that color of the tie he was wearing when you could see it for yourself, and would even deny that he was wearing one if you pressed him. And the scary part was that you couldn't tell if the man knew he was lying and didn't have moral shame, or if he really believed the shit he was shoveling. Anyway, the vice president had been in politics long enough to cover his ass. He said to the president, "Sir, I'm afraid that I will require this order in writing."

The president wasn't surprised. He said, "I figured you would say that. Write it up and email it to me. I'll sign and return it."

The vice president thought the better of the proposal. He knew that the president would sacrifice him if it would save face for the president, and it would be like the man to leak the email that contained the order and then say, "See, the vice president originated and sent this order." He said to the President, "Sir, I'm afraid that the original needs to come from you."

The President was frustrated. He slapped his desk and almost shouted, "Alright, damn it. You'll have it in five minutes." With a wave of his hand, he said, "You're dismissed. Now get to work." Five minutes later, an email arrived in the vice president's in box, and the message the vice president had insisted on was there. He read the message. Satisfied with it, he saved in on a thumb drive and forwarded a copy to his personal email, just in case the message mysteriously disappeared, which had happened on many occasions. The vice president began making calls.

The result was that every major television network except for one suddenly quit reporting on the story within the next half hour, and the AP and other major news outlets began pulling stories from their websites. The sudden change was noticed by the public, and the one network still reporting the news began receiving messages and calls saying the other networks had gone silent on the matter.

The CEO of that one network still reporting the story had received a phone call from the vice president, but he had never liked the vice president, or anyone in his administration. When the call came in, the CEO pushed the "record" button on his desk phone. The vice president first asked politely that the network cease coverage, but the CEO flat out refused. The vice president wasted no time. His next statement was that he would make damn sure that the story of his wife's mental health struggles went public, and if that wasn't enough, he would release the details of the divorce the CEO had survived 15 years earlier. The CEO was pissed off. He shouted at the vice president, "You threatening son of a bitch. You leak what you want about me and my family. But let me advise you that I have a few nuggets on you and the president. You want to play hardball, say when. I'm loaded for bear, and you can kiss goodbye any political future you thought you had."

The CEO slammed the phone down, and immediately picked it up again and called his chief editor into his office. When he arrived, he handed printouts of seven emails from department heads to their staffs ordering the raid on Ned's house. He said, "Work with Sara on this. I want her in front of the camera with this within fifteen minutes. She has the story. She received a call from a source an hour ago saying that the house that was raided belongs to an American hero, not a terrorist. She is verifying ownership and background right now. If the story is true, we are about to release the biggest bombshell this country has seen since Watergate."

The chief editor was reading through the materials. He audibly whistled through his teeth, then jumped from his seat and said, "Holy shit. This is huge. I'll gather an entire team to assist Sara and we'll go on the air shortly." He turned and ran from the room. Fifteen minutes later, the CEO watched from the control booth as Sara Shepherd broke the news live on camera. The CEO smiled in satisfaction. As he listened to Sara's nearly breathless delivery, he felt chills at how dramatic her delivery was. She had been a rising star, but this was going to catapult her into fame.

But all the while, the CEO felt uneasy about something he couldn't quite put his finger on. Why had the White House tried to quell the story? Why had the vice president himself called and threatened him. It wasn't the first call he had taken from the White House, and it wasn't the first time he had been pressured to quell or change a story they didn't like. He had been shouted at and cursed, but this was the first time they had leveled an outright threat. So they were clearly trying to hide something, but what? He walked back to his office determined to find out.

Twenty minutes later, Sara paused for a commercial break. A member of her support team ran to her and said, "Sara, there is a woman on the phone who said she talked to you earlier about your story. She says she has more, and she says she needs to talk to you right now."

Sara shouted to the producer that she had to take this phone call, that it was big and to buy her some time. The producer pulled in two other anchors who had been watching the production, and told them to editorialize about the situation until Sara returned. It was almost an inconsequential comment by one of them, but it was the first domino to fall of the larger story. The middle-aged man said to his female counterpart, "You know, there was a similar story that broke last night in Colorado. The national media reported it earlier today, but it was overrun by this story. The two situations sure sound similar. I wonder if the two events could be related?"

In a few minutes, Sara was back. She said, "Folks, I can only tease you with this since we haven't yet corroborated the story, but we have received some recordings of phone calls between people at the highest levels.

"Again, we are trying to verify the information, but we were just sent recordings of phone calls that incriminate several people, including the White House, with illegal acts and worse, that the raid we have been reporting on was performed solely for political retribution to, pardon my words, kill the source of the information. Literally. Stay tuned. We'll pass along information as we get it."

That was picked up by the wire services, and the information spread across the world within minutes. It was then that the other TV networks felt compelled to resume their coverage, and Kara was making sure that she handed each of them an incriminating nugget that would be but a piece of the puzzle.

*****

In the diner in Colorado, Kara overheard someone sitting at the counter say, "Hey, will you turn up that TV? Something is happening." A waitress obliged, and Kara and Sam listened as the cable news station reported on the very information she had just emailed.

Kara whispered to Sam, "This is incredible! I email information, and a few minutes later it's on TV. This whole thing appears to be working. I just hope Ned and Jimmy are OK."

They watched the news and asked the waitress to refill their cups with the brown liquid that barely passed for coffee. Sam continued his analytical monitoring of the information he garnered from the TV news reports, and what he gleaned from Kara's status updates. As Sam heard something of note on the television, he would mention it to Kara. One such instance was when a White House spokesman repeated the story that the Virginia raid was to roust a known terrorist, and that any rumors to the contrary were false.

Sam told Kara about it, and she said, "Well, I'm just going to have to give the media the information they need to prove the White House is lying through their teeth." She started tapping keys on her laptop, a look of determination on her face.

Five minutes later, she said to Sam, "I can't find property ownership records or tax records of Ned's Virginia home. Could it be listed under another name?"

Sam said, "It probably is. In fact, I think I remember that Ned mentioned that."

Kara said, "Well, did he mention a name of the listed owner?"

Sam said, "No, he didn't. Do you know any of the aliases he used in his work?"

Kara thought for a few minutes, but could come up with nothing. She racked her brain and had almost given up hope when she remembered their college days when Ned had mentioned a sister that had died in an automobile accident on the way to her high school prom. What was the sister's name? She started running different names through her head, trying each on to see if it fit the situation.

After searching every name she could think of, she said to Sam, "I can't find it. This is like trying to open a bank vault by guessing at the combination. It could be under any name, real or otherwise. And the way the county records system is set up, I'm not sure I could find it if I owned the property.

Sam sat there thinking for a few seconds, then asked, "Was Ned ever married?"

Kara said, "No, not as far as I know."

Sam asked, "Did he have any living relatives?"

"No."

Sam asked, "Was there anyone significant in his life that you know of, like a fiancé or steady girlfriend, or maybe a dependable friend?"

Kara said, "I dated him for a couple of years in college. Maybe we would have amounted to something, but I broke it off because I wanted to be unattached. It was just before graduation and I knew that the two of us had very different lives to live. He was already talking with the CIA, and I knew he wanted that career.

"It looked romantic to him, or he thought it was a way he could have a positive effect on the world, I'm not sure. But I knew he wanted it, and I was terrified of that kind of life. So I broke it off, and I didn't see him again for more than fifteen years. Then we ran into each other in Washington on one of his visits there, and we had a great time together. It was as if we had never parted, but the reality was that Ned was deeply into CIA activities. He couldn't talk about what he was doing, and I didn't want to be part of the shadow world. In that way, it also was as if we had never parted, that time had stood still for us while it rushed by for everyone else."

She stopped talking, but Sam could see that in some ways she regretted their life decisions. He asked, "So, as far as you know, you are the most significant living person in Ned's life?"

She thought for a moment. "He has friends. There's Jimmy, and there are others, around the world there must be others.

Sam said, "Search your name."

Kara looked surprised. "There is no reason to ... why would he ... it couldn't be."

"Search it."

Kara reluctantly typed in her name. She held her hand in the air, suspended above the enter key, then finally pressed it. The computer ran its search.

In the state of Virginia, there were three results under the same name as hers. One was her home in Alexandria. She didn't know the counties in western Virginia very well, so she did searches on Virginia county maps and their location in the state. Through a process of elimination, she isolated the county to what she thought was the location of Ned's property.

There was one Kara Allyson listed in that county. Kara's face turned white, then red as she blushed a little. Sam noticed the change in Kara's expression. He asked, "Are you OK?"

Kara took a deep breath and said, "You were right. Ned's property is listed under the name of Kara Allyson. He registered the property in my name."

She continued reading the screen. "And he used my social security number. How the hell would he get my SSN? … Never mind. Forget I asked that."

Sam was smiling.

Kara began typing, and a few minutes later she emailed the information to her media contacts.

The major networks were the last to pick up this new information, but the one leading the story, the one showing on the TV in the diner, reported it, although they gave the caveat that they were still looking into the matter.

Kara monitored the websites of the main news services and TV networks, keeping her finger on the pulse of the whole situation. Two of the main cable news channels seemed to be blatantly backing up the White House. The three major networks were trying everything they could to minimize the story and they were doing only bare bones reporting on anything associated with the Virginia raid.

As Kara's latest information began to sift through the filters of the media organizations, the story was again gaining steam across the media. The White House changed its tack to compensate. They amended their story. They were sticking with the terrorist claim, but now saying that Ned had been a great servant for the United States during his prime, but he had turned to the dark side and was now acting for terrorist organizations. They went on to say that Kara, the listed owner of the house, was missing from her post at NSA and they suspected her of selling sensitive information to Ned, who in turn used it in his terrorist activities.

She mentioned this to Sam. He sat silent for a moment, then asked, "Can you break into the CIA's system, and do a new search on NSA records to see if there has been any recent mention of Ned?"

Kara said, "NSA is no problem. I'm not sure I can get into the CIA system, but I can try."

She began pecking away on the keyboard. Fifteen minutes later, she said, "Bingo!" I not only got into the CIA systems, but I also got into Ned's file. This is a treasure trove.

I'm going to copy these files before someone figures out this information is out there. Government records have been known to disappear when someone in power wants them gone."

Ten minutes later, Kara copied parts of Ned's files and began dropping excerpts into a Word document. After she had two pages of bullet pointed information that cited examples of Ned doing dangerous things that made America safer and diminished the chances of war in other parts of the world, she typed an introductory paragraph that briefly summarized who Ned was, explained the name on the property records, and suggested that readers continue on for proof that the home raided last night in Virginia was not that of a terrorist, but that of a hero. She emailed the information to the media contacts, and as soon as she hit the button, Sam said, "Now that you're finished with that, I have a question."

Kara said, "OK, fire away."

Sam said, "Who is the listed owner of Ned's Colorado house?"

Kara smiled and said, "I don't know, but we are about to find out."

Chapter 23

Ned stepped quickly through the vault door and into the still-dark outer tunnel of the mine. They were still 50 feet from the true entrance. Ned swung his rifle from side to side as he scanned for hostiles, and continued walking forward. Best to be a moving target. Jimmy followed a few seconds later. As he turned to push the vault door closed, someone jumped from behind it and hit Jimmy in the forehead with a rifle butt, knocking him to the ground, but not unconscious.

The young SWAT team member holding the rifle shouted, "They're here! I've got them."

Ned didn't hesitate. He scrambled back toward the soldier, and with his own rifle, swung the butt into the barrel of the SWAT guy's rifle, sending it tumbling from his hands. Ned didn't know who the soldier had yelled to, but he was going to help Jimmy, and their best escape might be right back into the tunnel through the still-open vault door.

The SWAT man was probably in his forties, and Ned could tell by the bulge in his belly that he was civilian, what Jimmy had referred to as a toy soldier. Not a professional in Special Forces tactics or fitness routines. But the man showed no fear. He lunged at Ned reaching for his throat. He bull rushed, hoping to bowl Ned over and subdue him. "This guy must be a cop," Ned thought.

As the man lunged, Ned, who was used to Special Forces tactics and exercise routines, side stepped and swung his boot into the man's oncoming knee. There was a loud pop as the knee joint gave way, and a loud scream as the pain seared into the man's brain.

Ned heard a yell from the entrance to the mine. "Hey," the voice shouted, "You're under arrest. Raise your hands over your head."

Ned heard the instructions and heard boots running on rock, two pairs of them, as they sprinted into the mine. Ned had a more immediate threat, and jumped on the downed man's back.

Ned jammed the man's face into the rock floor and reached down to the man's right hip holster. Ned ripped the pistol from the man and slid the pistol in between their bodies and out of the view of whoever was approaching.

Before Ned could roll over, there were two SWAT members standing side-by-side, their rifles pointed down at Ned's head. One of them said, "Roll over onto your back, and keep your hands where I can see them."

In the Nano seconds that passed, Ned came up with his plan. He rolled away from the soldiers and onto his back, which freed his arm, which also freed the soldier's pistol. Ned fired into the face of the soldier standing to the left. Before the other man could react, a rifle butt swung into the back of his knee, immediately arching him backward. The soldier fired off a three-round burst that bounced off the rock roof of the mine and into the still open vault door. Ned could hear the bullets bouncing down the tunnel behind him.

Jimmy, who had regained his senses, had swung his rifle into the standing soldier's knee, and before the soldier hit the ground, Jimmy was on top of him. Jimmy wrestled the man's rifle away and slung it to the side. Jimmy slammed the man's head into the rock ground three times to disorient him.

Ned jumped up and grabbed the man's pistol from its holster and turned his attention to the man he shot. That one was no longer a threat. He turned back to see Jimmy throwing haymaker punches into the other man's face, one after another. After a few more punches landed, Ned said, "I think you immobilized him, Jimmy."

Jimmy stood up, bent over with his hands on his knees and breathing deep gulps of air. Ned reached down and grabbed the man's handcuffs. He rolled the man over and handcuffed the man's hands behind him. Ned then stepped over to the other soldier and wrestled his handcuffs from beneath him. Ned snapped one of the cuffs around the dead man's wrist, and the other to the chain on the cuffs the other man was wearing.

Ned stood up and looked at Jimmy, who was wiping blood from his face. The rifle butt had opened a two-inch cut in Jimmy's right temple. It was bleeding profusely. Ned dug into his pack and pulled out the remaining gauze and cloth tape. He held the gauze in place over Jimmy's wound and wrapped the tape tightly around Jimmy's head to slow the leakage.

Once Jimmy was sufficiently bandaged, each man turned and began stripping equipment from the two SWAT men. Each man had a knife, a tear gas grenade, a rifle, pistol and a radio transmitter.

Ned said, "Those rifle shots had to ring through the hills."

Jimmy said, "Being in the tunnel will help some by directing the noise in one direction, but someone, somewhere heard them."

Ned turned and pushed the vault door closed and locked it, then looked out of the tunnel. He said, "It looks like it's pre-dawn. There is some light in the eastern sky, but still mostly dark out. Let's go while we can."

They walked the remaining yards to the mine entrance, on guard for any additional surprises. Seeing no one else, they began their jaunt through the forest. They had gone a hundred yards when they heard on the radio a transmission inquiring about gunshots. A few seconds later when no soldiers had replied, a voice said, "Base, this is unit One. I am one hundred yards from the house. No gunfire to report."

The voice on the other end said, "Probably just a local hunter. A new order has come down from high demand. All units are to withdraw to base immediately. If bogies are encountered, consider them hostile and dangerous and work under free-to-fire orders. Repeat, new order is to withdraw to base camp immediately."

Ned and Jimmy looked at each other, wondering why a retreat had been ordered. Ned said, "They are pulling back, which means they will be heading the same direction we are. Free-to-fire is a license to kill and an instruction to eliminate any threat they encounter." Jimmy said, "Right, and we are the threat. The heat is on. Let's go!"

They jumped over the creek at the bottom of the first mountain and began the long trudge up the other steep hill. When they were about halfway up, they heard someone from near the mine. There was a shout, followed by a burst of three rounds. A few seconds later, there was a loud bang.

The radio came to life with a transmission. "Base, this is unit one and unit two. We have encountered the bogies in an old mineshaft. We have fired on the hostiles, and have thrown a live grenade into the shaft. We believe the threat has been neutralized. Stand by."

Base replied, "Roger that. Standing by."

Jimmy looked at Ned and said, "Damn. They killed their own soldier, or at least tried to. I wonder how they'll explain those hand cuffs."

Ned said, "Sure enough. Let's move before any of these trigger-happy toy soldiers run into us."

It was daylight when they arrived at the paved road bordering Ned's property. They were lying side-by-side in the rhododendron beside the road assessing the situation before dashing across. There was heavier traffic than either of them had seen on this road.

Ned said, "This is a popular place this morning. I counted four SUVs with TV channel logos, and what was that, three satellite transmission trucks?"

Jimmy said, "That was my count, too, plus a few others that looked like Feds. I suppose the shit has hit the fan."

Ned said, "It looks that way."

They waited until no vehicles were in sight and none could be heard before making their dash, Ned first, Jimmy following five seconds later.

They jogged through the forest to the road where they had been dropped off the day before.

When they arrived at the bridge where it crossed the stream, Ned said, "Let's go down to the stream and clean up a bit. We look like we've been on the front lines in Iraq, with both of us earning Purple Hearts for our efforts."

They waded into the cold stream and washed their faces. They each removed their shirts and washed away as much of the blood as they could. They climbed up the bank by the road and wrestled themselves into their wet shirts. Ned looked at Jimmy and said, "We still look like hell, but at least we don't resemble characters in a bloody horror movie."

Jimmy laughed and winced from the pain the laughing caused. He raised his hand and touched the wet bandage on his forehead.

Ned asked, "How's your head?"

Jimmy said, "Swollen and sore, but I've suffered worse. It's nothing compared to your wound. How are you holding up?"

Ned said, "I have decided not to let it enter my mind. We don't have the luxury of being slowed by superficial wounds."

Jimmy dropped his hand from his head and said, "No, we don't. I guess we best get walking. It's probably three or four miles to the little store we saw on the way up here."

They turned and began striding toward the store, sticking to the edge of the forest. They had gone about a quarter of a mile when they heard a vehicle coming down the road behind them. Ned turned and looked, and said, "Not law enforcement. Looks more like a local."

Jimmy turned and looked at the old green Ford 150 pick up truck. He said, "That's a local, all right, and one I'm familiar with."

The truck pulled up beside them. Jimmy walked out of the edge of the forest and stuck his hand through the passenger window, shaking hands with the driver. Jimmy stood and turned to Ned and said, "Jimmy, meet my cousin Huldon. Let's get in."

Jimmy slid into the middle of the bench seat, and Ned sat beside him at the window. Huldon appraised them and said, "You boys look like hell. I heard you two were bloodied, but you look like you'll live. Still breathin'."

Jimmy said, "How'd you hear that?"

Huldon said, "One of our men saw you come out of the old mine shaft and kept his glasses on you. He was on top of the next ridge and heard shots coming from near the mine. He radioed me and described the two of you. He had his rifle on the two soldiers that came to the mine after you left. He said they were the closest ones to you, and he was going to take them out if they got too close."

Jimmy said, "So you knew we were walking down this road?"

Huldon said, "Naw, but my man said you crossed the road from your property, and I reckoned you were headed over here. I figured you had a car stashed somewhere, but thought I might be able to give you some help if you needed any."

Ned said, "How far away from the mine was your man?"

Huldon said, "About three quarters of a mile, I reckon."

Ned raised his eyebrows and said, "That's a long shot. Could he have hit one of them had he needed to?"

Huldon laughed, turned and spit out the window. He said, "I guarantee you he could have hit them. I've seen him hit a flying crow with a rifle from two hundred yards. That boy grew up in these hills, and he takes down deer from nearly a mile. Seen him do it more than once."

Ned said, "Well, tell him we thank him for looking out for us."

Huldon nodded and said, "Where you boys headed now?"

Ned said, "Not too sure about that. We need to get to a phone or, better yet, a secure computer. We need to get a message to someone as soon as we can."

Huldon hit the gas harder and said, "I'll take you to my house. We have an encrypted computer there and you can send anything to anywhere in the world, and even the NSA won't be able to tell where it came from or figure out the contents of the message."

Ned smiled and said, "That'll do fine."

After a couple of miles, Huldon said, "Did you know you boys are famous … at least Ned is. They haven't mentioned you, Jimmy."

Jimmy said, "Famous? Who hasn't mentioned me?"

Huldon slapped his leg and said, "The news people, boy. They're talking about it on every channel now, how SWAT teams raided the home of an innocent man because he had proof of the president hisself committing crimes, along with a bunch of those other sumbitch politicians in Warshington. Couldn't happen to a bigger bunch of assholes, I say. Some of the networks are doing spotty reports on the situation, but one has this story on non-stop, the one with that looker they have for a reporter."

Ned asked, "Which one?"

Huldon said, "Fox."

Ned made a mental note of the network and looked over at Jimmy and said, "Looks like Kara has been at work."

Jimmy said, "Then we better get these account numbers to her ASAP."

Huldon looked over and said, "Account numbers? You boys come into some money recently?"

Ned said, "We're about to, if it goes right. And so are you. You've helped us along the way, and you'll be rewarded for it."

Huldon looked at Ned and said, "Don't need no money. Life is fine here in the hills just like it is."

Ned smiled at Huldon and said, "Then how about your organization. I suspect you could use some more cash to educate people and buy supplies and facilities."

Huldon smiled and said, "Yep, I expect we could at that. But don't spend it all. You're gonna need some to fix your house up. It appears them feds shot a missile into your house and left nothin but ashes. And they're saying you also had a house in Colorado that got burnt up, too."

354

Ned felt a sinking feeling. "Shit. I hope Sam and Kara are alright."

Huldon said, "Ain't heard nothing about those names."

Ned asked, "How far you say it is to your house and this encrypted computer?"

Huldon said, "About seven miles from here. We'll be there shortly."

They rode in silence until Huldon stopped the truck in front of his house, which was more a rustic cabin until you looked closely. Huldon had built it with his own hands. It was constructed of huge poplar logs with ornate overhanging eves and hand carved, heavy oak doors and window frames.

Ned said, "I see the carpentry gene runs through the family."

Huldon said, "She's not big, but she's mine and I don't owe a dime on it. Come on in, boys."

Ned sat at the computer, which was on an old wooden table Huldon had made. Before beginning work on the computer, Ned admired the table, which was held together with dowels and pegs. It was simplistic, solid and beautiful. Ned asked, "Huldon, did you make the furniture?"

Huldon said, "I made every stick of furniture in this house, and most of what Jimmy owns. I didn't use one screw or nail, and I made it to last."

Ned looked around the room admiring each piece. The countertops were large, four-inch thick pieces of cherry or chestnut with live edges. The tables were the same, and they were stunning in their simplistic yet complex beauty.

Ned turned his focus to the computer. He created his message and clicked on the send button. He sat there hoping for a reply so he would know the whereabouts of Kara and Sam. He didn't have to wait long, although it seemed like an eternity.

Kara sent a reply that read, "Got it. I'll handle transfers right now. Rushed as time is scarce. The rats are beginning to run. Are you OK?"

Ned replied, "Fine. Handle your mission, then we'll catch up. I am anxious to learn how you fared."

Ned stood from the computer, felt the throbbing pain in his side and said to Huldon, "You know of a doctor who could come up here and sew up our wounds?"

Huldon said, "Sure do, one of our best members. I'll call him." Huldon walked onto the front porch and made a phone call. He came back into the cabin and said, "He'll be here in thirty minutes. You boys have a seat at the table and I'll fix ya some food."

Huldon worked at the gas stove, spatulas ringing against cast iron skillets and the cabin filling with smells of coffee, ham steaks and scrambled eggs. Huldon filled a pitcher with cool water from the sink and carried two glasses over and set them down in front of Ned and Jimmy. Each man filled his glass, quickly emptied it and re-filled. The water was cool and sweet mountain spring water.

Ned continued to admire the furniture and the craftsmanship in the cabin's interior. He said, "Huldon, I am really impressed with your carpentry skills."

Huldon said, "Well, you want me to make you some, or build you a house? From reports I get, you'll need some. There's not much left of your house save maybe the foundation and a few ashes."

Ned said, "Between you and Jimmy, I think I would be in good hands. But I have a few more things to accomplish and I need to survive before I start planning for a new house."

Jimmy said, "If Kara accomplishes what she's doing, money sure won't be a problem."

Help Me

Chapter 24

Kara knew that she had little time left. The first two of the eleven accounts she accessed had been emptied in the last few minutes. He third one had a balance of $321 million. The fourth had nearly three times that, and the remaining accounts had what totaled a whopping $27 billion.

She moved the money to the first set of parking accounts, then moved it again, then four times more until she created a trail that would take someone a good while to trace.

Her mission complete, she sent another message to Ned. "Transfers complete with 9 of 11 successes. We're unharmed and in hiding. Awaiting your status and instructions."

Ned replied, "Relieved to hear of your wellbeing and good fortune. Proceed to designated rendezvous. Will follow after a few more tasks."

Kara shut down her laptop and began sliding it into her backpack. As she did so, she said to Sam, "Time to fly. You ready for some beach time?"

Sam smiled and said, "Nothing would suit me better. I'll go to the payphone and call the pilot. I'll meet you in the truck."

Two hours and fifteen minutes later, Kara climbed into the right seat of the Leer's cabin, and Sam sat in the jump seat behind her and the pilot. The pilot went through his checklist, checking each item on a printed booklet. He put the booklet in its place, looked over at Kara and said, "You two ready to spend some time on an isolated island with unspoiled beaches and great fishing?"

Kara smiled, "So that's where we're headed?"

The pilot said, "I'm flying you to Charleston, South Carolina, but I'm not your last stop. You have a boat ride after you de-plane. Ned's friend has a house is on a little island off the coast of South Carolina."

Kara smiled. Sam turned to Kara and mused, "I wonder if you own property in the Carolinas, too."

*****

The doctor sewed up Jimmy's forehead first, which required 17 stitches. Ned's wound was more complex. The doctor worked on him for a half an hour, using several syringes of Lidocaine and more than 40 stitches, so many that the doctor lost count. He said to Ned after he finished, "This is going to hurt for a couple of weeks, but the bullet didn't contact any muscle or bone, so you won't have structural issues. Keep it clean until it heals over. You will need to have the external stitches removed in about two weeks. That's longer than usual, but since the wound is in a place that moves and stretches, we need to give it more time to fully heal. The internal stitches will dissolve, so no action required for them."

Ned handed the man several $100 bills, which he resisted. Ned insisted, finally saying, "If you don't want the money, donate it to someone who needs it." The doctor accepted, said his goodbyes and drove off, leaving Jimmy, Huldon and Ned alone in the quiet cabin.

Jimmy broke the silence, asking, "Ned, what's next?"

Ned scratched his chin and said, "We are going to pay a visit to someone in New York for a little chat. After that, we're going to disappear."

Jimmy said, "Disappear to where?"

Ned said, "Someplace warm with pristine beaches and good fishing. We'll eventually head for the Caribbean to visit some bankers, but for now we're heading to the southeast."

Huldon said, "What can I do to help?"

Ned said, "We need a vehicle and I need to call my pilot and set it up."

Huldon said, "There's a Tahoe in the barn you can drive. If you need to leave it somewhere, give me the location so I can retrieve it. We have connections with pilots that can fly with the best of them and keep their mouths shut. When do you want to leave?"

Ned said, "Tonight. We need to get some sleep, so I would appreciate a place to lay down for a few hours."

Huldon said, "In yon room; first door to your left. What time you want to hit the road? I'll have some dinner ready before you head out."

Ned looked at his watch and said, "We'll leave at seven."

Huldon said, "I'll have food ready at six."

Ned stood and walked toward the room. He heard Huldon say to Jimmy, "You take the room across the hall from him. I'll stand watch and wake you if anybody approaches."

*****

Ned awoke to the aroma of a venison roast and vegetables. Huldon treated them to a fine meal and handed them the keys to the Tahoe once they had finished. During dinner, which was excellent, Jimmy asked, "You mind filling me in on our plan?"

Ned looked at Huldon and said, "Huldon, I would rather not talk about this in front of you. I want you to be able to tell anyone who asks that you don't know where we are or what our plans involve. I hope you are OK with that. I promise you it is in your best interest."

Huldon said, "Fine by me. I'd like to hear about it afterward, if you think it'll be alright. But I can tell you that I meant what I said about rebuilding your house and furniture. You can count on me to help in any way I can, with the re-building or anything else. It was good enough for me that Jimmy vouched for you, but I see what you've been doing these last few days, and I know where your heart is. I'm with you."

Ned said, "But there's one more thing I need from you."

Huldon said, "Name it."

Ned said, "I need to know where I can buy a couple of prepaid cell phones."

Huldon said, "Hell, the closest place that sells those is thirty miles from here. But you don't need to go there. I have five of 'em in my emergency "Go" box. Take as many as you need." Huldon got up from the table and came back with three phones.

"Three enough?"

Ned said, "Three is plenty. I thank you … for the phones and for everything else."

Huldon winked at him and said, "Patriots have to look out for each other."

After they finished eating, Ned thanked Huldon for his help and the fine food, and they walked to the vehicle. When they drove onto the pavement, Jimmy said, "OK, what are we doing?"

Ned said, "We're going to see the man at the top of everything. We are going to drop in on Bedekowski."

Jimmy asked, "What makes you think he'll see us?"

Ned said, "As soon as I tell him that we've drained his accounts, he'll usher us in. Nothing is more important to the man than money and power, and one begets the other. He'll see us."

Jimmy smiled, but that quickly grew into a frown. He said, "I hope you plan to go armed. From the little I know about Bedekowski, once they get you inside their first impulse will be to torture you until you give their money back to them."

Ned said, "I agree that that will be his instinct, but I am going to tell him that I don't even know the account numbers. The only the person who can move the money back to him will do it after I tell them, in person, and I'll only do that if, and as long as, he complies with my demands."

Jimmy slowly nodded his head. "I don't like this. That man is ruthless. To him, you are nothing more than the key to his money. Once he has the information, he'll kill you. Hell, he might even kill you on the spot for nothing more than revenge. What if he doesn't let you walk out of there?"

Ned looked over at Jimmy. "That's your role. You're going to watch my back, but you'll be doing it from a building three blocks over, and you'll be doing it while on live TV."

Jimmy's eyes opened wide. "What the hell? Me on TV? And just how do you intend to make that happen?"

I'm about to call the largest cable news outlet in the world, and I'm going to talk to the woman who has been reporting this, Sara Shepherd. I'm going to arrange an interview with you, and you're going to tell the world where I am, and you're going to say it over and over until I walk into the studio."

Jimmy whistled through his teeth. "I think I am more nervous about being on TV than I am being tortured and killed by these people. In fact, I might prefer the latter."

Ned smiled and pulled off the road. First he called his Virginia pilot and arranged an immediate flight to New York City. The he called the news channel and asked for Sara Shepherd. He had to explain who he was to more than one person before one of them finally said, "Sara is on the air. She will call you back during her next break ... which is seven minutes from now."

Ned said, "This conversation will be off-air, but two of us will come in tonight for live interviews."

Sara Shepherd called Ned's cell phone seven minutes later. She was excited but wary, and asked Ned a series of questions about who he was, his history, his property, how he had escaped the raid and some of his accomplishments with the CIA."

Ned was amused that she already had so much information, but he answered her questions and established his credibility. He said, "Look, I have a meeting tonight in New York just a few blocks away from you. While I am in the meeting, Jimmy Rogers, who is my neighbor and partner, and who has a distinguished military career, will be in your studio telling our story. Look him up. He has been with me throughout this ordeal, and he can answer any question you have. He will be there at 10 p.m. I will arrive 30 minutes later, and I'll talk with you as long as you want."

Sara agreed to the arrangement, and they signed off. As Ned turned the truck into the same airfield they had used to fly to Colorado, Ned turned to Jimmy and said, "If she asks about Kara or Sam, tell her you've never heard of them. If she asks who has been sending her the information, tell her 'people who want to save our country, the same people the men in power have been trying to eliminate before they release more information, and they have much more.'"

Jimmy said, "Anything else?"

Ned stopped the truck inside the hanger where it would remain out of sight. He turned off the ignition and left the keys in it. Said, "You know how it works. We don't want anyone to know where we are going, where we will live … if we live … and we don't want anyone to know where we put the money. If it feels like you shouldn't share information, if the hairs on the back of your neck stand up, don't share it. Now I have to call Bedekowski." He looked up a number in his black notebook and called. As he had with the news organization, he had to speak with someone below Bedekowski.

Ned said to the man who answered the phone, "This is Ned Harrison. I will be paying a visit to Mr. Bedekowski at 10 tonight. I will be alone and unarmed. He must clear his calendar for the twenty minutes I will be in his office."

The voice protested, saying Mr. Bedekowski sees no one without an appointment. Ned stopped the man by saying, "Tell him to look at his bank accounts. I moved more than $20 billion of his money into secret accounts. Only I can get his money back to him; no one else. And one more thing, if I don't walk out of his office by 10:20 unharmed, he will never see the money again, never. And just so you know, I don't know exactly where the money is, so I couldn't reveal that if I wanted to."

The skeptical voice said, "Sure, buddy. And why should I believe you?"

Ned said, "Because Bedekowski's bank accounts are empty. Go look. I'll be there at 10."

Ned hung up the phone.

Jimmy paused and asked, "Are you sure this will work?"

Ned looked over at Jimmy and said, "Hell no I'm not sure, but this is the best solution I can come up with. There are but four of us and we can't bring down the most powerful people in the world with only us. We have to have help, and we have to make sure a spotlight is shone brightly on these people and what they are doing, and we have to keep the spotlight focused on them until they can be brought down and removed from power by the very system these people have manipulated and corrupted."

Jimmy said, "Safety in numbers, then. The more people that know about this, the more people that know about us, the safer we will be."

Ned said, "Exactly. Now let's go make you famous."

They boarded the plane and the pilot pushed the throttles forward until the plane left the ground, destination New York City.

Chapter 25

Jimmy walked into the studio at 9:55. There was an intern and two security guards waiting for him in the lobby. They whisked him quickly into an elevator, down a hall and into a brightly lit makeup room. The makeup artist, Dominique, a woman in her early thirties whose Nordic complexion belied her exotic name, winced at Jimmy's appearance. Jimmy's clothes were dirty and torn, and the bandage on his forehead shone like a flashing light. Dominique approached Jimmy carefully and was shaking her head slowly as she muttered expressions of hopelessness. She stared at Jimmy for a long moment, appraising her options, when Sara Shepherd dashed into the room. She took one look at Jimmy and snapped at Dominique, "Don't touch him. I want him just the way he is. His look of war weariness ads credibility."

Dominique expressed relief and backed away. Sara said to Jimmy, "Come with me. We have five minutes to cover a few facts, then we're on the air."

She turned and walked out of the room. Jimmy could hear her quick footsteps as she hustled down the hall toward the studio. Dominique said to Jimmy, "You better hurry. She's a fast mover and waits on no one."

Jimmy jumped up and began to jog down the hall behind Sara. She led him into the control room and pulled two rolling chairs over to the corner. She slid close to Jimmy and looked him dead in the eye.

Sara said, "Tell me your name and some reason I should believe anything you say."

Jimmy said, "I'm Jimmy Rogers, Special Forces, U.S. Army, retired. In the last 24 hours I've traveled halfway across the country, walked several miles through mountains full of armed SWAT teams, made it through an abandoned mine shaft we could have been lost in forever, and snuck into and out of a house that was being watched by teams of armed men and fleets of flying drones.

I barely escaped the house before it was blown to smithereens by our own U.S. Government, and my friend and I had to go back through the mineshaft and exit it into the mountains. That's when I got this wound, which was the result of a well-aimed rifle butt. And now I am in New York about to go on TV for the first time, and I think I would rather be dodging live ammunition."

Sara looked at Jimmy, her eyes growing wider, and said, "This is a great story. I wish I had this very moment on tape. No more questions. I don't want to miss any more jewels."

Jimmy said, "What I just told you is but a hint of the bigger story, a story that is bigger than anything this or any other network has ever told."

Sara smiled, thrilled at the career boost she was going to earn from this. Someone shouted to Sara, "One minute!"

Sara said, "Jimmy, come with me. We're on the air in one minute. I'll introduce you and ask you a few basic questions to start the interview. You say what ever you think is pertinent. I'll step in and guide you if you drift, and I'll prompt you with questions when I need more information. Got it?"

Jimmy said he did, and added, "Now remember, there is a bigger story behind all of this, and my friend Ned Harrison will tell most of it, although everything I will talk about leads to that.

Sara smiled again. They were taking their seats at a large glass table in the studio. Attendants rushed to Jimmy and slid a microphone into his shirt. A few seconds later, the set cleared and Sara, in a professional coolness that Jimmy had rarely seen in civilians, introduced Jimmy and asked him, "Jimmy, people have no idea what you've been through the last 24 hours. Could you tell us about it?"

Jimmy told about flying to Virginia at the last minute and the dash through the mountains to the house right under the noses of SWAT teams from several organizations.

Sara interrupted him and said, "It is being widely reported that the SWAT teams attacked the house because known terrorists were there. How do you respond to that?"

Jimmy said, "That's what corrupt politicians want you to think, but that's not at all what happened." He paused and asked, "Did you know that more than 31 federal agencies have SWAT teams, and that they raid the homes of U.S. citizens fully armed, even if the charge is as mild as an unpaid fine or misdemeanor? And did you know that over the course of the last four years, 81 U.S. citizens have been killed in those raids even though those people had not been charged with – much less convicted of – a crime? Now let me ask you something."

Jimmy paused a full three seconds to let the information sink in. He said, "Let me ask you if, from what you've experienced at the department of motor vehicles, or the post office, or with the IRS or the EPA or any other part of the government, what do you think the chances are that these SWAT teams are tightly controlled and operate efficiently or effectively, or even within the law?"

Sara squirmed a little, then said, "Why don't you tell us, Mr. Rogers."

Jimmy said, "That house in Virginia that the SWAT teams blew up last night is … was … owned by my friend and neighbor, Mr. Ned Harrison, who just so happens to be an American hero. He isn't a terrorist, that's a bunch of bullshit some politician came up with to cover his ass."

Jimmy cited a few of Ned's heroic accomplishments during his career with the CIA, and he explained how Ned had become an enemy of those who wish to destroy the country for ideological and personal gain, including Russia, China, Cuba, and apparently, some of our own politicians who are supposed to be acting on our behalf rather than working against us.

Jimmy said, "And before I move on, I want you and everyone around the world to know that Ned Harrison is at this very moment in the New York Office of the most corrupt man of any and the man funding most of these corrupt politicians, Mr. Bedekowski. The address is 45381 North Avenue, just a few blocks from here." He paused for a few seconds before repeating the name and address.

Jimmy continued. Left to his own devices, Bedekowski would kill Ned before letting him out of his office, but Ned has some leverage that I hope saves his life."

Jimmy pulled a piece of folded paper from his pocket and changed the course of the conversation by citing examples of politicians who had received money for political favors. After he mentioned senators and congressmen and gave detail on each transaction and resulting political favor, Sara interrupted him. She said, "Jimmy, these politicians will deny all these allegations and say you are making this up to get yourself off the hook."

Jimmy said, "And I am on the hook for what? I haven't been charged with a crime of any sort, and neither has Ned Harrison, who will join us shortly. I am not on any hook. I bring this information forward for three reasons. First, I love my country and am tired of seeing it pilfered and abused by greedy, dishonest and power-hungry politicians of all parties and persuasions. Second, I am tired of watching our freedoms disappear and seeing citizens who fear their own government more than any of our enemies abroad. And third, the U.S. government, who I risked my life for in Iraq and Afghanistan before retiring, has declared all veterans enemies of America. I'll say that again. The government who had us fight in foreign lands, who shoved us in front of the enemy's guns and bombs, now considers us to be enemies of our own country. Now ask yourself, 'why would they do that'?"

Sara began to shake her head slowly from side to side. Jimmy continued, "Because they know that we know how to protect ourselves, and we have seen from afar what politicians are doing to citizens of the United States, as corrupt government officials have done to their own people in Iraq, Afghanistan, Russia, Cuba and on and on. When the president says that he wants a civilian force as strong as and as well funded as the U.S. military, he told everyone in the world that he considered the citizens of the United States to be an enemy as equally threatening as the Chinese, Russians, Al Qaida and North Korea."

Jimmy paused again to let that sink in. He broke the silence by saying, "Our own president considers each of us, not only veterans, but every citizen who simply goes to work everyday to put food on the table for his family, he considers all of us to be his enemy. Why? Why are we his enemy?"

Sara said, "Why do you think he considers us enemies?"

Jimmy said, "Because he knows he is doing things that do and will harm us, things that we won't like if we ever wake up to what he and his ilk are doing and what their plans are. You have seen the reports of Homeland Security buying millions of rounds of hollow point ammunition. Just this year they bought enough rounds to supply the army for an eight-year active battle, and this is for Homeland Security to use on its own citizens? And it's not only Homeland security, the Post

376

Office, Forest Service, the EPA, IRS and even the Department of Education are arming up."

Sara said, "But Homeland Security says the ammunition is for training purposes."

Jimmy said, "Remember I served in the Army. No federal agency or arm of service is using hollow points for training because they cost nearly five times more than conventional rounds. Either they lied, or they made a change in their purchasing practices that cost the American taxpayers five times more than it should have."

Sara said, "But back to our story. You leveled some serious accusations of illegal actions by politicians and you offered specific evidence. Where, may I ask, did you get that information?"

Jimmy smiled and said, "I got the information from the same place the government gathers and stores information on every American citizen. In fact, I got the information on government officials *from* the government. You see, the NSA has this information. They know every phone call, email, text or letter you have ever sent or received. They know who all your contacts are. They know every tollbooth you've passed through, and they know where you are while carrying a cell phone, or where you drive your car. They know every banking transaction you've ever made, everything you've purchased or sold, and they know what you read and what websites you visit. They know everything, and the sad part is that America has become a police state just like the Soviet Union, Cuba and China. Maybe worse, if we indeed do enjoy a technological advantage."

Sara chuckled and said, "Well, except the Soviets and Chinese murdered millions of people as they took full control of the citizenry."

Jimmy said, "That's correct. The U.S. government hasn't killed millions of its own people in their own country, but they do have SWAT teams that raid people's homes and kill some of them, just as they burned up those people in Waco, Texas a few years back, and just as they tried to do at Ned Harrison's house last night. If we had been ten seconds slower getting out of the house, there would be no trace of us.

AND," he raised his hand to keep Sara from straying from the subject, "Remember that Homeland Security and other federal agencies – agencies that shouldn't even have weapons and SWAT teams – just purchased enough ammunition to shoot every American citizen more than five times. Each person alive in the U.S., including all women and children, could be shot with five rounds *by our own government*."

Sara looked at the camera and said, "Folks, we'll be right back with Jimmy Rogers after these messages."

After the cameras were off, Sara bent over and took several deep breaths. One of the studio assistants ran over to her and said, "Sara, are you OK?"

Sara said, "Yes, just terrified."

The assistant said, "But Sara, you have the biggest story of our lifetimes. Why are you terrified?"

Sara said, "Because if this is all bullshit, I'm finished. And if this is all true and we don't bring the people in power to their knees, I am dead." She stood and collected herself and said, "But besides that, I'm fine."

*****

Ned waited fifteen minutes in the dark shadow of a building entryway, observing the entrance to Bedekowski's building. No one had come or gone, but there was a man hiding in the shadows at the corner 50 yards from Bedekowski's building. There was another man to his right on Bedekowski's side of the street. That man sat on a stoop pretending to read the paper, but he was either a lookout for Bedekowski or he was the slowest reader alive. He hadn't turned a page or scrolled down on the page he held in front of him. Ned appraised the two men as best he could from his position. He assumed they were both armed. The one to his right looked like FBI, or he could be ex-FBI and now working for Bedekowski.

Ned couldn't tell much about the other man since he stayed tucked around the corner most of the time, so he considered him to be the worst of them: Big, strong, fast and armed.

At 9:59, Ned stepped from the shadow and walked briskly across the street so the men couldn't cut him off, if that was their desire. Neither man moved, but both watched his every step. Ned stepped into the front door and walked directly to the elevators in front of him. There were two men in the lobby, one on each side of the room in the corners nearest the street. Anyone who entered would have to turn to each side or walk into the room and turn around to get a good look at each.

Ned noted the bulge under the men's coats where each carried his firearm. Neither man moved, just watched, until Ned pushed the button for the elevator. Ned saw one of them talk into a radio, and both of them began to walk toward him. The men stopped five yards behind him, alert and ready.

The elevator opened and two men in dark suits stood in a corner of the elevator. Neither had his hand on his weapon, but they had their arms bent and ready should they need to pull their weapons.

The man on the left in the elevator asked, "You Harrison?"

Ned said he was, and the man motioned him onto the elevator. As soon as the door closed, the man said, "We have to search you. I'm sure you understand."

Ned nodded, and the other man stepped behind him and frisked him. The man said, "He's clean," and backed into the same corner he came from. The men didn't say another word until the elevator stopped on the top floor and the door opened. The man who initially spoke said, "Straight ahead and through the double doors. Someone will be out to escort you momentarily."

Ned looked at him and asked, pointing to the other man, "He mute, or just dumb."

Ned saw the man he pointed to perk up, which indicated that the man wasn't a trained professional who had been scrubbed clean of any reaction that could take away his focus, or at the very least, he was an undisciplined man in spite of his training. Ned noted that as a weakness he could exploit if necessary.

The man who had spoken said flatly, "Straight through the double doors."

Ned stepped through the double doors and into a large room with marble floors and walls, and sparse, modern furnishings that looked European. Ned noticed cameras in each corner, a single, heavy black door on the right wall and a small window on the far wall that didn't open. Ned knew he had just walked into a potential mausoleum, and that he was being watched.

Another man in a dark suit entered the waiting room from the door to his right. He was a large man who looked professional. He approached Ned and said, "Walk through the door and sit."

Ned said, "You're not joining us?"

The man didn't answer, only pointed at the door. Ned walked into the large, marble office with blacked out windows. The man who just retrieved him followed and walked to the back of the room. Ned could no longer see him without turning around.

A small, bald and ugly man sat behind a green marble desk that had only a phone on it. Ned grabbed one of the small wooden chairs that were arranged on the guests side of the desk. He moved the chair, which seemed to bother Bedekowski. Ned turned the chair so that Bedekowski was 60 degrees to his left, and the man in the back of the room was 60 degrees to his right. Ned didn't speak, only observed.

Bedekowski said, "I believe you have something that belongs to me. Exactly how do you propose to return it before you leave this office … if you leave this office."

Ned said, "I don't propose to return it to you now, and I will be leaving this office in exactly 18 minutes or you will never have your money again."

Bedekowski released a wicked laugh that sounded forced and a bit frantic. Ned was learning just how important money was to the man.

Bedekowski said, "Then I'll call in my men and we'll pull your fingernails out with pliers. If you don't comply then, the real fun will start. I've been dying to try out a new water torture technique we learned from America's best interviewers in Afghanistan. You'll love it."

Ned said, "You don't have enough men to hold me here, or at least you don't have the right ones, especially this clod in the back of the room, and you aren't in charge here, Bedekowski. You know the Golden Rule … 'the one who has the gold makes the rules.' And in case you've forgotten, I have the gold – your gold – although I suspect that the origins were less than above board."

Bedekowski lost his laugh and his wicked smile. They were replaced by a determined, gritty glare that was rife with nothing less than hate. Ned said, "Tell me, Bedekowski, I'm trying to decide. Which is it you hate worse, losing all your money, or losing control."

Bedekowski's face reddened, and after a futile attempt to maintain his composure, he slammed his hand on the marble desk and shouted, "You give me my money or I'll kill you."

When Bedekowski banged his hand on the table, it made no more than a slapping sound. Bedekowski was now feeling the pain of a collision between a soft hand and the hard marble.

Ned smiled and said, "The intimidating sound you intended from slapping the desk pales in comparison to the pain you now feel. I recommend you find another method of trying to scare people. As for killing me, that is the one sure-fire way to ensure that you will never see your money again. If I don't walk out of this office in exactly … " Ned looked at his watch, "17 minutes, your money will automatically be distributed through a complicated pathway of more than 100 accounts until it lands in the accounts of 12 American charities and patriotic organizations. The transfers have already been set up, and only someone seeing me walk out of here unharmed will prevent that. You have one way, and one way only, to get your money back."

Bedekowski tried to regain his composure and asked as calmly as he could, "What is it you want?"

Ned smiled and said, "That's more like it. I have three things for you to do. First, you release a statement to the three alphabet networks, and to CNN and Fox, and to the AP and the New York Times. You statement will say ... get out a pen and write this down." Ned waited until Bedekowski complied.

Ned continued, "It will say 'I, Mr. Bedekowski, have been buying politicians in America and other countries, to advance communism in this country and others. Included in those illegal transactions are the current president and vice president of the United States, as well as the majority leader of the Senate and the Attorney General. My end goal has been to convert all countries to communism, and to have one central government to run the entire world."

Bedekowski was steaming, but he was still writing. Ned continued, "There are many other politicians I have paid off and many federal agencies I completely control. Detailed evidence will be released to news organizations separately, and the evidence is indisputable.

"In retrospect, I see that my efforts were wrong. I am leaving the country immediately, and will cease any further political involvement."

Ned sat watching Bedekowski, who was gritting his teeth. Blood vessels in his temples were bulging as if they would explode, and his face was a deep red. Bedekowski finished writing. Ned said, "Have your man make a copy. I will walk out of here with the original." Ned looked at his watch. "I will leave here within 11 minutes, so get moving."

Bedekowski motioned to his man, who walked up and took the paper into another room to make a copy. While he was gone, Bedekowski said, "I am going to find you, make you wish you were dead, and then refute everything. You'll wish you never knew my name."

Ned smiled again and said, "Two minutes ago, we released our first batch of information to the media that directly implicates you in numerous federal and state crimes, up to and including murder. Believe me, you had best waste no time getting out of the U.S."

Bedekowski laughed and said, "You fool, I own the media and I own the legal system. You're a dead man."

Ned said, "Oh, I beg to differ. You own most of the media but not all of it, and the same goes for the legal system. But even if you did own all of it, all governments are but a small collection of rulers that keep their people in check through fear. Every leader in the world, including you, knows that if the masses rise, it's all over for you. And guess what. The masses are rising, and by tomorrow night, the uprising will be growing, and it will continue until the likes of you are eradicated, strung up in the public square. You are wasting time, and you don't have much left."

Bedekowski was struck as if by a hammer. The secret was out, the one that rulers held close in hopes that their vulnerability would continue unchallenged. Ned Harrison was right, and Bedekowski knew his time was running out.

Bedekowski said, "What about my money?"

Ned said, "Off the top, we are keeping $500 million. Since you were behind building the power structure and the agencies that destroyed my house, I'm going to re-build at your expense, and the rest is for new houses for my friends."

Bedekowski interrupted and said with a satisfied smirk, "Two of your houses. The Colorado structure was also obliterated."

Ned said, "OK, we are keeping an additional $200 million for houses. Anything else we need to add to the ledger?"

Bedekowski's smirk disappeared, and he went silent. Ned continued, "You destroyed the careers of two fine people who were public servants, and they will live a fine life of retirement, at your expense. You came after me with intent to kill and endangered the life of my friend and neighbor. Therefore, you will be contributing to the funding of our retirements to the amount of an additional $500 million. Consider it a donation to our pensions."

Bedekowski began to look as if the blood was literally draining from his face. He looked progressively pale, and he seemed to shrink as time went by.

"From the balance, we will contribute 25 percent of the remainder to charities of our choice. I figure you are what, 75 years old? We will return what remains of your money by wire transfers … in annual installments. I figure you have as much as 20 years left, so if you do as I told you, each year we will transfer one twentieth back into your accounts … as long as you are alive, minus the twenty percent we will contribute to charities of our choice each year."

Bedekowski began to protest. "You already gave to charities!"

Ned said, "That's right, we did, and you are going to get into the habit of habitual charitable giving, just like you should. Tick tock. We're almost out of time, so you best listen closely."

Bedekowski's smirk returned, and he waived his hand in the air and said snidely, interest alone on my money far exceeds anything you will take, so worse case under your terms, I still end up with billions of dollars."

Ned said, "I'm glad you brought that up. Everything we've talked about comes directly from the principle. The interest, all of it, will be distributed to groups and individuals who support and fight for the preservation of the United States Constitution. Our goal is to rebuild all the destruction you and your minions have done to the American system. We will help the citizens regain the power the Constitution reserved for them, and we will help restore the balance of power so that the government fears the people, as was the design of our founding fathers, rather than the citizens fearing the government, which is the system you have built, aka tyranny.

Bedekowski laughed. "You are an idealist whose time has passed! You have forgotten that I still own the media, the universities, a good portion of the Supreme Court, and I also own the president of the United States, both current and the incoming. You see, a certain South Carolina senator is about to re-enter the race, and since we defeated your kind's effort at voter ID, and we can manipulate electronic voting results at will. I'm sure that at this very moment the sitting president is sending people to take you down in a very public way."

Ned laughed himself, and said, "I don't think so. First, I suggest that you get on your way to the airport as soon as I dismiss you, and if your airplane can pick up cable news channels, I suggest that you tune in. You're about to get a bitter, harsh taste of reality. We only have one minute left, so shut up and listen or we keep all your money.

"If you become involved in politics in any way … and I mean any way … the installments will stop and we will take anything you have left. And not only that, we'll find you and you'll wish you weren't alive. And there's one more thing. If any harm comes to me or any of my people, even if it's an accident, the installments stop, we seize your remaining money and we find you and make you pay with pain and suffering."

Bedekowski yelled, "But you or your people might be killed in an automobile accident or something I have nothing to do with."

Bedekowski's man returned with the copy and handed Ned the original of the statement. Ned took the paper but his gaze stayed on Bedekowski. Ned said, "Then you will be a poor man, Bedekowski."

Ned took a small piece paper from his pocket. He said to Bedekowski,

Now, fax this statement to the number on this paper. Now. If you don't send it, the deal is off and we keep all your money."

Ned stood and walked to the door. The man looked at Bedekowski wondering if he should take Ned out. Bedekowski reluctantly said, "Make sure Mr. Harrison has safe passage out of here. Call off the dogs. As much as I hate the man, Mr. Harrison is valuable to us. I'll send the fax myself."

As Ned opened the door, he heard Bedekowski pick up the phone and say, "Get the plane ready. We're going to Switzerland … immediately."

Ned rode the elevator with the same two men as before, and he walked right past the two men waiting in the lobby. He left the building unharmed, and turned left. As he walked past the man with the newspaper, he said, "Better start reading the want ads. Your boss is about to leave town for good, and he's very low on cash."

Ned walked to the end of the block, turned left around the corner where he saw a young man texting someone. Ned said to the young man, "Could I please make a short phone call on your phone? It's an emergency, and I lost my phone."

The young man thought for a few seconds, and said, "Sure, but make it quick and don't try to run off with it."

Ned dialed the ten digits. A man picked up the call after one ring and Ned said, "Get the plane ready. We'll leave at midnight for South Carolina; same airfield where we picked up Sam a few days ago."

Ned ended the call and handed the phone back to the young man. He thanked him and walked quickly to the building housing the news network where Jimmy was still on camera. Ned walked into the lobby and was greeted by the same two security guards and assistant that escorted Jimmy. They took him to the same makeup artist, who looked at Ned in his dirty clothing. She shrugged and said, "Well, you're not as bad as the last guy. At least you don't have any bandages on your face."

Ned said, "I appreciate your craft, but I'll stay as I am."

Sara Simpson ran down the hall, grabbed Ned's arm and said, "You're Ned Harrison?"

Ned told her he was, and she started pulling him down the hall. She said, "We're on in 45 seconds. Holy shit, what a night this has been."

Ned said, "It's about to get a whole lot more interesting. Check your fax machine and look for a statement from a Mr. Bedekowski."

Sara asked, "Who's Bedekowski?"

Ned said, "The power behind the throne. Get the fax and I'll tell you everything."

Sara said, "Hold it until we're on the air. I want the world to hear this."

As the man behind the camera was counting down, Ned was thinking about Kara and how anxious he was to see her. He wondered if they could put all this behind them and get to know each other again without so much complication. As the man behind the camera said,

"Three, two, one," Sara introduced Ned to the audience and said to him, "Let's go back to the beginning. How did this all start?"

Ned thought for a second and said, "It all started in South Carolina when a woman looked at me with terror and pain in her eyes and said, 'Help me!'"

***

Ten minutes into the interview, Sara interrupted and said that the president had just released a statement that denied any affiliation with Bedekowski, and that no one was more of a supporter of the Constitution than him. And even though he was in the latter stage of his second term, the senator from South Carolina would soon announce that he was re-entering the race, and that he was in full support of and would continue the policies and dramatic progress made by the current administration. She turned to Ned and asked, "Mr. Harrison, do you have any comment on what the president said?"

Ned smiled and said, "Yes, I do, and I suspect that both the president and the senator from South Carolina will change their tunes within the hour. Let's start with the president. As you are all now aware, the president used the IRS and every federal agency he could think of as weapons to silence, and in his own words, 'punish' his opposition. He also illegally spied on every American to determine who was friend to him and who was foe. He intercepted and recorded … and stored … all of our communications of any type. He also tracked us through our cell phones and our automobile GPS systems, tollbooths and more, and he used the NSA for all of this data theft and storage."

Sara said, "Yes, we've talked about most of that tonight."

Ned said, "Yes you have, but many news outlets have covered for the administration by denying it or writing it off as the paranoid fantasies of right wing nut cases. The president and his minions are smart, as is the real power behind the throne, Bedekowski. They were smart enough to recognize the power of the information they could access through our own intelligence organizations, and they used those systems *against* the citizens, rather than to defend them. They added to that information and power source when they took over our health care system.

"Now, not only could they access intimate personal health information on everyone in the United States, but they could use the information to their advantage, and they could control anyone's access to care. They had everything they needed now to have full control of the people, our wealth, and the boundless resources of the United States. But they got a bit too confident in their control over our country. They seemed to forget that if they were able to penetrate our communications, our private conversations, that just maybe, someone could access theirs. I want everyone to listen to this." He bent forward toward the camera.

"They stored every communication you have had, except some in-person conversations. They even listened to some of those through listening and video recording devices they have installed in public transportation and in public places. They even have broken into your homes and watched and listened to you through your computers and other electronic devices."

Ned paused and looked at the camera. "I know this sounds farfetched and more like a James Bond movie than reality, but it is real. It is real." He paused.

"BUT, they seemed to forget that they themselves have proven that no system is impenetrable. Now listen carefully. We penetrated *their* systems, and we accessed *their* conversations. We have duplicates of every electronic conversation they had, and we kept records of everyone who holds a political office and anyone they had conversations with. And fellow Americans, the level of corruption throughout our political system is shocking, even to me, who has seen the most corrupt governments on the planet."

Sara interrupted. "Ned, you started in this direction after the president's announcement. Is what you are telling us directly related to the president?"

Ned said, "Yes. In addition to his blatant disregard for the law pertaining to immigration, dispatching our troops into battle or worse, sending our best fighting troops to deal with a deadly disease in Africa when they are not trained or equipped for such a mission, or the president making whimsical changes to laws whenever it suits him and using federal agencies to destroy American citizens, we have recordings of the president's conversations, including ones where he ordered those federal agencies to take illegal actions. He also demanded payoffs, took orders from Bedekowski, and conspired with numerous politicians, including the current majority leader of the senate. They even discussed their plans to deal with several people who ended up dead in public parks and in plane crashes. Now let me be clear, they discussed the people in cryptic language, and that will have to be dealt with in a court of law before they are proven guilty of murder, but there is no doubt that they have their hands very deep into a very dirty and corrupt cookie jar."

Sara started to break in, but Ned waved her off. "Now let me talk about the senator from South Carolina who is considering re-entering the race for president. I personally witnessed him shoot the woman who begged me for help. She died from her wounds. Not only did I see it happen, but I also have a spent shell casing from the murder weapon, and in fact, have the murder weapon, which is a pistol registered to the senator. It also bears the senator's fingerprints. I recommend that the senator focus his energies on his upcoming murder trial. If the police don't file charges, I will press them myself. He will not be our next president."

Sara finally said they simply had to break for commercials. She wiped tears from her eyes, and looked at Ned. "Are you one hundred percent sure of all of this? You have all the evidence? You have the murder weapon and you witnessed the senator shooting that woman?"

"Ned said, "Yes, it's all true, and ..."

Sara interrupted him and said, "Save it for the camera." A crew member walked over and said, "Sara, our feed is now being picked up by every other cable news network, as well as so many local affiliates across the country I can't give you a total. The three alphabets and their owned channels are still refusing to acknowledge it. I suppose they are going to go down with the ship of their political brethren, but the local affiliates are deciding to bypass them."

Three minutes later, Sara gave a quick recap to her viewers, and asked Ned if he was rock solid positive of the validity of what he was saying. She added that over the last years the playbook of the people in power has been to first destroy the reputation of the messengers, and with it their credibility. Was he prepared to endure the attacks?"

Ned said, "My teammates have sent to you, or will in the next hours, our personnel files, mine and Jimmy's. I mean the deep cover records that require the highest clearance. You will get everything on both of us before anything can be changed in our files."

"I expect you to cull the files and redact anything that could endanger people fighting for our country, such as CIA or military names, finger prints, social security numbers, techniques, missions, that sort of thing. People have a right to know who we are and what our pasts were. And they should know the unvarnished truth, not some spin or false information designed to ruin our credibility and protect those corrupt individuals who will do anything to stay in power. And as you are learning, these people will do anything, anything, to stay in power.

"To answer your question, we have solid proof of everything. We will begin sending you some of the communications we discussed tonight. In fact, it's probably been coming in all night. It's a massive amount of information, and there is so much incrimination, it's going to rock our country, and with it, the world."

Sara asked, "So, you are certain that the information you have and will provide us will take the president from office and end the careers of several politicians, including the rumored candidate from South Carolina?"

Ned said in a deliberate, carefully paced tone, "These politicians and the people behind them, like Bedekowski, have fought their entire adult lives to have and keep power and the money that comes with it. They will keep fighting. They will say anything and do anything they can think of to retain their power. They already tried to kill Jimmy and me, and they won't stop until they are all in jail or dead.

"For a time, their focus will continue to be centered on keeping power. But soon, their focus will become fighting to stay out of prison, or out of reach from the very angry citizens of the United States."

Sara said, "This has been a very chilling night. As I am, I suspect that many of our viewers are rocked by these revelations."

Ned said, "It is, indeed, chilling to learn that the very people we trusted to protect us and our country have actually been our worst enemies. And while it is shocking to some, it has been obvious to others for years. You and I have both heard many people sound alarms only to be brushed aside and labeled conspiracy theorists or 'nut jobs.' But this is different. We have evidence; lots of it, and it is damning at an astounding level. If what people know right now about what our own government did to us isn't enough to shock people into reality, the information we are providing certainly will. Much of the information is in the form of emails between corrupt individuals, including emails that were claimed to have been 'lost,' such as those between the White House, Justice Department and The Department of State. And even more damning are the voice recordings of the conversations these people had. They can deny email authorship or create lies to cover themselves, but they can't convince anyone of their innocence when we play recordings of them, in their own voices, conspiring to commit crimes, ordering them or bragging about crimes they already committed. And as a reminder, those recordings include our sitting president and the majority leader of the senate, and many, many others, including leaders at the Federal Reserve, IRS, EPA, State and BATFE."

Sara said, "Ned, this is an amazing night, and if you haven't stopped to think about it, you have been at the point of the needle of the injection of harsh reality so many people say our country was in desperate need of. You will be hated by some, and a hero to others. What is your biggest worry?"

Ned said, "I have two worries. First I worry that the citizens of the United States will ignore this or assume that someone else will fix everything. I ask everyone right now; please don't rely on someone else to take responsibility.

"Be responsible for your own freedom and for that of your children. Educate yourselves using multiple sources. Demand voter ID so that your vote counts and some unscrupulous person doesn't vote numerous times, which has been happening at sickening rates. If you use voting machines, review the results to ensure that it is registering the vote you intended. Protest, peacefully but in mass. Remember that government workers, including leadership, are your employees, not you theirs. Resist when necessary, and once you've educated yourselves, vote.

"My second worry is that the power vacuum this shockwave is likely to create will be replaced with violence and the worst of the worst taking over. Don't let that happen, people. It's your country. Yours. Cherish it and protect it from those who will serve themselves rather than serve you and the United States."

Help Me